BATS IN THE BELFRY

THE CASES OF DAN SHAMBLE, ZOMBIE P.I.

KEVIN J. ANDERSON

EBook ISBN: 978-1-68057-570-5
Trade Paperback ISBN: 978-1-68057-571-2
Dust Jacket Hardcover ISBN: 978-1-68057-572-9
Case Bind Hardcover ISBN: 978-1-68057-573-6
Audiobook ISBN: 978-1-68057-574-3
Library of Congress Control Number: 2023946062
Cover design by Miblart
Vellum layout by CJ Anaya
Published by
WordFire Press, LLC
PO Box 1840
Monument CO 80132
Kevin J. Anderson & Rebecca Moesta, Publishers
WordFire Press Edition 2023

Printed in the USA
Join our WordFire Press Readers Group for
sneak previews, updates, new projects, and giveaways.
Sign up at wordfirepress.com

PRAISE FOR KEVIN J. ANDERSON'S DAN SHAMBLE, ZOMBIE P.I.

"Sharp and funny; this zombie detective rocks!"

—PATRICIA BRIGGS

"A dead detective, a wimpy vampire, and other interesting characters from the supernatural side of the street make Death Warmed Over *an unpredictable walk on the weird side. Prepare to be entertained."*

—CHARLAINE HARRIS

"Master storyteller Kevin J. Anderson's Death Warmed Over *is wickedly funny, deviously twisted and enormously satisfying. This is a big juicy bite of zombie goodness. Two decaying thumbs up!"*

—JONATHAN MABERRY

"A darkly funny, wonderfully original detective tale."

—KELLEY ARMSTRONG

CHAPTER 1

When my vampire half-daughter drew a breath to sing, her fangs flashed in the stage lights. Since Alvina had been turned when she was ten years old, they were just cute little fangs, and her grin made them even less intimidating. The kid loves to sing.

I felt proud as we watched the recital in the cathedral. Standing with her fellow members of the Banshee Tabernacle Choir, Alvina belted out the words, though her voice was lost amidst the howling of young werewolves and the shrieking of harpies. These vocalists had all made the final cut, but that cut must have been made with a dull knife.

My ghost girlfriend Sheyenne and my lawyer partner Robin Deyer also watched the performance, fully supportive of the little vampire girl. At Chambeaux & Deyer Investigations, we were an extended family. Robin is the most dedicated firebrand lawyer in the Unnatural Quarter, fighting for the rights of monsters everywhere, and I'm undeniably the best zombie P.I. (because I don't have any competition).

The Banshee Tabernacle Choir performed in the vault of a large cathedral that had been revamped into a performance hall and community center. Across the floor of the echoing hall, rows of metal folding chairs held proud parents of all persuasions and species.

Watching from the metal folding chair next to me, Officer Toby McGoohan wore a blue patrolman's shirt, because he had to walk his beat as soon as the singing was over. Yes, we were all here for Alvina's recital.

The choir had two dozen members, all dressed in white shrouds designed by the group's founder, a loud banshee named Sheila. When Sheila had been forced to resign because her powerful voice kept shattering the cathedral's windows, she was replaced with a much calmer director, a troll named Sally Allan.

Sally was attractive enough for a female troll, which means she was not attractive at all. Her blocky reptilian face looked like a dinosaur sculpture that had rolled around in a rock tumbler. Her serrated ears reminded me of the fins of a largemouth bass. But she had perfect pitch and a good attitude toward the young singers, and they liked her as their choir director.

As the performance continued, Sally strolled around the fringes like a mother hen, raising scaled hands to conduct her protégés, building their music into a battering ram of notes, some of which actually belonged together. Harmony went by the wayside in favor of enthusiasm.

I had attended some of Alvina's practice sessions, so I was prepared for what I heard, but my joy was not diminished. Alvina's smile said it all. She was cute as a button with her blond hair in pigtails, her blue eyes wide and sparkling. In her face, I could see hints of her mother Rhonda, back when I had considered Rhonda beautiful. But Alvina was Alvina, and I loved the kid with all my heart.

She got the rest of her good looks from me, a ruggedly handsome detective. I may be a zombie, but I'm well-preserved. I know the kid gets her intellect and insight from me, although McGoo insists otherwise.

He's my best human friend, and it's also possible he's the kid's biological father. About a fifty-fifty chance, we figure. He and I each had a fling with Rhonda at about the same time, so we'll never know, since paternity tests don't work on the DNA of a human who was turned into a vampire.

It doesn't matter to us, because we're both Alvina's half-daddies, and two half-daddies adds up to more than one Rhonda—who is, thank God, long out of the picture.

In a lull between verses, McGoo said in a loud whisper, "Al can certainly sing, Shamble. She gets it from me."

The chorale built up louder and louder to the point where it almost worked, many unnatural voices along with a handful of human boys and girls, who got along just fine with the monster children and sang their hearts out. Surrounded by monsters, the human parents looked considerably less comfortable than their kids.

The shrouded choir stood directly beneath the cathedral's bell tower. As the singing got louder, though, the choir director lifted her jagged earflaps, disturbed by something. She turned about, narrowing her slitted eyes toward the audience on the folding chairs. She stalked around the edge of the performance area, as if ready to accuse the gathered parents. I figured someone must have forgotten to turn off their cellphone.

Sally's nostrils flared as she prowled past the lines of chairs. Even as the choir continued, she grumbled deep in her wattled throat, "What's that noise? That high squeaking noise? Surely you hear it?"

I couldn't hear anything but the caterwauling of the choir. She marched off.

The music grew even more dramatic, building toward a loud finale, and the powerful operatic tune sounded familiar. It was from a movie soundtrack—several soundtracks in fact, always used during epic battles with huge armies clashing, knights riding in on horses or starships colliding.

"I know that from a movie," I whispered to Sheyenne, trying to impress her with my knowledge about musical compositions.

She turned her glowing face toward me, her full lips curved in a smile. "That's from *Carmina Burana*, Beaux. A classic cantata by Carl Orff."

"Orff?" I asked.

The werewolf singers howled louder.

My forehead wrinkled enough to pucker the bullet hole there. "I don't think I ever saw a movie called *Carmina Burana*."

The dramatic music was a perfect accompaniment for how upset the choir director was. Even more agitated, Sally turned her attention up to the vaulted ceiling and the open belfry high overhead.

When the chorale was over, the choir members caught their breath with a sigh and a giggle. One of the werewolf boys howled in triumph, along with a few shrieking banshees and moaning ghosts. Robin, McGoo, Sheyenne, and I joined in the thunderous applause.

McGoo's freckled face was flushed with adoration. "Al has a good set of lungs and the voice of an angel."

"She gets it from me," I said.

He scoffed. "You, with any musical talent? I don't think so. You should hear me sing in the shower."

"No," I said, "I shouldn't."

Clearly distracted, Sally stepped in front of the choir and raised her hands for silence. "Next, we have a fine a cappella performance of another classic work from our specially trained singing group."

Alvina came forward with a werewolf boy, a teenage vampire boy, a wavering ghost, a thin zombie, and two human girls about twelve years old.

I used it as an excuse to applaud again.

The choir director continued, "This song will be immediately followed by our tentacle dance troupe."

One section of the audience hooted and cheered and burbled, clearly the parents (or at least the generative spores) of the tentacle creatures.

When she saw they were ready, Sally gestured to Alvina and her companions. "And now, our a cappella performance of ... the 'Hokey Pokey.'"

Alvina looked right at us, then started off with her bright voice, before she was joined by the vampire boy, the ghost, and then the rest of the group. "You put your right hand in. You put your right hand out."

The Banshee Tabernacle Choir's select singers harmonized wonderfully.

"And you shake it all about!"

The zombie sang a deep bass, and the werewolf growled a constant undercurrent that somehow worked.

Though I was captivated by their performance, I noticed Sally slipping away toward the staircase that led to the high bell tower. Her fanlike ears were erect like satellite dishes looking for a signal, as if she heard something no one else could.

Alvina and her a cappella troupe knew what they were doing, though, and they held their own. Beside me, McGoo sang along with the words.

"And that's what it's all about!"

They finished the "Hokey Pokey," drowned out by appreciative cheering, and moved right into an a cappella version of "Monster Mash," another crowd pleaser.

When they finished, Alvina and her group bowed in their shrouds, but looked around uncertainly because the choir director hadn't returned from her determined errand up in the belfry.

Fortunately, Sally's assistant, a supple salamander woman, stepped into the awkward silence to introduce the tentacle dancers.

Five spotted, gelatinous critters scuttled onto the cathedral floor, flopping across the stone tiles. The salamander troupe master set out a boom box, then waved her soft, fleshy hands. "Presenting the Eldritch Dance Crew!"

The little amoeba-like creatures had a variety of stretchy, floppy limbs. Some reminded me of octopuses squashed under a truck tire, and others were like sunny-side-up eggs with whiplike extensions. They waved and twirled colorful ribbons on sticks.

The salamander troupe master switched on the boom box, releasing the thrumming beat of techno dance music. The tentacle creatures thrashed and flailed, snapping their ribbons like colorful whips in the air. It was like an explosion in a confetti factory, but fun nevertheless. McGoo swayed to the boom box beat.

Standing with the rest of the choir, Alvina kept her attention riveted on the performance. No one seemed to notice that the troll choir director hadn't made a reappearance.

And then she did, in a big way.

Serendipitously timed as a grand finale to the tentacle dance, the huge bronze bell in the tower rang with an explosive *BONG!* The concussion resounded throughout the cathedral.

The Eldritch Dance Crew waved their ribbons and pranced in a circle under the bell tower.

As the clamor of the bell diminished, it was replaced with a scream as the choir director plummeted down from the high belfry. Her oddly musical yell stopped as abruptly as a cymbal clash when she hit the wide floor with a splat— right in the middle of the Eldritch Dancers, squishing two of the tentacle creatures in a grand finale.

The protoplasmic creatures squirmed, reshaped themselves, and slithered away.

Sally did not.

Everyone else started screaming.

CHAPTER 2

The Unnatural Quarter is filled with so many strange and unexpected happenings that you get used to them after a while. Still, a troll choir director falling from a belfry is not an everyday occurrence.

The monsters in the audience panicked, and the human parents lurched away so fast they knocked over their metal folding chairs. The resulting clatter startled them even more.

The audience bolted from the splatter pattern. Many rushed to rescue the shrouded choir members. Eldritch tentacle parents squiggled forward to wrap appendages around their offspring, covering them in protective ooze.

Sheyenne and I raced to intercept Alvina, who stood in shock. Her innocent smile was gone, her charming recital ruined. Robin shouted for the audience not to panic, but they did not follow instructions well.

McGoo turned around, surveying the cathedral for suspects. "We have to find out who did this, Shamble." He approached the body.

Taking Alvina's arm, I pulled her to Robin. "You and Sheyenne get her to safety."

"This sucks," Alvina said.

"There'll be other recitals, honey," Sheyenne said.

Robin hurried the girl away. "Your singing was beautiful, but all these screams might damage your hearing."

McGoo and I moved toward where Sally Allan was sprawled on the floor like a broken monster mannequin that had fallen on top of a bag full of raspberry jam. "Better call an ambulance," I said.

"Better call the coroner," he said.

"I was being optimistic."

He studied the victim, then looked up to the tower high overhead. "You think she just slipped and fell from way up there?"

"The bell could have startled her off the edge," I said, "but I don't believe in coincidences."

"I believe in a lot of crazy things since the Big Uneasy, but that is too much of a coincidence."

The Big Uneasy had occurred more than thirteen years ago, when a virgin librarian had cut her finger on a page of the original *Necronomicon* under a full moon during a rare alignment of planets. This truly cosmic event had returned all sorts of monsters and legendary creatures to the world. Thanks to a recent case, I now knew there was much more to the Big Uneasy than the public story, but those details didn't matter now. Unnaturals were here to stay, and they wanted to live their lives and be productive members of society. They were welcomed in the Unnatural Quarter.

But being hurled from a high belfry to disrupt a choir recital wasn't a welcome sign at all.

Standing next to the smashed troll body, I gazed up at the bell tower. I'd watched Sally slip away to climb the stairs, distracted by strange noises that only she heard. I nodded toward the belfry. "We have to go up there, McGoo."

He wiped a hand across his sweaty forehead. "I was

afraid you'd say that, Shamble." He usually wasn't reluctant to dive into a crime scene.

I reached into my sport coat and was reassured by my trusty .38. McGoo had his police special revolver and his police extra-special revolver loaded with silver bullets. "Don't worry, McGoo. Whoever's up there, we can take him."

He sighed. "No, Shamble. I was thinking about all those stairs."

We raced up the first flight of steps, then walked up the second flight, trudged up the third, and plodded up the fourth until we reached the summit of the bell tower.

The belfry was open to the air so the peals of the great bell could ring out across the Quarter, announcing the hour, or maybe a furniture sale from a paid sponsor. The bell was silent, but I could hear high-pitched squeaks and fluttering wings—not pigeons or other birds, but scores of bats, like a cloud of giant mosquitoes. They squeaked as they circled in terror, or maybe it was just a mating dance.

We moved forward, looking for suspects at the top of the tower. A walkway circled the entire belfry, with arched window openings to the outside air. A stone railing on the inside blocked the long fall to the cathedral floor below (though not well enough, as Sally Allan could attest). Feeling unsteady after climbing all those stairs, I gripped the waist-high rail to stabilize myself.

The lowering afternoon sun filled the belfry with shadows, offering places to hide. We both drew our weapons as we cautiously advanced. If a perp happened to be lurking up here, McGoo was panting too hard to give chase.

I spotted the dark demonic figure first, silhouetted

against the slanted light. He sat on one of the arched window ledges, facing outward. His large batlike wings were folded against his back, relaxed.

I raised my .38.

McGoo pointed his revolver and braced himself to fire. "Don't move. UQPD! Identify yourself!"

The figure didn't move, thus following the first half of McGoo's instructions. In fact, he didn't twitch, flinch, or even acknowledge our presence. He just kept staring at the view.

It was a large gargoyle on the ledge, his legs dangling out in open air.

"I said don't move!" McGoo shouted.

"He's not moving," I pointed out.

We approached cautiously. The gargoyle gazed out at the endless streets and rooftops of the Unnatural Quarter. He didn't even glance at us.

"Turn around, and come down from there!" I shouted, since I couldn't let McGoo hog all the intimidating lines for himself.

Still nothing.

We tiptoed closer. More bats squeaked around us, flitting closer and then flurrying away.

When at last we entered the gargoyle's peripheral vision, he swung his weathered gray-green face toward us, and his bright yellow eyes widened in surprise. His mouth had plenty of fangs, like any respectable gargoyle, but he didn't lunge at us or make any threatening moves. "Hello," he said in a rasping voice. "Didn't see you there."

McGoo kept his revolver extended. "I said freeze! We identified ourselves."

The gargoyle's brow furrowed as he concentrated on McGoo's lips moving. He shook his head and tapped his pointed ears. "Sorry, can't hear you."

I saw that he had hearing aids stuffed into each ear.

"Deaf as a post—spent too much time next to the loud bells. And these hearing aids are crap." He adjusted the controls until the earbuds emitted a thin squeal, and he quickly turned the volume off.

"We have some questions to ask you," I said.

McGoo stood beside me. "The obvious question being, did you throw the choir director to her death?"

The gargoyle shook his head. "Can't hear you, sorry."

McGoo took out a notepad and a pen from his pocket and scribbled, *What's your name?*

The gargoyle squinted, took the pad and wrote, *RUSSELL.*

My turn. I wrote, *Did you witness the murder? Did you have anything to do with it?*

Russell read the words two or three times and looked up at us. He spoke out loud. "What murder?"

Exasperated, McGoo took the pad back, writing, *Just now! The choir director fell to her death from up here.*

The gargoyle read the continuing dialogue and flipped the page for a clean sheet. He wrote with his clawed hands. *Sally? Oh no! I like when the choir performs. I can hear the music up here—or at least I can feel it.*

McGoo and I looked at each other, and I took the pad next. *Sally Allan came up here during the concert. Did you see her? Did you see anyone at all?*

Russell nodded slowly to himself and handed the pad back. "Don't need that. Yes, I saw her. She was looking for something, and I could tell she was annoyed. But I didn't talk to her—I can't hear, you know."

McGoo's nostrils flared. He wrote in bold letters, *Did you kill her?*

Russell seemed horrified. "No! I was just enjoying the fresh afternoon air. I like looking at the city from up here. I'm in my own world, a little slice of heaven."

I said aloud to McGoo, knowing the gargoyle couldn't hear me. "Apparently his little slice of heaven doesn't have murders in it."

Russell gazed out at the city again and flapped his batlike wings, upset.

I whispered unnecessarily to McGoo, "I don't think he did it."

"There's no one else up here, Shamble."

Police sirens wailed in the streets below, along with the coroner's wagon and an ambulance, which someone must have called for thoroughness.

McGoo pocketed his notebook. "Don't leave town, Russell. We'll need to ask you some more questions."

The gargoyle blinked at him. "What?"

McGoo pulled the pad back out and wrote it down.

Russell nodded. "Sure. I'm always here, taking in the view, feeding the bats."

I looked over the edge into the cathedral vault below, where Sally lay sprawled. On the scene, moving with frantic intensity, the coroner's squad of ghouls circled the body, taking photos, inspecting it from all angles. They obviously enjoyed their job.

One of the evidence-tech ghouls took out a pack of bright sidewalk chalk and demonstrated a flair for homicide investigation by using an array of colors, swapping one fat stick for another as he outlined the fallen body.

I turned away from the gargoyle and joined my BHF. "We better get down there, before they mess up the evidence."

McGoo sighed. "At least we're going *down* the stairs this time."

CHAPTER 3

Taking over the formal case for the UQ Police Department, McGoo managed the coroner ghoul techs, while my priority was to make sure Alvina, Sheyenne, and Robin were safe.

In the office, the kid hung up her choir shroud on the peg usually reserved for my fedora. Sally had been a supportive mentor, encouraging her to sing, boosting her self-confidence —not that my half-daughter needed any extra confidence.

Shaken, she hugged me, and I hugged her right back. I said, "I'll help McGoo solve the case, kid. We'll find out what happened. Promise."

Sheyenne joined the group air hug, then flitted into the kitchenette to make Alvina a cup of hot chocolate. There, she encountered the malicious graffiti invectives of the persistent black mold that grew on the walls. Short-tempered from what we had all been through that day, she snapped at the fungal stains, "That's enough from you! Your mother's spores wouldn't grow on cheese."

She drifted back out of the kitchen, stirring the hot chocolate.

Alvina accepted the mug and sipped contentedly, while she distracted herself with a workbook of homework assignments.

In her office, Robin poked among several legal briefs she

was working on, but I could tell she was upset. She had faced fierce rivals in many courtrooms. She had been insulted, threatened, and excoriated by opposing counsel, and she was usually unflappable. But Sally's death right in front of everyone was a different matter.

I explained about Russell the hearing-impaired gargoyle, whom McGoo would be interrogating down at the station. In her office, Robin looked up from her case paperwork. "Maybe I should go along and help. I'm fluent in GSL."

I noticed her documents were upside down, so she hadn't really been reading after all. "What's GSL?" I asked.

"Gargoyle sign language?" Alvina piped up.

"The G is more comprehensive than that," Robin said. "It includes goblins, gremlins, golems, and ghosts, in addition to gargoyles. I got certified, because I figured it might come in handy for certain clients, though I haven't had a chance to use it."

"Are there actually deaf ghosts?" I asked.

Sheyenne drifted close enough to give me an air kiss. "The world has many remarkable things, Beaux."

"I'll follow up with McGoo to see if they need any help at the station."

ANY DAY THAT STARTED OUT WITH A POSSIBLE MURDER, suicide, or terminal clumsiness was not going to end well (even if it included a charming a cappella performance of the "Hokey Pokey").

Naturally, I needed to collect my thoughts over a beer in the welcoming gloom of the Goblin Tavern, my usual watering hole. By unspoken agreement, or just plain force of habit, McGoo came there as well.

I found him on his barstool nursing a happy-hour pint. Another beer sat in front of my seat, and I was glad he had already ordered the first round. It's one of the many reasons he is my best human friend.

"Hey, Shamble," he said without enthusiasm.

"Hey, McGoo," I replied with an equal lack of excitement.

Normally, we would sink our teeth into cases like a gnashing, carnivorous horde, but this one was more personal. "How's Al doing?" he asked.

"Kids are resilient, and vampires are resilient, so vampire kids are doubly resilient." I took a sip of my beer, then wiped the foam from my cold, gray lips. "Alvina's already been through so much and bounced back."

Nodding, both of us said in the same breath, "Rhonda."

Lubricated by several more gulps of beer, McGoo filled me in on the further questioning of Russell, using notepads and a GSL interpreter who worked for the UQPD.

"His hearing aids functioned better in the station," McGoo said. "The squeaky feedback was gone."

"Did he give you any clues about Sally's fall?"

McGoo shrugged. "Nothing to go on. We released him and told him to keep in touch. It's a big belfry, and he's not very aware of his surroundings when he sits next to the bells. There could have been a bachelorette party up there, and he probably wouldn't have noticed."

I tilted my fedora to cover the bullet hole. "So, you're pursuing that bachelorette party angle then?"

"Funny, Shamble." He snorted and finished his beer.

"I've got a better one for you—a Chupacabra walks into a doctor's office, and the doctor asks, 'Why the long face?'"

At least the joke didn't require me to respond.

When it was time for another round, we had trouble getting Francine's attention. The salty old bartender usually had a mother hen's awareness of her customers, ready to keep them refreshed and happy, but she was preoccupied.

Francine had been through much unpleasantness in her life, with multiple unhappy marriages. She had weathered them all, and the weather definitely showed on her face. Tonight, though, she had applied bright lipstick and even eyeshadow.

We all knew the reason for the makeup, as well as her distraction.

A dapper old vampire was sweet on Francine, making polite and complimentary conversation, chuckling at her jokes. Night after night, he sat on a barstool, nursing his drink, and they would chat whenever she wasn't busy. He had slicked-back iron-gray hair, features that might once have been dashingly handsome, but the expiration date had long since passed. Nonetheless, he still came across as suave, maybe because of the intrinsic glamour that vampires possessed.

His real name was César Marici, but McGoo and I had nicknamed him One Fang, because his left canine remained a normal human tooth, noticeably shorter than his other fang. Francine often talked about him when he wasn't around, and we could see she adored him. The dapper vampire was well past his prime, but Francine was no spring vulture either, and they made a connection.

Knowing the bartender had been unlucky in love so

many times, I was surprised she was willing to try it again. What did psychologists say? The definition of true romance is banging your head against someone else's heart again and again and expecting a different result.

César finished his scotch and rattled the ice cubes around in his glass. Francine refreshed his drink, and as soon as she finished serving One Fang, McGoo raised his empty pint glass and I raised mine, trying to snag her attention while we had the chance. Several other bar patrons did the same.

Francine dashed about, pouring and mixing drinks like a whirlwind. She was always efficient, but this was downright impressive. Clearly, she wanted to get back to her casual chit-chat.

She brought us two foam-topped beers. "Here you go, gents," she said in her raspy, cigarette-damaged voice. "Put them on the same tab as before?"

McGoo nudged me. "No, add all four of them to his. I'm on a cop's salary."

I snorted in defeat. "At least you get a salary! My line of business isn't as reliable. The cases don't solve themselves." I let out a sigh. "And the clients don't always pay the bills."

"You need an enforcer, Shamble—some big, snaggletooth giant to deliver late notices. That would be effective."

An enforcer? I recalled a group of blood beasts on whom I had served eviction notices not too long ago. I'd heard they were looking for work.... "I already have Sheyenne for that. I try to maintain a cordial relationship until things really get out of hand."

Just then things did start to get out of hand when four rowdy gremlins in grease-stained mechanic's overalls bustled into the tavern. They chittered, joshed, and punched one another, a group of friends just off work. One was Wrex, the owner of the repair shop that had serviced Robin's ailing Pro Bono Mobile. The other gremlins were his mechanics Winkin, Blinkin, and Todd. The four gremlins jostled up to the bar and hopped onto high stools not far from me and McGoo.

After taking their seats, they joked and poked at a hairy dark object the size of a small grapefruit, which was clipped by a carabiner to Wrex's overalls.

I leaned over, curious to see the thing. It was a small, wrinkled head with discolored flesh. The rubbery lips twisted in a snarl as it opened and closed its mouth.

Startled, I said, "That's a head!" thus proving my well-honed detective abilities.

Wrex grinned at me with his needle-sharp teeth. "A *shrunken* head! A shrunken zombie head, special edition."

"Shut up," said the head.

Winkin, Blinkin, and Todd giggled. "It's so cute!"

Wrex's face lit up with recognition. "Hey, you're Mr. Shamble. Good to see you again." He lowered his voice. "How's the car? Satisfied with our wrexing?"

Robin's battered old Ford Maverick had finally given up its last gasp a few months ago, forcing us to take it to Wrex's Auto Repairs. The gremlins had done more harm than good, "installing damage," but in the end we'd gotten our vehicle back, with certain improvements made to the engine, added power as well as increased noise (at no extra charge).

"It's still functioning," I answered with a hint of relief. "The accelerator is a little touchy."

"Those engines can really roar! Good for a high-powered chase, I bet!" Wrex said.

"But bad for parallel parking. And the gas mileage is about half what it used to be."

"I can install an extra tank to make up for it," Wrex offered. "Minimal charge."

But I declined. We only drove the vehicle around the Unnatural Quarter, and I preferred to walk anyway, since I needed to exercise my stiff limbs.

"Brains!" said the zombie shrunken head. "Tiny brains!"

One of the gremlins—Winkin, I think—stuck his finger close to the shrunken head's mouth. It gnashed and snapped, but Winkin yanked his finger away, giggling.

"Where'd you get that thing?" McGoo asked. "Never seen anything like it."

"At the auto repair shop," said the surly little head. "Lots of gremlins there."

Wrex flicked the side of the miniature head with his finger. "They're collectibles, taking the Quarter by storm. Many people want them. I got mine from a street vendor—it's like a pet."

Francine came to take the gremlins' drink order and spotted the shrunken head. Her face lit up. "That's grotesque and bizarre! Just the right kind of knickknack."

"Kris!" growled the head, apparently mistaking Francine.

Other bar patrons came to have a look at the shrunken head. Wrex fondled it, bobbing it up and down on the carabiner until the little head said, "I'm dizzy...."

Even César joined the group, maybe to be closer to

Francine. He seemed more interested in her delighted expression than in the shrunken head itself.

"Isn't it adorable?" she asked him.

"Most adorable shrunken head I've ever seen," One Fang agreed. "I didn't know you wanted a pet."

I finished my second beer, while McGoo was still nursing his. I got serious again, thinking of the choir director's fatal plunge. I had seen enough death myself— including my own—but this one presented a mystery to solve, and I owed it to Alvina.

I swung down from the barstool. "Let me know if you learn anything more about the case, McGoo. I'll help if I can."

Nearby, Wrex and Todd were feeding peanuts to the shrunken zombie head. It seemed voraciously hungry, but when it chewed, broken peanut debris fell from the bottom of its decapitated neck.

I knew Alvina wanted a pet, but this demonstrated one of the main reasons I hadn't said yes: owners always had to clean up their pets' messes.

CHAPTER 4

For a little guy, the imp made a grand entrance. The office door popped open with a burst of wind, demonstrating a flair for showmanship magic that imps are known to possess. "I'll bet you can help me!"

Sheyenne floated up from the receptionist's desk and put on her "meet the new client" face. "We're always glad to assist in either legal or investigative matters. Dan or Robin would be happy to discuss your case."

"I wager they will be!" With an offhanded wave behind him, the imp closed the door with a nudge of wind.

He had bright green skin and stood barely three feet high. His head was bald, but his chin sported a goatee plaited in a thin braid. He wore a blue shirt, tiny blue jeans that looked as if they'd been pulled off of a Chucky doll, and pointed satin shoes. A stained grocer's apron covered the front of his outfit.

I went to greet the visitor, since Robin was in her office preparing to present a legal brief for a tombstone misspelling lawsuit. A very grave case: When rising from the Greenlawn Cemetery, a zombie had discovered to his horror that his name was incorrectly and embarrassingly engraved into the granite headstone. EAR L. THROMBINS. Apparently, none of his family members had bothered to proofread. Now the indignant Earl (rather than Ear L.) wanted the typo rectified, even though he was no longer using the plot or the headstone.

That meant I was taking point with the impish potential client. I extended my hand and offered him a cold smile. (Due to my body temperature, my smiles are always cold.) Clients who seek us out are desperate in one way or another, and I try to put them at ease before we dig down into the craziness that lies ahead.

"Pleased to meet you, sir. I'm Dan Chambeaux, private investigator." I paused, recognizing him. "Haven't I seen you at the grocery store?"

The imp scuttled forward and extended his little green hand. "Yes! My name is Barney. My brother and I own the neighborhood grocery, one of the last brother-and-brother general stores in the Quarter."

"So, what seems to be the problem?" It had been a slow month for cases, and I was eager to start solving something, especially from a paying client—which would keep Sheyenne happy, too.

Barney said with a groan of dismay, "I didn't know where else to go! I'm being cheated, and it's cost me a pretty penny."

"I'll bet," I said.

"No—I bet! I bet too much. It's the bane of my existence."

I gestured him toward my office door. "Come in and have a seat, so we can discuss further."

Normally, we'd use the conference room for an intake meeting, but Alvina was in the middle of a home-school project that took up the whole table. Her homework was supervised by me, Sheyenne, McGoo, Robin, or anyone else who could help grade her work. Ever since the vampire girl had moved in with us, she'd been homeschooled, although we were starting to doubt that was the best choice for her.

The old desk in my dingy office was piled high with manila folders—cases to ponder, bills to wrap up, a collection of yellowed clippings. The imp followed me with frenetic impatience.

I moved files from the seat of the extra chair, but Barney was much too short-statured to sit comfortably, so I found two thick phone books to use as a booster seat. I was proud of the discovery, because nobody used phone books anymore, but I'm old school in a lot of ways.

The imp hopped onto the stack, sitting much taller now, though his braided chin beard still barely cleared the desk.

I slumped into my chair and casually picked up the World's Greatest Detective mug. Scum and brown coffee stains covered the bottom of the mug. I'd been averse to brewing fresh coffee recently because I was intimidated by the boorish black mold on the wall.

With perfect timing, Sheyenne flitted in and snatched the cup out of my hands. "Could I get you something to drink, Mr. Barney?"

"Bourbon?" The imp glanced at me. "You're a gumshoe, a noir private eye. You must have bourbon?"

"I play against type. I'm a beer guy."

"Oh." Disappointed, Barney tugged on his braided beard. "Do you have a beer, then?"

"Not in the office."

"I guess coffee will do," he said.

"I'll brew a fresh pot." My ghost girlfriend had no fear of dueling with the mold. She flitted away.

Bending my stiff arms, I placed my elbows on the desktop, leaning forward to face the little imp. "So, Barney, who's cheating you? I can bring in my lawyer partner, if we need legal advice. Tell me the whole story."

"I need a detective to expose a crime! I keep losing at the nightmare races. There is something fishy going on at the Underground Downs."

I wasn't sure I understood the problem. "Plenty of people lose at the nightmare races. It's the nature of gambling."

"I bet there's more to it!" The imp wiggled on the stack of phone books. "My bookie is taking advantage of me. He's rigging the races, somehow. You know how many crashes and accidents happen on the track? When I confronted my bookie after losing another wad of money, he said that there are winners and losers—and I'm just a loser."

He let out an indignant huff and crossed his little arms over his chest. "But he was also supportive and encouraging, because he doesn't want to lose a good sucker—I mean, a good customer."

I shook my head. "You'll need to give me more than that. Betting is never a sure thing."

Barney's green skin darkened. "The only sure thing is that I'll lose, again and again! I look at the odds. Sometimes I take big risks, and sometimes I'm really conservative. Every time the result is the same. My horse loses—usually because of unforeseen circumstances."

"Unforeseen circumstances? Don't the nightmares just run around in a circle, and whichever one goes around the circle fastest wins the race?"

Barney was impressed with my deep understanding of

the sport. "Look at the track's track record. The monster horses swerve into the wrong lanes way too often, or they trip, or buck their jockeys, or have some other accident. No matter what, I lose all my money every time." When he huffed again, a breeze stirred the papers in my office. "And my bookie keeps it all."

"Sounds like you need a different bookie," I said. "Or a different strategy ... or maybe a different sport. Have you tried Fantasy Football?"

"My bookie has other clients, too, and they all lose! Somehow, it's rigged. He's cheating, I know it—and I want you to investigate how."

I advised him that bookies were not technically legal, even in the Quarter. But I had seen cockatrice fighting rings and golem mud wrestling, so nightmare races didn't seem that much out of line. "It might be hard to prove, Barney, but I could definitely look into the matter."

Sullen, the imp tugged at his grocer's apron. "My brother tells me to stop gambling, but I know I've got one big win in me! I could never try another sport. I grew up around the races. I love the animals." He let out a wistful sigh. "There's nothing so majestic as a coal-black nightmare, or the thunder of the hooves on the track, the smell of hay and fresh manure in the stables."

Sheyenne breezed into the office, and I moved the folders aside so she could set down two fresh cups of piping-hot coffee. I took a sip, which scalded even my numb gray lips. Barney gulped it down like a shot of tequila, and steam wafted out of his ears.

The imp would not be distracted from his nostalgic musings. "My dream was to be a jockey, not a grocer! I tried and tried, but I never made the cut. I failed because of my deformity." His shoulders sagged.

Sheyenne paused at the office doorway. "Oh? What deformity?"

Barney raised both little green hands, exasperated. "Why, I'm too *tall*, of course!"

"Ah," I said. "It was hard to tell with the extra boost from the telephone books." I reached across the desk to shake his hand. "I promise I'll look into any discrepancies in the nightmare races. If there's something to this, I'll find it."

"I wager you will." Barney wrote down his bookie's address, then stormed away with a satisfying rustle of wind that scattered junk mail and telephone message slips from Sheyenne's desk. The office door swung shut, but the imp politely buffered it so that it simply clicked into the jamb.

I cracked my knuckles—then worked my fingers back into place—ready to get started on a new case.

CHAPTER 5

When Sheyenne caught the angry black kitchen mold teaching Alvina how to spell—with entirely inappropriate words—she'd had enough. "I'm going to wash that mold's mouth out with bleach!"

The vampire girl followed her into my office with an innocent and curious expression. "But what do those words mean? I like to learn new things."

"That is not something I intend to teach you, honey," Sheyenne said.

Alvina sounded disappointed. "Fine, I'll just look them up on the internet."

I glanced at the files on my desk, but knew I would find no answer to the problem there. Sheyenne put her ectoplasmic hands on her shapely hips. "Beaux, what are we going to do?" I could see the red tinge to her glow.

"Bleach sounds like a good start." Sheyenne had already tried everything to eradicate the surly fungus, but she could always find more caustic substances. Renfeld, the building super, had ignored our repeated requests to clear out the mold with fresh drywall.

Sheyenne continued, "Think of all the horrible conspiracy theories and misinformation that fungus is teaching her! The rot will get into her brain. She needs real instruction."

Alvina batted her eyelashes.

I knew what Sheyenne was going to bring up. I said, "We're each taking our turn homeschooling the kid. I like spending time with her." I winked at Alvina, and she winked back.

"So do I, and so does Robin. Even McGoo does his part," Sheyenne said. "But Alvina needs to be with unnatural children her own age, or at least her own level of maturity."

"I want to have more friends," said my half-daughter. "That wouldn't suck. And there's extra credit classes, special lecturers, and all kinds of subjects!"

"She'd kick their butts on the grading curve," I said. "Not only can she sing, she gets her brains from me."

Sheyenne gave me a doubtful expression.

Robin had researched local homeschooling recommendations, curricula suggestions, and obtained all the highest-rated textbooks: readers' guides, workbooks, syllabi, teacher handbooks. As a team, we had guided Alvina through mad-scientist chemistry experiments and the politics of evil geniuses. We studied the history and repercussions of the Big Uneasy, which had occurred after the kid was born; she'd never known a world without all the monsters unleashed.

For the past two weeks, Alvina had taken over our conference room with arts and crafts materials. For sociology class, she was making a diorama of an ancient culture, using putty, modeling clay, popsicle sticks, cardboard, pipe cleaners, and construction paper to recreate Ancient Egypt. It was ambitious and downright cool, and when she finished,

I promised to take her to the Natural History Museum so she could show it to Ramen Ho-Tep, a former pharaoh of Ancient Egypt (who never let anyone forget the fact) and current docent in the Egyptian wing. Alvina had certainly earned an A, but the accomplishment seemed hollow if she had no other student projects to compare it to. Sheyenne was searching for upcoming student science and history faires, where Alvina could exhibit it.

"I want the kid to meet her greatest potential. I can only imagine the great things she'll do." She had already overcome many challenges in her younger years, before McGoo or I even knew that one of us had a daughter.

"I want to go to a real school," Alvina said. "I've heard it doesn't suck, and the homework is going to be so easy."

"We're way ahead of you," I said. "Robin's already requested the paperwork to get you enrolled."

Serious, Alvina crossed her arms over her chest. "But we can't let classwork interfere with me helping you solve cases."

"Chambeaux and Deyer couldn't do it without you," I said.

The vampire girl beamed. "And I should get extra credit for each major criminal we put away."

As if on cue, McGoo strolled into the offices, as he often did when he was bored with his beat. "Hey, Shamble." He greeted Sheyenne and then Robin as she emerged from her office carrying a folder and a pile of paperwork. He saved his biggest grin for our half-daughter. "Hey Al! You always brighten my day."

"I usually sleep in a box during the day," she said, "but they're letting me stay up late."

"Sounds like questionable parenting to me." He gave me a teasing glance. "I always make sure you get into your air conditioner box by sunup."

She giggled. "No you don't."

"Good thing you're here, Officer McGoohan." Robin stepped forward with her folder. "I finished some forms, and we need your signature."

"What, am I cutting Shamble out of my will?"

I groaned. "You actually have enough possessions that you need a will?"

"Even thirteen years after the Big Uneasy, the probate system is still a mess," Robin explained. "Everything becomes muddled when the decedent returns from the grave. Good thing Dan didn't have any heirs contesting his estate."

"I dug myself up before anyone had time to file paperwork," I said.

"Others aren't so speedy about it," Robin said. "I've seen cases where zombies are so rotted by the time they rise from the grave, their dental records and fingerprints are all messed up, and the beneficiaries have already spent the estate money. Then it's only their word against a slurring zombie."

"I'm leaving my fortune to Alvina anyway," I said. "There, you all witnessed it. No need for paperwork."

Robin narrowed her eyes. A lawyer never wanted to hear that paperwork was unnecessary.

"Does that mean I get your coffee cup after you're dead?" Alvina said, making a move toward my office.

"Not so fast, kid. I can get you one of your own."

McGoo turned to Robin. "But seriously, folks—what sort of legal paperwork do you have for me?"

Robin smiled as she revealed her surprise. "This young lady has just been accepted into Nosferatu Academy! I filed the documents last week, and I received approval. It just needs parental signatures." She extended the paper to McGoo.

He lowered his voice and looked around warily. "Does that mean we have to find Rhonda?"

Robin shook her head. "You two are her legal guardians now. That's all we need. The school is thrilled to have Alvina as a student, especially after I made the case for her." Nobody wanted to stand in the way of my firebrand partner.

Alvina blinked in disbelief. "I'm really going to school? That doesn't suck at all."

Robin continued, "Nosferatu Academy is a well-respected institution with a broad advanced curriculum that caters to all sorts of unnaturals, particularly exceptionally gifted students like Alvina. They even have a special-education unit for humans, though there aren't many of them in the student body."

"They're probably afraid they might become actual student bodies," McGoo said.

Robin had him sign the bottom of the completed form, then handed it to me. As I picked up a pen with my stiff fingers, she said, "Student safety is paramount, and Nosferatu Academy has strict standards. The educational environment is a pressure cooker with so many different monsters studying for exams, feeling the stress of term papers and blood tests. For that reason, before Alvina can attend classes, they require her to have a full evaluation from a licensed therapist."

"I get to go to therapy!" Alvina cheered. "I know people who've gone to therapy. It sounds like fun."

McGoo was defensive. "There's nothing wrong with our little girl."

"Just an assessment," Robin said. "Nosferatu Academy is conscious of the potential risks in having a student body that combines all different types and temperaments of unnatural children. Many unnaturals have long-standing racial enmities, and ADHD is rampant among young monsters— Attention Deficit Horrific Disorder."

"The kid will pass with flying colors," I said. "She'll charm the pants off any therapist."

I paused to consider the situation, though. Not only had Alvina just seen the choir director fall to her death, she was dealing with the typical problems of a maladjusted kid who was turned into a vampire at age ten. I didn't think it was a bad idea for her to have a session or two with a qualified shrink.

"If Al is seeing a therapist, then I'm going along as her half-daddy," McGoo said.

"Two halves make a whole. We'll both go," I said.

CHAPTER 6

Using her mad skills dealing with phone trees and voicemail, Sheyenne secured the next available appointment with unnatural therapist, Dr. Eva Schrank—in less than a week. To a kid eager to start school, it sounded like an eternity, but I explained to Alvina that official paperwork moves more slowly than even a shambling zombie.

That evening, as usual, I went to the Goblin Tavern. The cases don't solve themselves, but conversation and commiseration with my BHF can lead to unexpected connections. Then again, sometimes it's nice just hanging out and having a beer.

As we sat on our usual barstools, McGoo filled me in on his investigation of Sally Allan's death—which didn't take long, because he hadn't made any progress. For my part, I told him about my new imp client and his suspicions that a bookie was manipulating the nightmare races.

"I always wanted to go see the races," McGoo said. "I admire horses ... maybe because I'm such a *stable* person."

"Ugh," I said instead of laughing. "That was like taking a bite out of a big horse apple."

Wrex and his three gremlin mechanics sat at the bar drinking brewskis, clinking bottles together, and playing with

Wrex's grotesque shrunken head. The head snarled back, "Die! Die! You'll all die!"

One Fang was at the bar again. In fact, I couldn't remember the last evening he hadn't been there. Overly attentive, Francine kept his scotch properly filled, although he nursed the drink for an incredibly long time. César (I had to keep reminding myself to use his real name) seemed a little nervous and kept looking at his watch.

I elbowed McGoo. "What do you think is going on with One Fang? He's squirming like his underwear is too tight."

The dapper vampire glanced at his watch yet again. Francine talked with him, but for once she didn't have his complete attention. I took the opportunity to signal her for another round of beers.

The older gentleman had a paternal aura, as if he drew his glamour from a Norman Rockwell painting of a friendly doctor treating a freckle-faced kid. While Francine poured us two more pints, César looked at the tavern door and brightened when the door opened. He rose from his barstool.

A pale, gray-skinned young banshee entered. Moist black hair, stringy and tangled, drooped down the side of her face. She had a long jaw and hollows under her eyes. Her garments were damp and tattered—the usual outfit of a banshee—and she raised thin, skeletal arms.

Her gloomy appearance did not seem the sort to inspire a happy welcome, but One Fang was delighted to see her. "Here we are!" He raised his voice. "Hello? Everybody! May I have your attention?"

Francine gave him a curious look.

He smiled to show his one long fang as well as the shorter human one. "Francine, my dear, I know how you love unusual and memorable things, and I have something special to show how much I adore and appreciate you."

The tavern patrons fell into a hush. Francine seemed mortally embarrassed, but her lips curled in a small smile. "What are you doing, César?"

The old vampire gestured toward the banshee, who glided forward and tilted her chin up. Her depthless black eyes were filled with never-forgotten pain, as well as a repertoire of showtunes.

César said, "This is Sheila, my dear—from the banshee singing telegram service, with a special gift from me to you."

McGoo leaned closer to me and whispered, "That's *the* Sheila, the first choir director before Sally!"

"That didn't turn out well." I stifled a groan. "Now she's got a singing telegram service?"

The banshee spread her gaunt arms, and her wet, tattered garments rippled as she twirled. She tossed her stringy hair back and opened her mouth. In a warbly and grating voice, she said, "This is for Francine, with love."

Bewildered, the bartender let out a shy giggle. César seemed pleased by her reaction to his romantic gesture.

Then Sheila began to sing.

After sucking in an audible lungful of air, the banshee crooned deep notes that ascended the scale into drawn-out words, "Only You." She launched into a full-throated, full-volume rendition of the 1955 hit from the Platters.

César beamed—until the sonic waves hit him and knocked him back a step. The notes rose and wailed, piercing and vibrating.

McGoo slapped his hands over his ears. Francine staggered away.

Wrex and the gremlins ducked down from their barstools and crawled under the bar as if an air-raid siren had gone off.

Sheila was fully into her song now, giving it her all. Some of the werewolves in the tavern started howling to accompany her song, but the banshee drowned out their caterwauling.

I plugged my fingers in my ears, but the music vibrated through the hole in my forehead until it gave me a migraine.

When Sheila reached the song's crescendo, numerous liquor bottles burst behind the bar. The low mirror cracked, then shattered. The row of cheap vodka bottles broke first, followed by the mid-range alcohol. Finally all of the ornate and expensive bottles of top-shelf booze exploded. Shards flew in all directions, as if Sheila was using the bottles for musical target practice.

Covering her ears, Francine threw herself to the sticky floor in order to dodge flying glass. My pint shattered, and I groaned at the waste of good beer. McGoo was in the middle of gulping his own drink when the glass broke in his hand.

When the singing telegram was finally over, we were all half deaf. Leftover shreds of notes resounded in the air, accompanied by tinkling shards and dripping alcohol.

Sheila bowed. "Thank you very much."

Devastated, One Fang held onto his barstool, weak kneed.

Francine got back to her feet, her expression shifting from annoyance to outright anger. She whirled on her would-be suitor. "César, what have you done? Look at all the damage!" She groaned in dismay at the jagged remnants of bottles from top shelf to bottom shelf, all the smashed drinks and glasses along the bar. Even the pints and tumblers in the little dishwasher beneath the bar had broken.

"I ... I wanted to do something special for you, Francine," he said.

"Special? Like a bull in a china shop!"

"I didn't mean for this—"

"You didn't think it through! You're too impulsive, César. What did you imagine would happen if you brought in a banshee singing telegram?"

"But ... it seemed quirky and unusual. I was sure you'd like it."

"Ask me how much I like it after I spend five hours cleaning up this mess!" She surveyed the ruined bar and hung her head. "Go! Get out of here." She waved her hand and turned her back on him in disgust. "Everybody out! The Goblin Tavern is closed for the rest of the evening." Francine grabbed a broom, exasperated to see the wreckage across the floor.

"I wouldn't want to be in One Fang's coffin tonight," McGoo muttered. Together, we backed away.

I shook my head. "Nothing says 'romantic' like an extravagant but ill-advised gesture."

Hearing me, César perked up. "Yes, exactly!"

Wrex and his three gremlins scuttled along the bar, trying to get Francine's attention. "Hey, is this *free* broken glass? We'll take some of it off your hands."

"Out!" Francine shouted. "All of you, out!" She furiously started sweeping up the smashed bottles. "I need to be alone right now."

One Fang lost no time darting out the door and disappearing into the night.

CHAPTER 7

Barney avoided giving me his bookie's name, but I had the address, a small office on the top floor of a rundown three-story building. Considering the sketchiness of the profession, it was possible the bookie didn't want to spread his name around.

As soon as I entered his unmarked office door, I discovered the real reason, an unusual reason.

"I'm Batman," said the creature.

And he was. Literally.

His voice was a high annoying squeak, but the cramped office emphasized the fact that he was huge. And a bat. The bookie's broad shoulders were covered with bristly brown fur. He wore a vest with pockets, tailored to accommodate his dark leathery wings. His face was sharp, as were his long teeth. His beady eyes were black beneath an incongruous green accountant's visor, as if to shield his eyes from unpleasant numbers. His ears were large echo scoops, the better to funnel sound.

"You're Batman?" I asked.

He sat behind a rickety desk cluttered with newspapers folded to the racing section. Multiple lines were circled in red or scribbled out in black. Receipts were impaled on a sharp spindle on the corner.

"Yes—Batman." He leaned forward, and I could hear the

squeak of nails and loose wood in addition to the squeak of his voice. "But I can't use the name publicly." He paused to stress the importance of his words. "Trademark issues."

"I can believe that. DC Comics protects their trademarks very vigorously."

"As you can see, though"—he raised his arms, which were connected to the leathery membrane of his wings, almost in a parody of a caped crusader costume—"it's a true statement. I am a bizarre hybrid created by some aftereffect of the Big Uneasy."

I removed my fedora and stepped into the cramped office. "The Big Uneasy caused a lot of decidedly strange things." The obvious ones were werewolves, vampires, ghosts, and zombies—like me—but the human imagination had concocted innumerable things that went bump in the night, including oddball mixes like the bookie in front of me. "I think they're called mashups."

"Monster mashups," answered the not-officially-Batman. "Avoiding trademark infringement, I was going to call myself Man-Bat instead, because that also fits perfectly." He opened his mouth to show the needlelike fangs. He inhaled through a smashed nose that only the spouse of a vampire bat could love.

"Nice thought, but you'd get in trouble for that, too," I said. "The name Man-Bat is also trademarked. A lesser character—in fact, he looks a bit like you—but that name's already taken."

Fortunately, my lawyer partner had given me a solid grounding in subtleties of the law. And I used to read a lot of comics.

The bookie's leathery wings and arms sagged. "I know.

It's a real identity crisis for me—DC has all variations covered, including Batgirl and Batwoman. But I found a loophole."

His laugh came out as a shriek that felt like a screwdriver stabbing my ears. I never wanted to hear an argument between this guy and Sheila, the banshee singer. He stood from his desk and rose to his full height, which showed just how fearsome and intimidating he could be. "I am *BatGN!*" He lowered his voice. "For Gender Neutral."

"Glad we finally got that resolved." I hadn't expected the mere introductions to be so long and convoluted—and we were only half finished. "I'm Dan Chambeaux, zombie private investigator." I extended one of our business cards. We had them printed up by the thousands from a quick-print shop run by elves.

BatGN took the card with his clumsy webbed hands, then dug into his vest pocket and pulled out a twenty-sided die, like something used in a Dungeons & Dragons campaign. He rolled it on the cluttered surface, squinted down at the numbers to make out what he had rolled. I thought of the phrase "blind as a bat."

The bookie looked up at me and declared, "I'll bet you're here to place a bet."

"Actually, I'm here to investigate the placing of bets. I represent a dissatisfied customer of yours."

BatGN squeaked. "A loser, you mean."

"Even losers have legal rights."

"I have many clients, Mr. Chambeaux—respectable clients, people who understand the risks of placing a wager. They're happy when they win, and they always imagine something nefarious when they lose."

As he talked, I had a chance to look around the office. His office walls were covered with framed photos of legendary black horses with blazing eyes, spiky manes, and smoke coming out of their nostrils. Each one was ridden by a determined imp jockey. I wasn't a race fan, but I'd heard of some of the prize thoroughbreds like Seawitch Biscuit, Pharaoh's Curse, Hoof 'N' Mouth.

Next to a potted plant stood a black rocking horse. The toy looked even more fierce than the actual nightmares in the racing photos. I pictured BatGN rocking furiously back and forth while flapping his leathery wings as he imagined himself at the head of the galloping herd.

The bookie rolled the twenty-sided die again, then scooped it up and put it away. "Hmmm, easier odds in this case." He rolled a regular six-sided die, reconsidered, and just flipped a quarter, which landed heads-up on the desktop. "I know who the whiner is. It's the imp, right?"

"Yes, sir. Barney engaged me to look into your practices."

"Look around all you want." BatGN raised his arms and spread his wings. "Barney's one of my regulars—never met a bet he didn't like. And he's had a long unlucky streak. Almost a perfect track record of picking losers."

I couldn't go back to Barney with such a weak explanation. "He says that many of your other clients also have a habit of losing."

The man-bat's large ears flared. "That's the nature of the game—you win some, you lose some. The odds get even."

"Maybe if Barney won more often, he wouldn't be so suspicious."

I had looked into the imp's claims, and I did indeed find frequent mishaps and unusual circumstances that happened to occur with the exact horses that Barney had wagered on. Those nightmares would stumble and throw their jockeys, or rear up as if being attacked by invisible demons—and in each instance, all the invisible demons at the racetrack had an alibi.

BatGN made a squeaky, scoffing noise. "They're *nightmares*—lightning fast, but with a thunderous temperament." He waved a wing toward the framed photos on his wall. "Some real beauties there."

As he listed some of his favorite steeds, I heard a disturbance from the ceiling—flapping wings, squeaking sounds.

"Is there something on the roof?" I asked.

BatGN's large ears flared, and he turned his flat snout toward the ceiling. "I should get up there. It's feeding time for my pretties."

"Feeding for what? And what do they eat?" In the Unnatural Quarter, those are sometimes dangerous questions.

"I keep my battery up there."

"I've never heard a battery make sounds like that. Nine volt? Solar battery? Car battery?"

"No." The bookie flared his hideous nostrils. "A *bat-tery* —you know, like a rookery or a pigeonry, but for bats."

"Oh, like a bat coop," I said. "I guess everybody needs a hobby."

He adjusted the green visor on his head. "Have you ever been to the races yourself, Chambeaux? A fine sport. Get some first-hand knowledge."

The mutant bookie reached into the desk drawer, making me wonder what sort of dice he would pull out next.

Instead, he presented me with a couple of passes. "Next Saturday, treat yourself and some friends at the Underground Downs. A handsome zombie like you must have a girlfriend."

"Ghost girlfriend." I wasn't sure if Sheyenne needed a physical ticket. "And a kid, if you've got a spare pass."

He gave me three. "Here, have a good time."

"Thanks, Mr. GN."

"Call me Bat." The bookie exuded squeaky charm. "Just don't say Batman." He adjusted the green visor over his beady eyes. "Care to make a bet yourself, to see how it works?"

"I'll stick with secondary research." I put the fedora back on my head as I heard another flurry of squeaks and chittering from above.

I wanted to leave before the bookie began his feeding chores.

CHAPTER 8

When I showed off our free tickets to the UQ Derby—affectionately known as the "Ucky Derby"—Alvina was thrilled. "I love horsies!"

Under normal circumstances, the little vampire girl should have had Saturday singing lessons, but practice was canceled due to the lack of a choir director.

Sheyenne was also very pleased by the idea. "Let's call it a date," I suggested.

"We could start before Saturday, Beaux." She snuggled her glowy form next to me. "I have some errands to run. We could go for a walk now."

Alvina still had a few finishing touches to put on her Egyptian diorama. She wanted to use gray pipe cleaners to make mummy figures for extra credit. "I'll stay here—Robin can watch me. Later on, I've got a game of tic-tac-toe with the kitchen mold."

Sheyenne refused to let anything darken her mood.

Outside on the sidewalk, I extended my elbow, and she slipped her ghostly arm through mine. It was a beautiful gloomy day, with a chance of miasma later in the afternoon.

We passed the long-shuttered Zombie Bathhouse, which had briefly reopened as the Recompose Spa, before tentacle monsters rose up from the sewers and ate all the clientele. We passed the former Parlour BNF (Beauty, Not Funeral)

Salon, which had also closed down after a hairy mess of a case. Now the space was the offices of financial and estate planners.

"So many memories," Sheyenne said with a wistful sigh. "You've had a lot of cases."

I nodded. "So many changed lives. So many bankrupt businesses."

"I think of them as adventures."

She had some mailing to do at the post office, a Wanted poster to put up, and overdue client bills she intended to serve personally. This had all the hallmarks of a good day.

We were about to cross the street when a gray-skinned orc in a neon green crossing-guard vest over his spiked armor held up a clawed hand to make us stop. Then he threw his full body bulk into the middle of the street, blocking traffic.

Tires shrieked as a massive garbage truck ground to a sudden halt. Packrat creatures hanging on the truck chattered at the delay. In the truck's noisome back compartment, squirming maggot helpers took advantage of the delay to take inventory.

After the orc crossing guard used his clawed hand to threaten oncoming traffic, he showed his rotted splinters of teeth and gestured toward the opposite corner. "Come on, kids!"

A troop of rambunctious little vampires, werewolves, and zombies dressed in gray-plaid school uniforms hopped and skipped along the crosswalk. When they safely reached the other side, they thanked the orc guard.

Sheyenne was smiling. "They're from Nosferatu Academy."

I pictured my half-daughter wearing the same uniform.

"She'll be happy to go to school with other kids." Even so, my heart was heavy. "She's growing up so fast."

Actually, Alvina wouldn't physically grow up at all. As a vampire, she would look like a ten-year-old girl forever, and the consequences had already sunk in for her. It got her down sometimes, but she used her "I Was a Teenage Vampire" blog to bare her feelings and get things off her mind.

"She'll do just fine," Sheyenne said.

Over the next hour, we tracked down the addresses of three former clients so we could deliver past-due notices. Despite Sheyenne's polite ringing of the doorbell and my impolite pounding on the door, nobody was home, or at least not ambulatory. Maybe I would need to hire the blood-beast enforcers after all.

"Unnaturals can be just as unreliable as humans," Sheyenne said, deeply disappointed.

This part of the Quarter had shops, outdoor cafés, spell emporiums, hookah dens, and upscale eateries, as well as the lowbrow Ghoul's Diner. On street corners and down side alleys, earnest vendors stood at tables hawking tie-dyed shrouds, floppy hats for sensitive vampires, even sequined gloves for those who wanted to protect their cadaverous skin and remain stylish.

A mummy was selling bootleg VHS videotapes that seemed as old as he was. Two tattooed zombie rappers displayed their own music CD, but the boom box playing their sample tracks only discouraged anyone from buying the music.

Walking past a narrow alley, we heard shrill, echoing voice. "Helllppp mmmeeee! Helllppp mmmeeee!"

Instantly on alert, I touched the gun in my pocket. Down in the shadows of the alley, I saw a smiling necromancer behind another vendor table. The overlapping, agonized voices came from an array of shrunken heads on display. "Helllppp mmmeeee! Helllppp mmmeeee!"

"Brains! Tiny brains!"

"You'll all die!"

"Where's my body? I miss my neck."

I let out a sigh of relief. "Oh, it's just those creepy zombie shrunken heads."

The vendor's printed tablecloth displayed the large, bold words, GET A HEAD IN LIFE.

"Helllppp mmmeeee! Helllppp mmmeeee!" the shrunken heads said.

Both disturbed and fascinated, Sheyenne put a ghostly hand up to her mouth. "That's horrible."

I remembered the excitement in the Goblin Tavern when Wrex showed off his shrunken head. "They're quite a novelty item in the Quarter."

Sheyenne clucked her tongue. "I'll never understand some people."

"Couldn't agree more," I said.

Sooner or later, McGoo would surely want one.

The necromancer vendor raised his hands to snag our attention as we approached down the alley. Now I recognized his olive skin, heavy eyebrows, handlebar mustache, and the prominent gap between his front teeth. "Alterro?"

Sheyenne also knew him. "Oh, you're from Spells 'N ' Such."

"Great to see you two!" He was exuberant. "Everyone

knows the Unnatural Quarter's most famous zombie P.I. and his lovely office manager! You've used my services before." He looked darkly disappointed. "I wish you had shared some of your fame and fortune with me, however. All I needed was a testimonial for my mail-order spell service, maybe even a mention of me in one of your novels. I would have gotten so much more business."

"They're not actually my novels," I corrected him. "Just ghostwritten adventures loosely based on our cases."

"Publicity is publicity." Alterro waved his hands to show a star tattoo that proved he was a member of the Necromancers' Guild and a hashtag tattoo to show that he did most of his work online.

"Brains! Tiny brains!" yowled one of the shrunken heads, which set up a chorus from the other heads. It wasn't clear if they were demanding brains or bragging about the size of their own brains.

Sheyenne was spectrally queasy. "Who would want one of these? They're hideous."

"The perfect macabre souvenir of the Unnatural Quarter," Alterro said. "Excellent for conversation or decoration—the most ghoulish knickknack you'll find in the Quarter. Would you like one today, Miss Sheyenne?" He leaned forward, lowered his voice. "Maybe two? They'll make a real conversation piece, because you won't be able to shut them up."

"You shut up!" said one of the heads.

I pulled Sheyenne away. "No thanks."

"I'm just trying to make a living," Alterro insisted, but his voice had a whining tone. "I've put up a store on eBay, and

I'm trying to get people to sign up for my spell subscription service, but times are hard."

"*You* think times are hard?" said one of the shrunken heads.

"Where do you get them?" I asked. "Shrunken heads don't just grow on trees."

"I fell off a truck!" a surly head snapped.

Alterro waggled a stern finger. "Oh, I can't reveal my sources."

Uncomfortable, Sheyenne and I walked away. As we departed, one of the heads called, "Have a nice day."

CHAPTER 9

irecting the Banshee Tabernacle Choir was not a plum job, and the position was wide open (now that the predecessor was a big red stain). With the sessions canceled for the foreseeable future, Alvina was bored and gloomy. She played tic-tac-toe with the black fungus on the wall, then upped the stakes to a game of hangman, which became disturbingly gruesome.

"I'd be happy to give you lessons, honey," Sheyenne said. "If you wanted more practice."

I smiled at Alvina. "She does have a good set of ectoplasmic lungs, kid." I'd first met Sheyenne as a lounge singer at the Basilisk Nightclub, where she'd won my heart with a special rendition of "Spooky." We were both alive then, and we had a wonderful fling. What should have been a romance for the ages was cut tragically short when we were each murdered. Still, love conquers all.

"But I want to be with the choir. And my friends." She loved being around other musically talented (or at least musically *interested*) unnatural children.

"I know." I tousled her hair, jostling her pigtails back and forth.

Then, like a miracle, a new choir director was found, and we received notice that practice would resume that afternoon. "This doesn't suck!" Alvina said.

"It doesn't suck at all, kid." I glanced at my watch in relief. "In fact, I'll take you there in person."

"Instead of walking, will you drive me so we can get there right away?" Alvina asked. "The Pro Bono Mobile goes really fast now."

Wrex's gremlins had installed augmented engines in case of an emergency, although I doubted choir lessons would qualify as an emergency.

I lifted the set of keys from the wall hook. "Only the best luxury limousine for my little diva."

"Yay, now we'll have time to stop for ice cream on the way," Alvina said.

Yes, I spoiled my half-daughter, but nobody was going to arrest me for it. "There's always time for ice cream."

Sheyenne started filing the unpaid bills as we left the office. "I wonder who they found to be the new choir director."

"It must be someone with great talent and patience," I said, closing the door behind me.

We kept the lime green 1972 Ford Maverick parked on a nearby side street. With its crumbly rust patches, it looked decaying and decrepit enough to fit right in. Alvina opened the squeaky passenger door and jumped into the seat, chatting about ice cream flavors she wanted to try. Vampire metabolism had altered her taste for many human foods, but a little girl and ice cream were always a good match.

When I started the car, the engine rumbled, grumbled, and roared like a threat, but I found it comforting, a sign of confidence. "Buckle up, kid."

Once Alvina did so, I tapped my heavy foot on the accelerator, and the engine roared like a nightmare stamping its hooves and ready for a race. After driving across town, we stopped at the treat stand. I convinced the kid to try pistachio ice cream, but I declined having a scoop of my own. Since my tastebuds are pretty weak these days, delicate flavors are wasted on me.

Mercifully, it was only three o'clock when we arrived at the cathedral for choir practice, so the great bell's *BONG-BONG-BONG* ended quickly enough. I imagined Russell up in the belfry, enjoying the clamor. I decided I'd go talk with him again while Alvina was at choir practice.

She bounded up the stone steps, wrapping the shroud around her waist and shoulders, dressing up for practice. At the tall door, she pleaded with me to join in the lessons and sing beside her, but I begged off, since I couldn't carry a tune even in a body bag. From inside, I could hear melodious singing by the few choir members who knew how to sing, and ear-grating noises from those who didn't.

Alvina hurried inside, greeting her friends. As my eyes adjusted to the gloom, I noted that the folding chairs had been put away after the disastrous recital. In the center of the performance area, the splat pattern had been scrubbed clean, though I could still see the faint remnants of the colorful chalk outline.

The monster choir members were lined up in their usual places, wrapped in cheerful shrouds. Alvina took her position, joining in with the chorus.

Then I spotted the new choir director, and froze. She was a generous-sized woman with generous curves, bright red lipstick, and an enormous personality. She had ebony skin, though her name was Ivory—the diva lounge singer from Basilisk, who had briefly been a suspect in my murder, years ago.

Ivory sang along with the children, belting out her own variation of the chorus and adding a rich, bluesy undertone to the "Monster Mash."

Ivory was a vampire with a capital V ... and vain with a capital V. She had a full voice and the ego to go along with it. The crowds loved her singing, but disliked her volatile moods, because Ivory would capriciously decide she didn't feel like performing that night. She had caused great misery and consternation for Travis the nightclub owner, and he'd been close to a nervous breakdown from the stress (before a tentacle creature had crushed him in an alley, but that was a different story).

When Ivory simply didn't show up, Travis had offered the stage to his cocktail waitress, Sheyenne—who had a singing voice that made the customers shivery, especially me. The audience loved Ivory's replacement—thus, there was no love lost between her and Sheyenne.

Now finishing the "Monster Mash" chorus, the vamp woman turned around as if for applause and spotted me. Her big brown eyes widened, and her gaze skewered me like wooden stakes. Her lips spread in a smile that strained her lipstick. "Why, sugar, you came to hear me sing again!"

It was too late to duck away without being seen. "This little girl is mine, and I came to hear her sing. I, uh, didn't know you were the new choir director. Congratulations on the job, though Sheyenne will be disappointed to hear about it."

Ivory's eyes lit up with fire. "Oh, is that poor girl still around? Does she still think she can sing? How sweet."

Alvina glanced back and forth between me and Ivory, frowning. She knew nothing about our history.

I tried to back away. "I'll let you get back to work, Ivory. Be sure you take care of Alvina here. She really missed coming to choir practice."

"Of course, sugar! I'll take care of her as if she were my own little darling." The big vamp cooed as she bent over a puzzled Alvina. "Aren't you cute? I could just eat you up!"

Alvina flashed her fangs at Ivory, which made the big vamp chuckle. Stepping back, she gave me a coy look. "You're welcome to stay and watch, enjoy the view." She wiggled her backside. "And the music. We're going to step it up a little." She turned to the eager young choir members. "Y'all will be singing more than those boring little ditties that are easy to teach."

"Or the movie soundtrack songs," I said, "like *Carmina Burana*."

Ivory raised her voice. "We're going to learn sexy torch songs, so you can all grow up to be lounge singers. The opportunities are endless."

It was a good time for me to sneak up the stairs to the belfry, out of sight.

CHAPTER 10

As I plodded up the stone stairs, my footsteps were buoyed by the rising voices below. Ivory had the choir warm up with an unsettlingly sultry rendition of the "Hokey Pokey" before teaching them a deep-throated, crooning version of "Stormy Weather," followed by "Heart and Soul."

I reached the top of the belfry, greeted by the single crash of the bronze bell on the half hour. A *BONG!* resounded, and I staggered back, clutching my fedora so as not to lose it over the rail. I spread my feet apart and braced myself. It was a long, long fall from the belfry down to the cathedral floor below—as Sally had discovered.

Recovering as the enormous bell thrummed into silence, I brushed the front of my sport jacket with its stitched-up bullet holes and squared my shoulders. Time to look around.

As before, bats darted and swooped like hyperactive swallows. Breezes whistled through the window arches. Far off, I could see the warehouse district with ugly buildings that housed innumerable nefarious activities, then the strip-mall zone, divided by canals that stretched like straightedges. The Quarter had a few parks here and there, the Greenlawn Cemetery, and the water-reclamation lagoon. Fog drifted down some streets, while other areas were sunny and humid for unnaturals who liked that sort of thing. It's good for a detective to get a high-level perspective.

Russell sat on a different ledge with his back to me, and I wondered what sort of insights he was getting from the view. Paint stains marked the backs of his folded wings, old letters that were mostly faded away. He probably had a tough time reaching back there with a scrub brush.

I approached the gargoyle with caution, so as not to startle him and make him fall from the tower. The defective hearing aids were in his ears, but he hadn't heard me arrive. I extended my arm and waved to get his attention. Finally, he swiveled his head, opened his fanged mouth in a polite smile of greeting. Russell was ugly, but no worse than most gargoyles.

I shouted, "Hello, Russell! Do you remember me?" Frowning, he tapped one of his ears, so I raised my voice further. "I'm Dan Chambeaux, private investigator. Can I ask you some questions?"

Russell shook his head and tapped his other ear.

This time I had come prepared with a pocket notepad of my own. I jotted down the words. He took the pad in his clawed hands and wrote, *Nice day, isn't it?*

I agreed and scrawled, *Just like any other day. I'm still working on cases.*

Bats flitted around Russell, trying to get his attention. Several perched on his head, shoulders, and folded wings. He brushed them off, shooing them away. "No treats today. I'm fresh out!"

The bats squeaked with displeasure, but Russell was deaf to it.

I wrote on the notepad. *I see some words painted on the back of your wings. Were you in the Big Uneasy Day parade last year?* I thought I remembered seeing something like that before.

Russell spoke aloud. "Yes! I marched with the Dixieland band. Had a welcome message painted on my wings. *Happy Big Uneasy Day!* Sometimes, I rent out my wingspan as billboard space. It's an easy job, except for when I can't scrub the paint off."

Two bats flitted close to me, but they realized I wasn't going to give them treats either. I noticed tiny, silvery adornments somehow attached to their furry chests or necks, but the creatures didn't stay still long enough for me to see what it was.

Wincing, Russell tapped on his left hearing aid, then plucked it out and held it in his palm. Shrill, high-pitched squeals came from the earbuds. "Damn things. They don't help a bit up here."

I nodded, which was an all-purpose response. I wrote down, *Have you had the hearing aids checked? Should you get new ones?*

Russell said, "Oh, they work fine. I just can't hear anything."

The sounds of the choir drifted up from below—Ivory leading the group through "Cry Me a River." I hoped Alvina was having fun.

Russell swayed back and forth, humming to himself. He extended his batlike wings. "I like the music."

I wrote on the pad, *How can you hear the music?*

He gazed across the Quarter. "I can feel the bells. I can

sense the vibrations of the songs." Even though his hearing aids continued to squeak annoyingly, he pushed them back into his ear canals. "I've got the music in me."

"I've just got formaldehyde in me," I said.

CHAPTER 11

The certified shrink assigned to evaluate Alvina for school was Eva Schrank. As a psychologist, her name was not meant to imply past tense.

After Sheyenne set up the appointment, we checked out Dr. Schrank's credentials on her website, provocatively named, "The Unnatural Quarter Is Crazy!" We went over reviews from previous clients, touting great successes. "I don't want to murder people anymore, and it's a relief!" and "The voices in my head now provide pleasant conversation," and "As a shrink, Dr. Schrank shrank my problems until they were of manageable size." The last was from HappyZombie23.

As we got ready to take Alvina to the therapist's office, with Robin staying behind to handle any office emergencies, McGoo showed up in uniform, as if to impress the therapist. "Let's see who's psychologically disturbed today! Is it you, Al?"

"Probably *you*, half-daddy."

"We're all a little disturbed," I said. "That's why we all get along so well."

THE MEDICAL BUILDING HAD UNNATURAL DENTISTS, optometrists, and dermatologists, as well as Dr. Schrank. As we stood in the lobby studying the tenant listing, the door to the dermatology clinic opened and a warty, leprous brute lurched out, clutching a tube in his peeling hands. Behind him the clinician called, "Use that cream twice a day and let me know how it works. See you in two weeks."

Alvina pointed to the therapist's name on the roster. "She's in office 3 1 3. I want to run up the stairs."

McGoo looked at me. "After that belfry, I've had enough stairs."

"We'll take the elevator, kid." I stabbed the button with my finger.

I could tell Alvina wanted to burn off nervous energy. As soon as the elevator doors opened for us with a polite *ding*, she bounded inside and pushed all the buttons for all the floors. "The stairs would have been faster," she said.

"Probably so," I replied.

The door to Suite 3 1 3 had a colorful sign showing a screwdriver and a hammer. *Do you have a screw loose? We have the psychological toolkit to help!*

"I knew she was a professional," McGoo said. "I just didn't expect a professional contractor."

We waited on a hallway bench for patient privacy. Just before our appointment time, the office door opened, and Alterro the mustachioed necromancer bustled out with a stack of leaflets for Spells 'N' Such. He called over his shoulder, "Everything's set, Dr. Schrank—just like I promised. Our motto should be, 'Think Small.'"

A voice responded from inside the office. "I've read your

money-back guarantee carefully, Mr. Alterro. I will hold you to high standards."

Surprised to see us on the bench, the necromancer ducked his head, as if we wouldn't notice him. He seemed embarrassed that we had seen him come out of the therapist's office.

"Hey, Alterro?" McGoo said. "What are you doing here?"

As the necromancer scurried away without answering, Sheyenne said, "Therapy is a private matter. It's not for shaming."

McGoo flushed. "I was just asking a polite question."

Alvina hopped to her feet. "Is it time for my appointment?"

Inside the therapist's offices, the chairs were soothing, pastel colors. Posters of hot-air balloons and kittens brightened the walls. Patients could recline on a long, leatherbound sofa, or they could choose a guest coffin or a sandbox filled with fresh dirt. Dr. Schrank wanted to make a variety of clients feel comfortable.

The therapist's desk—a sheet of plywood balanced on sawhorses—seemed incongruous with the rest of the decor. A large open toolbox rested on one corner, and pliers, drills, and mallets were strewn across the surface. Props for patients to work out their problems? A rusty coffee can held long nails, and a pair of canvas work gloves rested beside the patient ledger.

Alvina jumped onto the reclining sofa, squinching and squirming to find the best position. Her legs dangled over the edge. "Come on, sit here everybody! There's room for all of us."

Dr. Schrank gave us a pleasant smile of greeting from a rolling office chair at the therapy/carpentry table. She had a bland face, round eyes, sun-tanned skin, and a fluff of permed hair that looked like a tribble on her head. Instead of a professional business blazer, the therapist wore bib overalls as if she'd just come from a construction site. An incongruous crocheted shawl draped her shoulders and fell over the front of her overalls.

"Welcome to your first session," she said in a calm, welcoming voice. "You must be young Alvina, and these are your ... parents? Your family unit?"

"I'm Sheyenne, the office manager—I made the appointment." She leaned closer to me. "And I'm also Dan Chambeaux's girlfriend, which is my most important role."

"I'm Alvina's half-daddy," I said.

McGoo leaned forward on the therapy sofa. "I'm Al's other half-daddy."

Dr. Schrank gave a solemn nod. "Oh, I see. A nontraditional couple."

McGoo flushed so red the freckles on his cheeks disappeared. "It's not like that."

"None of my concern, unless your discomfort has any psychological effect on this little girl—which we're about to find out."

I straightened on the sofa next to the kid. "Alvina is a very happy, well-adjusted little girl. She lives with both of us ever since her mother"—I stopped myself from snarking words like "abandoned" or "dumped"—"uh, relinquished her into our custody."

"The girl spends time with both me and Shamble. We've

worked out a schedule," McGoo said. "And Sheyenne is like a mother to her."

"So is my lawyer partner, Robin Deyer," I said. "Alvina has a strong family network and support system."

Dr. Schrank shuffled the paperwork in front of her. "I see the young lady's applying for entry into Nosferatu Academy, a very selective school. I'll need to assess your attitude and outlook on existence. From the report, it seems you recently witnessed a terrible tragedy, Alvina."

"My choir director fell from the belfry," my half-daughter said, looking away. "It sucked, and I'm sad."

"As well you should be."

"But my half-daddies are a detective and a policeman, so they'll solve the case. Justice will be served."

I was very proud of her right then.

"Al's been through a lot in her life," said McGoo, "but she's resilient and has a great attitude."

The shrink raised her eyebrows, with her pen poised on the notebook. "And what do you mean by saying that she's been through a lot?"

Using only rosy language, the three of us took turns discussing the cases that Alvina had helped with. The therapist watched closely, more interested in observing the girl's reactions than in listening to the details.

Dr. Schrank said, "That's a lot of turmoil for a ten-year-old to process."

Alvina was indignant. "I'm really twelve by now, but because I'm a vampire I'll never look older than ten."

"Does that bother you?"

"A little, but I process my thoughts by writing it all down, and I help other people who are in similar situations."

The therapist's brow furrowed. "You mean other members of the Banshee Tabernacle Choir who witnessed their director's fall?"

"No, it's bigger than that," Alvina said. "I write a popular blog. 'I Was a Teenage Vampire.'"

"Oh, that's you!" The therapist ran a palm over the crocheted shawl that covered the front of her overalls. "Very sound advice, very mature. I thought it was written under a pseudonym."

"It used to be," said Alvina, squirming her butt on the sofa, "but I started putting my own name on it a few months ago. It helps me deal with my issues, even the fame I have from being part of a bestselling novel series."

"Fame? How are you famous?"

McGoo chuckled. "You must not read ridiculous popular fiction, Doc. Haven't you seen the book series that features me, along with Shamble? The Shamble & Die books. *Death Warmed Over, Working Stiff, Double-Booked*—I forget all the titles. It's about how I solve important crimes with my zombie detective sidekick."

McGoo must need therapy if that was how he viewed the series. "They're released by Howard Phillips Publishing," I explained. "Fictionalized accounts of some of our cases. Alvina has appeared in the last couple of volumes."

"And some of the short stories," she said.

"I'm not much of a fiction reader. I don't have the heart for it." Dr. Schrank pressed a palm to her bib overalls. "But I will review your blogs, young lady. They'll provide me with candid insight into your thought processes. It's a sign of a healthy personality that you can unload your troubles on perfect strangers."

"Sometimes I just need someone to talk to," Alvina said.

"Understandable. My motto is, 'Help every patient realize their problems are smaller than they seem.'" The shrink glanced directly at me. "I treat many zombie clients, Mr. Chambeaux, so they concentrate on their hearts instead of on brains. Perhaps you should make an appointment? I specialize in zombie problems."

"No problems here," I said.

The therapist pursed her lips. "That's exactly what someone in denial would say."

"It's also what someone without any problems would say," I countered.

McGoo pressed the therapist. "So, what do you think, Doc? Is Al ready for school? She's really looking forward it."

"I need to complete my assessment." Dr. Schrank smiled at Alvina, who hopped down from the sofa. "I'll contact you in a few days. If all goes well, you can come pick up my report and deliver it right to the school."

CHAPTER 12

Back at the offices, we debriefed Robin, who was sure the shrink would give Alvina a glowing report. Soon the kid would be taking Nosferatu Academy by storm.

Robin described a new case, a family of lava monsters filing a complaint against their neighbors, whose sprinkler systems sprayed water over the property boundary and harmed the fiery children. She was also studying permit requirements for a lagoon creature who wanted to open up a landscaping and irrigation service.

Later that evening, McGoo called with the best news of the day. "Hey, Shamble, Francine finished her cleanup. The Goblin Tavern is open again! You don't have to sit sad and alone in your apartment watching TV."

"I never sit sad and alone in my apartment watching TV," I said. "You're projecting, as the therapist would say."

"Anyway, meet me there and bring Al for a celebration. We can watch her throw darts again."

The vampire girl looked up from the table where she was drafting a new blog. "Can I? Please! I want another Shirley Jugular."

"A tavern isn't a place for a wholesome little girl to hang out," I said.

"Unless we call it family time," Alvina insisted, and I couldn't argue with that.

The kid and I left together at sunset, chatting in easy conversation. Alvina sang by herself, practicing the new torch songs Ivory had taught her. She did have a decent voice. I smiled down at her. "But can you sing the words to *Carmina Burana*? I recognized it from a lot of movie soundtracks."

"Which words?" Alvina blinked at me as if I were teasing her. "*Carmina Burana* has lots of words."

"You know, the part where they show knights fighting and horses galloping? All those dramatic operatic sounds."

She let out an impatient sigh. "Those are words." She demonstrated by singing incomprehensible operatic sounds as we walked along. But it was pretty.

We passed a vulture eating roadkill on a boulevard. A speeding car had squashed a furry critter of some sort, and two goblins with push brooms were trying to chase the vulture away. I couldn't tell if the goblins wanted to retrieve the body of a lost family member, or if they just wanted the meat.

At the Goblin Tavern, Alvina stopped singing and pointed across the street to a bus-stop bench where a dapper older gentleman sat wearing a wide-brimmed hat, sunglasses, and a sullen demeanor.

César—old One Fang.

Normally he would have been inside the tavern flirting with Francine, but now he gazed at the tavern door like a forlorn kid peering into a candy store.

"He looks sad. Should we go cheer him up?" Alvina said.

"I think he's in the doghouse, kid."

"Why would he live in a doghouse? He's a vampire—shouldn't he have a coffin to sleep in?"

"Not that kind of doghouse. It's something a grownup would have to explain."

"But you're a grownup."

"You're not old enough," I said.

She huffed. "I'll never be old enough."

"Then at least you don't have to worry about relationship problems."

Alvina trotted across the street to the bus-stop bench and plopped down next to César. "Hi there! I've just been to a therapist, and I'm supposed to find someone to talk to and unburden my problems. Do you need someone to talk to? You're frowning."

With a long finger, César pushed his lips into a bad smile, exposing his stubbier human fang. "Is it that obvious?"

"We've all got problems, mister."

"You're only ten," César said. "How can you have problems?"

"I'm not really ten," Alvina said, "but I'll always look this way. It sucks."

One Fang let out a dry chuckle. "Then you and I have opposite problems. I was an old fart when I was turned into a vampire, so I'll always look like this." He held up his liver-spotted hands.

"That sucks, too," Alvina said.

"Indeed it does, little girl."

"I got in a skateboarding accident, and they gave me tainted blood in the hospital. How did you turn into a vampire when you were so old?"

"I was a dentist with a long-established practice, ready to

retire," César said. "But not long after the Big Uneasy, I started taking unnatural clients. One rich vampire decided he wanted fancy veneers and fang extensions. I took him as a patient, but I didn't understand the risk. I was working on his mouth, applying the veneers, when the laughing gas hit him, and he started giggling. He bit down on my knuckles." One Fang lifted up his hand helplessly. "Presto, I turned into a vampire, so I'll forever be like this."

I joined them. "Sorry if Alvina's bothering you. She was just trying to cheer you up." I nodded toward the tavern. "I've seen you in there talking to Francine. Regular customer."

His shoulders slumped. "Former regular customer. I don't know if she'll ever talk to me again. I tried to do something to impress her, as a romantic gesture."

"Oh, I was there when the banshee came in."

"Who would have thought it would be such a disaster?" he groaned.

"Well, anyone who knows what a banshee does," I said.

"Sheila must have a terrible time getting insurance! After all that damage, Francine made me persona non grata. I miss her terribly. I thought we had a good thing going."

"Just give it time," I said. "Francine has been through far worse."

Alvina patted the old man's arm. "Don't be sad, mister. If you ever need someone to talk to, I'm here for you."

McGoo hadn't arrived yet, so I ordered a bubbly red Shirley Jugular and turned the kid loose throwing sharp stakes at the dartboard. I nursed my own beer, leaning my elbows on the bar surface.

Francine looked dejected. Some of the mirror shards had been taped back in place, and half of the top booze shelf was still empty. She had replaced the jar of pickled eyeballs on the corner and refilled the olives, but customers were sparse tonight. A couple of golems and a frog demon had come in expecting trivia night, but the tavern was so quiet they didn't stay long. The pool tables were empty.

When Alvina came back to the bar with her empty glass and asked for a refill, Francine did her bartender duty. "Here you go, squirt. Don't spill it on the floor. I can't afford another broken glass."

After she ran back to the dartboard, I said, "You know he meant well, Francine. It'll blow over."

"Thirty-five shattered bottles, fifty broken glasses and a ruined mirror ... and he *meant well*."

"He was flirting."

"That's no defense! My third ex-husband bought me a car when he was flirting."

I took a sip of beer and braced myself to give unsolicited advice. "Let me tell you something I've learned in life. Lovestruck guys can be just plain stupid."

She let out a raspy laugh. "Shamble, I've learned that *any* guys can be just plain stupid."

"Well ... sure. César seems pretty broken up about it. He knows he screwed up. He wants to apologize, but needs to figure out how. He's a retired dentist. He doesn't have the money to buy you a new car."

"It's not about the money—it's about thinking things through." She furiously rubbed the bar surface with a damp rag. "Besides, he's a well-paid retired dentist, and he could afford a car if he wanted to make a grandiose gesture. Just imagine how much that banshee singing telegram cost him!"

I looked at the empty shelves that should have held bottles of expensive liquor. "You must have insurance, though, right?"

Francine made a raspberry sound. "Insurance! I thought I had learned every insurance scam from my first and fifth husbands, but that banshee singer isn't covered by insurance. No one will write her a policy."

"She used to be director of the Banshee Tabernacle Choir," I said. "She was trying to do good work."

"Choir director is a hazardous job, too, I hear." She poured me another beer, on the house, and I knew McGoo would regret arriving late. "After all my marriages I'm wise in the ways of relationships—especially on how they fall apart."

"Don't give up too quick, Francine." I'd never seen myself in the role of relationship counselor before, but I needed to try my best. I couldn't forget the gloomy look on old One Fang's face. "Maybe after a few more days have passed, just hear him out."

Francine wasn't convinced. She looked up when two werewolf customers came in and seated themselves in a booth.

"Look, Shamble, I know César was trying, but this romance was doomed from the start." She walked over and put napkins in front of the two werewolves. Without giving me another glance, she started to mix them a pair of lemon drop martinis.

CHAPTER 13

The cases don't solve themselves—that goes without saying, as I've said many times. But they can sometimes be solved by wandering around.

To the outside observer, I might just be aimlessly walking along, chatting with shop owners, waving at former clients or patrons enjoying a hot beverage under the red awnings of a Talbot & Knowles Blood Bar.

Many zombies do shamble around without much purpose, like a Roomba covered with rotting flesh, but when I walk the streets, I always have a goal, even if it's just a vague one. A "Shamble amble" might seem pointless, but I'm absorbing details, picking up clues, making connections, observing life and commerce in the Unnatural Quarter.

Officer Toby McGoohan does the same thing when he patrols the streets, giving the denizens a false sense of security. He looks official in his uniform, but he's also just going wherever he likes.

Not surprisingly, we bumped into each other.

"Hey, Shamble. Been working on a hard case, needed to put a minotaur into Witness Protection." He adjusted his cap. "I couldn't figure out how he could keep a low profile—but then it hit me."

"What did you do?" My mistake was in taking him seriously.

"I made him ... invisi-bull!"

I sighed. "And here I was just having a nice walk, McGoo."

"I'm trying to put a spring in your step and a smile on that gray face of yours."

Since it had been McGoo's turn to watch our vampire half-daughter, I asked, "How's Alvina?"

"Comfy and happy. Ever since I got her a cardboard box to sleep in that matches the one at your place, there's less disruption when we switch."

I nodded. "We told the therapist she's a resilient kid."

"Al and I played checkers last night, and she is a tough opponent. She beat me game after game."

I was smart enough never to challenge her to a game of checkers. "The kid is a fiend for strategy."

McGoo sniffed the delicious aromas from a street taco cart run by a golem with a red checkered apron and a bandanna tied over his clay head. He was a flurry of motion at the little grill, chopping and scraping the meat and onions while tortillas warmed on a hotplate. The day's featured item on a chalkboard was "Traditional Mexican Specialty—Eyeball Tacos." Bowls held toxic salsas with varying levels of picante-ness.

We decided we weren't all that hungry. "Ready to stretch your legs, Shamble? I could use some help."

"Stretching keeps the rigor mortis down. What is it? Bank robbery, a fugitive pursuit?" We kept casually walking.

"I'm digging into the death of that choir director. Autopsy came back with pretty conclusive results."

I was happy to tag along, since I had an interest in the case. "What was the cause of death?"

His expression turned grave. "Falling. And then hitting the ground."

"Pretty much what I thought," I said.

"You're some detective, Shamble," he said, "but it's not the cause of death that's mysterious—it's the cause of the *falling*. That's what we have to figure out. I've got the address of Sally Allan's family. They live in a blue-collar neighborhood a couple of miles from here. I want to talk with them, try to understand Alice's state of mind. Right now, we have no idea whether it was suicide or push-icide."

"I'd like to meet them, too. I'll express my condolences." I pulled my fedora down farther on my head. "If it's a couple of miles, can't we take a patrol car? That's a long walk for you, McGoo—especially for a guy who had trouble climbing a few flights of stairs."

He snorted at me. "Look who's talking. You're plodding a lot yourself."

"I'm a zombie. I'm supposed to move slow." I picked up our walking pace. "In case you didn't notice, I wasn't even breathing hard by the time we got to the belfry."

"That's because you don't need to breathe."

I let him have the last word, then changed the subject. "You didn't answer why we can't get a patrol car."

"The fleet's been reduced." He frowned. "Budget cuts."

Thunder rumbled in the distance, and I could see knotted black clouds gathering over a section of picnic tables in Memorial Park. It was a family reunion of weather sprites, and they had been courteous enough to put up flyers suggesting that people have umbrellas handy on that day.

I decided to make the best of it. "It's a nice day for a walk anyway."

As we headed along and the downtown pedestrian traffic thinned out, a long tan sedan pulled up next to us. I glanced at it suspiciously, always wary that some bad guy could pull up and gun me down. Again.

This car wasn't just tan, though—it was flesh colored. And not painted, but rather *upholstered*, pale leather swatches clumsily stitched together with black thread, as if a set of coroners and taxidermists had had a party in an auto body shop. A taxi sign was mounted on the roof like a crown.

The driver's side window rolled down. A lanky skeleton sat behind the wheel wearing a gray cabbie's hat. He rattled a bony hand outside of the driver's door. "You boys need a ride? I'm the Dermi Taxi Service. We've got skin in the game!"

I looked at the skull's empty eye sockets, then glanced at McGoo. He shrugged. "Beats walking."

We both climbed in the back, and McGoo provided the address. "Don't worry, Shamble's a good tipper."

The cabbie introduced himself as Eric and drove off. He twisted the radio knob to increase the volume of the rap music he was playing and tried to sing along with the lyrics (which I couldn't understand).

McGoo lounged back in the seat as we cruised along. I noticed that the taxi's meter was modeled after a doomsday clock.

The Dermi Taxi lurched as the skeleton driver hit the brakes. Another car roared past us on the right with a hunchback flipping us the finger. The cabbie turned around to show us his empty eye sockets. "That guy was in my blind spot."

"Just get us there in one piece, Eric," I said.

"We guarantee that all passengers arrive intact," said the skeleton. "That's our commitment to you."

Eventually, the driver pulled up in front of a ramshackle duplex with several cars parked in the driveway. The home had a dead lawn, faded and patched siding, and a motley mosaic of mismatched shingles on the roof.

When I paid Eric, McGoo snatched the receipt and pocketed it. The cabbie handed each of us a business card. *Dermi Taxi: We have skin in the game—Eric Madrid, Transportation Guidance Specialist.* In his hollow, raspy voice, he said, "Call me if you ever need a ride. Always at your service."

"I've got my own car," I said, thinking of the Pro Bono Mobile.

McGoo glanced sideways at me. "It breaks down a lot."

I pocketed the card.

As the flesh-colored taxi spun away, McGoo and I headed up the sidewalk to the left side of the duplex. The Allan address.

The neighboring side of the duplex looked even more ramshackle, with garbage dumped on the lawn, trash cans at the curb, bicycles piled beside the garage, and cars crowded bumper to bumper in the driveway. I wondered what sort of tenants were even more slovenly than a troll family, until I saw the university stickers on the parked car windows. College students. That explained it.

The Allans' curtains were drawn, but the front screen door was open. The sounds of conversation and the hum of a TV drifted out. When McGoo pounded on the side of the screen, a voice from inside shouted, "Somebody get the door."

Another voice said, "Can't—I'm in my easy chair!"

"I'm in the kitchen."

"I'm doing homework."

"I'm on social media."

"Somebody get the damned door!"

Being more definitive, McGoo shouted through the screen. "It's the police!"

"Somebody get the door!"

Finally a troll teenager came to the screen, staring at his iPhone. He didn't even look up as he unlocked the door and swung it open. "Come on in," he said, turning his back on us. "There, I've done my part."

McGoo and I entered the crowded duplex. The noise of the TV diminished. "What do you want?" asked a burly man reclining in a La-Z-Troll chair. The footrest was propped up, and his horny toenails pointed toward the ceiling. He held a remote control in his clawed hand.

Another young troll—a girl, I think—sat at a dinette table working on math problems. I wondered if she went to Nosferatu Academy. The teenager wandered off to his bedroom, still staring at his phone, absorbed in his online activities. I figured he was one of the internet trolls I had heard about.

The mother troll emerged from the kitchen with a dishrag, drying a Corelle dinner plate with harvest-gold sunflowers around the edge.

McGoo pulled out his notepad as he introduced the two of us. "We're here regarding Sally Allan." I noticed his pad still had the previous conversation from our interview with Russell.

Gloom settled over the troll family. "Has something else

happened?" The mother stopped wiping the plate. "Has she been killed again?"

"Just the once, ma'am, but we're investigating her death," McGoo said. "We want to find some answers for you."

"No gravestone left unturned," I interjected, to reassure them. I hoped Sally's tombstone didn't suffer from typos like Ear L. Thrombins'.

"I thought she fell." The father didn't get up from the La-Z-Troll chair. "Sally was always clumsy, especially when she was singing."

"Just don't make *me* take singing lessons," whined the girl from the table. "I want to grow up to get a real job!"

The mother clucked her tongue. "I don't know why Sally was so interested in singing. She wanted to pursue a career in music, be a choir director."

The father clicked the recliner back another notch until he was almost supine. "Waste of time! Liberal arts!" He sneered. "Couldn't get a job, couldn't pay the bills—had to come back home and live with us."

"Now, dear," said the mother, "there's nothing wrong with a troll living in a dank, dark basement."

The father snorted. "This duplex doesn't even have a basement."

The teenage boy wandered past, still obsessed with social media. "I'm trying to get bad grades in school so I can get a good troll job, something acceptable."

"That's my boy," said the father.

"Being a choir director isn't acceptable?" I asked, remembering how much Sally had loved it. "What do you consider to be a good job for a troll?"

The entire troll family grumbled, as if the answer was obvious. "Bridges, of course!" said the father.

The girl piped up as she pushed her math homework away. "I want to work on bridges. Paint bridges! Scrape the undersides of bridges!"

"Sleep under bridges," said the teenage boy. "Cool."

"You're always welcome to come back home if you need to, dear," said the mother. "You can have Sally's room all to yourself."

"But your daughter was unusual because she wanted to sing?" I asked.

"And look what it got her!" snapped the father, still half watching the television. "She was always humming around the house, trying to cheer us up. Wanted to drag the whole family out to go Christmas caroling!"

The trolls groaned in unison.

"If she had to fall, why couldn't she just fall off a bridge, like any normal troll?" The father snorted. "I'm sad to have her gone, but ... why did she have to sing?"

"If she fell off of a bridge, she'd still be just as dead," I pointed out.

"It wouldn't have been so embarrassing," said the father.

McGoo turned the page on his notepad. "Did she have any enemies? Anybody who might have pushed her from a belfry?"

"I don't even know what a belfry is," said the troll mother.

"It's like a high bridge tower, but with a bell in it." I knew the comparison would help.

"Sally? Enemies?" The family members discussed the question, but none of them could think of a reason why someone would want her dead, even if she was a choir director.

The trolls perked up and expanded their fanlike ears as a faint thumping reverberated through the wall.

"It's those college kids," the father grumbled. "Always playing their easy-listening music around the clock!"

"At least there's good insulation between the two duplex units." McGoo cocked his ear. "You can barely hear it."

The trolls looked at him in disbelief. "Are you kidding? It's deafening!" The teenage boy jammed oversized earbuds into his ear canals.

"I hope that answers your questions," said the mother, setting the dry plate on the counter behind her. "I have to start dinner. You two are welcome to stay, if you can stomach it."

"What are we having tonight, Ma?" asked the girl.

"Spaghetti with roadkill, and some Spam."

McGoo turned quickly for the door. "No thanks, ma'am. Already considered an eyeball taco for lunch. If you think of anything else, let us know. We need to get going."

I followed him out the door. "And I have to pick up some groceries on the way back."

CHAPTER 14

As the only human in the office, Robin was in charge of the grocery list, making sure no one forgot to buy coffee, tea, or toilet paper. Sheyenne and I remembered what it was like to be human (and to run out of toilet paper). Robin asked to go with me on the next run, suggesting that I'm not a good judge of fresh produce.

I needed to go to the store for reasons of my own. Robin had a grocery list—I had a client list.

After visiting the troll family, I met her at the Chambeaux & Deyer offices and we went together. Our local food market had all the basics we needed, and we liked to support small businesses—especially now that one of the owners was a client of mine.

In front of Barney & Clyde, Imp Grocers, canned goods were on display in pharaoh-worthy pyramids. Moldy bakery items had special pricing, some marked down and some at a premium, depending on what sort of mold they offered. Big signs in the window advertised a special on Mystery Meat, various cuts at $2.99/lb.

Robin took out her list and coupons, then used her attorney focus to scan the other specials. "Dan, there's a buy one, get one free on the new Zom-B-Fresh product line. I'd like to spritz it around the office."

I couldn't forget the horrific scheme by Jekyll Lifestyle

Products & Necroceuticals, which would have dissolved the unnatural population. "Still not sure I trust the brand."

"The company's under new ownership, Dan. There's definitely a market for their products."

"Are you saying I have a particular odor?" I pride myself on being a well-preserved zombie, and I get a regular touch-up at Bruno and Heinrich's Embalming Parlor, but it's not possible to entirely erase the lingering odor of decay.

Robin crafted a strategically tactful answer. "There's nothing wrong with being fresh for our clientele, and the office staff. We should go the extra mile."

"All right, I'll try it. Just don't get the evergreen scent. It smells like a janitor's mop bucket."

Robin picked up a grocery cart from the outside corral and wheeled it into the store. The market's automatic glass doors whisked open to greet us like hungry jaws.

Barney & Clyde's was packed with groceries to serve a wide range of customers. Many aisles were so narrow they could accommodate only one cart at a time, which caused occasional traffic jams.

Holding her list, Robin looked around, studying the aisle markings: soft drinks, breakfast cereals, crackers and snacks, poisons, sorcerous paraphernalia (I was impressed that they could fit the word paraphernalia on a sign), as well as personal hygiene products, a pharmacy section, and a partitioned-off liquor wing for monsters over the age of twenty-one.

Before the Big Uneasy, the grocery store had carried only products for humans, plus an aisle for pet supplies. Now Barney & Clyde's Grocery was segregated by species:

zombies, werewolves, vampires, even a sundries section for ghosts.

I had shopped here for years, grabbing whatever items we needed. On previous trips, I'd seen the imp brothers stocking the shelves or working the cash register. We would give a nod of greeting, but were not actually friends.

Robin trundled off with her empty cart, and I promised to meet her at the cash register after I spoke to the imps.

"I won't be long," she said, and I knew she wouldn't. Unlike my ex-wife Rhonda, who would wander up and down every single aisle in a store in search of whatever struck her fancy along the way, Robin was a hunter and didn't waste time on impulse buys. She had a list.

Two ghoul teenagers and their lich girlfriends hung around the live-bait section, pawing through bins of maggots and earthworms. They glanced furtively around and slurped samples when they thought no one was looking.

In the far back of the store, the heavy swinging doors were propped open, and I could hear a commotion by the loading docks.

"Fresh?" shrieked a grating voice. "You call this fresh? I'm not paying for *fresh!* I want mealy, moldy, and mushy! The customers won't know the difference, and that's what they expect!"

I recognized that harpy.

"I've already discounted it for the bruises and rot, Esther." It was Barney's voice, with a hint of exasperation. "Same as every day. Albert never complained before."

"Albert is an idiot!" Clearly, the harpy waitress from the Ghoul's Diner was just as obnoxious behind the scenes as when she waited on her customers. "And *I* want this crap, so you can't say *nobody* wants it."

At the Ghoul's Diner, Albert always served up a foul tasting and gruesome looking mess, and now I knew where he got his produce. Since it was before the midnight rush, I guessed that Albert must be in the steamy kitchen concocting whatever he would serve all night long.

Barney sounded defeated. "All right, I'll throw in two pounds of Mystery Meat."

"Three!" Esther shrieked. "And it better taste good!"

"It's a mystery to me." Barney followed Esther out to the loading dock, carrying crates of moldy produce while she didn't lift a feather to help.

The other imp—Clyde—was working in the produce section, which had wilted greens, fresh Spanish moss (salad fixings preferred by bayou monsters), and watermelons. Clyde used a crowbar to pry open the wooden lid of a large crate from South America. The nails screeched as he pulled them out.

Unlike his brother's long braided beard, Clyde's beard was bifurcated into two pigtails. His bushy eyebrows were threaded with little gold rings. Like Barney, he wore pointy-toed shoes, kid-sized dungarees, and a long grocer's apron.

While Esther kept Barney busy, I took the opportunity to chat with Clyde.

He looked up at me as he lifted the lid off the crate. His brow furrowed, making the green skin of his forehead look like a shriveled cucumber. "You're that zombie detective."

"Dan Chambeaux—one of your regular customers. Barney told me about you."

He removed the top of the crate to reveal yellow bananas

—on top of which were four black, hairy tarantulas. Exposed, the large spiders twitched and backed away, bending their pointy legs in a defensive posture. Their beady eyes looked up at us.

Clyde jumped back and held up his hands. "What's this? Who put bananas in my crate of fresh tarantulas?" He slammed the lid back on the crate so he could deal with it later. "Sorry about that. My brother told me he engaged your services." He shook his head. "As if we can afford another expense, after all the money he's burned through!"

Since Barney was a client, I felt a need to come to his defense. "He wanted me to investigate his bookie. He thinks he's being cheated."

Clyde let out an exasperated sigh. "My brother always thinks he's being cheated. He just picks the wrong horses. The only times he wins is when he writes down his bets for me, and then I choose completely different horses."

"I'll bet," I said.

"Don't bet. It's never a good proposition."

Barney came back in from the loading dock, wiping perspiration from his green forehead. His pointy-toed shoes were curled up, as if offended by what he'd just been through. "Esther's worse than any nightmare I've seen at the Underground Downs."

Clyde commiserated. "Sorry, bro, but today was your Esther day. I'm stuck with her tomorrow."

Barney brightened when he recognized me. "Mr. Chambeaux! Do you have a report for me? What cheating have you uncovered?"

"I've interviewed BatGN, but I have no proof yet."

"I didn't ask for proof," Barney said. "I want you to accuse him!"

"All in good time." I explained my conversation in more detail, describing BatGN's responses to any suggestion of improper bookie behavior. Since illegal gambling was unregulated in the Quarter and seedy bookies were not required to abide by any upstanding code, it was difficult for me to make a case that would satisfy my client. I did tell him that I would be checking out the Ucky Derby the following day, and I promised to review suspicious activity at past nightmare races.

"I knew you were a good bet, Mr. Shamble!"

His brother let out a disappointed sigh.

Robin had filled her grocery cart with boxes of Unlucky Charms for Alvina, cartons of milk, mega-giga packs of toilet paper, Zom-B-Fresh air freshener, and a loaf of whole-grain bread. She caught my attention as she headed to the checkout line, and I said goodbye to the two imp grocers. I joined her at the cash registers.

The automatic glass doors slid open, and four figures staggered into the grocery. Their tattered shirts and pants were stained with mud or some other brownish substance. They were all barefoot, their toenails black and cracked. Their arms swung listlessly from side to side, and they bumped into one another as they lurched into the store.

They had no heads.

The headless figures plodded into a pyramid of pumpkin-pie filling and knocked over the cans. One bent down and fumbled to pick up the cans, but without a head he was unable to stack them again, so he just made a clattering mess. The other three headless figures blundered past the checkout lines.

Two moved in single file down the narrow canned-vegetables aisle, where a vampire housewife was pushing a cart full of red juice and cans of carbonated blood drinks. The headless zombies shuffled forward, but there was no room for them to pass, so they forced the vampire housewife to retreat to the end of the aisle. The blundering figures turned toward the produce section.

Clyde had unloaded the newly arrived tarantulas into a live arachnids terrarium and dumped the bananas into a garbage bin. He dodged out of the way as the headless figures marched past the potatoes and onions, straight toward a bin of watermelons on special.

One zombie raised a melon high and squashed it down onto the stump of his neck. He battered unsuccessfully to reattach the surrogate head until the watermelon broke and spilled wet red pulp everywhere.

A second headless figure had better success with an overripe cantaloupe and managed to balance the rind on a jagged vertebra.

The other two decapitated zombies went to the leafy greens and grabbed heads of iceberg lettuce and cabbage. The lettuce proved to be the best option, light enough to stay in place. Before long, all four headless figures had new heads —one cantaloupe, one cabbage and two lettuce.

Barney and Clyde shooed them out of the grocery store, realizing it would be a wasted effort to get the headless zombies to pay for the produce. "Don't come back until you have your own heads in place!" called Clyde.

"And your wallets," said Barney.

It was an empty demand, though, because without heads the zombies also had no ears.

After the chaotic distraction, Robin used all of her coupons, then folded the receipt and put it into her purse after marking off the items that were tax deductible.

I wished I had been able to give my imp client more of an update, but I hoped I would learn more at the Underground Downs tomorrow.

CHAPTER 15

And we were off to the races!

After a short delay.

I shambled in place, eager to go, while Sheyenne and Alvina finished getting ready. Robin had to stay in the office working on the Ear L. Thrombins gravestone typo case.

Alvina posted last-minute pictures on Monstagram along with a new "I Was a Teenage Vampire" blog. Meanwhile, Sheyenne packed a cooler with water bottles and snacks for the twenty-minute drive, including packets of blood gummies and brute rollups. In the kitchenette, as she zipped the cooler pack shut, she made a loud retort to the wall. "No, I won't place a bet for you!"

I poked my head into the kitchen. The black mold had written on the wall, $50 on Cloven Hoof. Ten-to-one odds!

"How does a kitchen fungus know about betting on horses?" I asked.

Sheyenne sniffed. "How does it learn any of that vocabulary?"

"And where is it going to get fifty bucks?" I glanced at the donation cup next to the coffeemaker and saw it was empty. "Huh, sneaky little—"

The wall fungus scrawled words that I would never speak aloud. I hoped Alvina didn't see them.

Sheyenne's form glowered. "You can rot in drywall for all I care." She snatched the snack pack and followed me out to intercept Alvina, who was inordinately curious to see what the black mold had to say.

"We'll look at it later, kid ... maybe when you're twenty-one." Even then, the words might still damage her vision.

The Pro Bono Mobile's rumbling, newly repaired engine gave us a feeling of power, and I had to be careful with the accelerator so we wouldn't hurtle into any nearby brick walls. Even so, I got us across town in record time.

The racetrack had fallen into disrepair and disrepute long before the Big Uneasy. But when the monsters had returned, a vampire entrepreneur named Vincent Galdi used ancient money to refurbish the entire complex. Galdi had identified a monster consumer interest in gambling. All the unnaturals felt lucky, since their very existence was a long shot, and wasted their money accordingly.

Galdi had redone the oval track and built a new set of bleachers covered by extensive black awnings to block hazardous sunlight. He had expanded the seats to accommodate all body types, including fleshy clusters of tentacles and massive ogre derrieres.

After I paid five dollars to a sunken-eyed parking attendant holding a bloody meat cleaver, we pulled into a dirt lot. I parked next to an old pickup truck with a bumper sticker that said "Unnatural—And Proud American."

Alvina sprang out of the car, and Sheyenne drifted right through the passenger door while I locked up. I adjusted my fedora as I followed them to the ticket gates. I handed our passes to an orc ticket taker who narrowed his yellow slitted eyes. "BatGN comps?"

I got the impression that the man-bat bookie was not held in high regard at the Underground Downs. "They're good, aren't they?"

"He always wants things for free." The orc ripped the passes in half and handed me the stubs.

"Can I keep them as souvenirs?" Alvina held out her hand. "Our first nightmare races as a family."

That made me feel oddly warm. "You're keeping a scrapbook?"

"I'll help you with it, honey," Sheyenne said. "I have pinking shears, and we can make pretty labels."

"And little heart stickers," Alvina said.

"Anything you want, kid," I said.

"Good! I want a hot dog." She bounded ahead into the stands before I could remind her that we had brought snacks.

Outside the main stadium, a row of computerized betting stations were used by a few werewolves and a gargoyle, but most of the gambling patrons were furtive humans with baseball caps pulled low over their eyes.

Even though we had free passes to the track, Alvina's hot dog and an arterial fountain drink cost as much as we spent at Barney & Clyde's Grocery store in a month. Hot dogs weren't nutritious food for vampire girls, but they weren't good for humans either. Who am I to ruin my half-daughter's childhood?

The large black awnings kept the bleachers in deep shadow. The seats were already crowded with boisterous unnaturals rubbing shoulders, pointing toward the racetrack in anticipation. A ghoul accidentally bumped into an annoyed orc, jostling him, and he shoved back hard enough to send the already-staggering ghoul sprawling.

I spotted the mutant bookie sitting on a high bench by himself, still wearing his green accountant's visor and his vest. The shaggy winged figure propped a notepad on his lap, and he had a small boxy device next to his ledger of bets.

Alvina noticed BatGN. "Oh, is he the one who gave us the free passes? He does look like a batman!" She began to wave at him. "Thank you, thank you!"

The bookie did not acknowledge me, but shifted his position so that all we could see were his big fuzzy wings.

Sheyenne guided the girl down a different aisle. "There's more uncomfortable benches down in the front, honey."

"When do the races start? I want to see the horsies! Can we go to the stables?"

"They're not open to the public just before a race," I said.

Alvina was disappointed. "Can I place a bet? That sounds fun! There's ten-to-one odds on Cloven Hoof."

Sheyenne frowned. "You've been talking to the mold again."

The kid giggled. "I hear things."

"And sometimes it's better *not* to hear them," I said. "Let's enjoy the race, dip our toes in first and see what it's all about."

Out on the track, a hunchback rider on a chocolate-brown thoroughbred cantered along the track, taking a practice lap to check out the turf. When he completed the loop, he raised a hand to declare the race ready.

The crowd noise was louder as the monsters grew restless. A frail mummy carrying a tray with soft drinks and deep-fried hearts worked his way down the bleachers, trying to find his seat. He blundered into the annoyed orc, whose big knobby knees took up most of the space between the bleachers, and he shoved the mummy out of the way, spilling cola all over the brown linen wrappings.

Down in front, Wrex and his gremlin buddies were waving their furry hands and chattering. "I hope they crash!" Wrex said. Winkin, Blinkin, and Todd all hooted with laughter.

"The best races are the ones where they crash," said Blinkin. "That's the most exciting thing about the races."

The spectators leaned forward, hungry. Up in his out-of-the-way corner BatGN watched everything like a hawk.

Hearing fluttering wings and high-pitched squeaks, I spotted bats darting around under the black awning. Several flitted into the open air above the track. Here in the Unnatural Quarter, bats were as common as pigeons.

An airhorn blared, and the restless monsters quieted down. A deep-voiced announcer said through the loudspeakers, "Welcome to this Saturday's running of the UQ Derby. Seven nightmares, the finest demonic horseflesh —ready to run circles for your entertainment."

A family of frog demons bounced on the bleachers, cheering. "Ayup! Ayup! Ayup! Ayup!"

The announcer continued, "Full details are in your programs. We have Frankensteed in lane one, Cloven Hoof in number two, Cactus in three, Etherial in the fourth lane, Pharaoh's Curse in the fifth, Dem Bones running in lane six, and Dead Last in the last lane."

"We should've bet on Cloven Hoof," said Alvina.

I nudged the vampire girl with my elbow. "Next time you can pick, kid, but we're using your allowance."

"You don't pay me an allowance."

"Well, you deserve one. Talk to Sheyenne."

Before the race began, the announcer requested respectful silence for the singing of the national anthem. A small-statured mummy emerged from beneath the stands carrying a black parasol to shade a dark-skinned vampire woman from the rays of the sun. Ivory sashayed out, expecting the crowd to roar with approval.

"Look, that's my new choir director!" Alvina said. "Ivory!"

Sheyenne was annoyed. "*She's* singing the national anthem for the Ucky Derby?"

"She does have a really loud voice," I said.

Ivory's deep, sultry voice boomed out through the speakers. "Thank you to all my beloved fans, and a special thanks to my boyfriend, my supporter, and my sugar daddy, Vincent Galdi." She waved at the darkened VIP box at the far end of the bleachers. "Thank you Goldfanger!"

The crowd responded with a lukewarm cheer as she continued to wave. Everyone knew the Underground Downs and the Ucky Derby would not exist without the largesse of the vampire investor. I hadn't known the big vamp singer was his arm candy, though.

"I wonder if she's got a stake in the races," I said.

Sheyenne's glow was tinged with a faint red. "I know where I'd like to put a stake."

Ivory inhaled a deep breath that filled her lungs, and she crooned out "The Star-Spangled Banner" with all the enthusiasm I'd expected. She wasn't bad, though I didn't mention that to Sheyenne.

When Ivory was finished and retreated to the VIP box, a loud bell rang, and the track gates opened. Nightmare steeds burst out like demons unleashed from hell, ridden by small-statured imps dressed in colorful silks and tight jockey caps. The monstrous coal-black horses were each the size of an armored military vehicle. They had blazing red eyes and manes that stuck up like spikes or spines.

"And they're off!" yelled the announcer.

The jockeys dug in their heels, and the nightmares pounded forward. Their hooves looked to be made of sharpened steel, and even though the track was dirt, they still struck sparks with every hoofbeat.

Over the thunder of the galloping nightmares, the crowd cheered. Bats swirled around under the awning and then flew out into the open air, as if startled by all the noise.

"As they run into the first turn, it's Pharaoh's Curse in the lead, followed by Cactus and Dem Bones, with Cloven Hoof taking up the rear."

"I told you we should have bet on Cloven Hoof," Alvina repeated.

"I'm not sure you understand how betting works, honey," Sheyenne said.

The imp jockeys bounced up and down as the horses raced ahead, pounding the turf.

"And as we move into the back stretch, Frankensteed pulls ahead, neck and neck with Dead Last." I could feel the excitement in the air, picking up on the enjoyment and the adrenaline, but since we hadn't placed a bet, I had no horse in this race.

"As we hit the clubhouse turn, it's Pharaoh's Curse, then Etherial, with Frankensteed and Dead Last giving it their all. And now for the homestretch!"

The black horses remained clustered together as they

headed toward the finish, though Cloven Hoof still lagged behind.

I glanced up to see BatGN marking down notes in his ledger. Then he worked his strange device, as if it were a calculator or a phone.

The crowd shouted encouragement to their nightmares. The bats darted around, swirling and squeaking over the track as the horses thundered along. The jockey riding Cactus twitched and flailed his hand over his cap. Neck and neck with Pharaoh's Curse, Frankensteed snorted, thrashed its head, then lurched sideways to slam into the adjacent horse. Yelling, the other jockey struggled to stay in the saddle.

Dem Bones reared up and pounded forward, while its jockey struggled to keep control. The crowd gasped in horror. Two ghouls in the bleachers moaned just for the sake of moaning.

Frankensteed's jockey slipped out of the saddle and tumbled onto the track, barely avoiding the sparking steel hooves. Even Cloven Hoof pounded past him.

Dem Bones and Pharaoh's Curse crashed into each other in the home stretch, and both tumbled out of their lanes, losing their rhythm. Cactus, Etherial, and Dead Last raced past them.

Left behind, the disrupted horses milled about on the empty dirt track. As the remaining nightmares reached the finish line, they were in a dead heat.

The announcer called out, "Aaaaand Dead Last is the winner!"

Some unnaturals cheered, others booed, and others growled and snarled, "Foul play!"

Down at the front row Wrex and his gremlin buddies squirmed and cheered. "Horse crash! Best race ever!"

CHAPTER 16

I was looking forward to the Goblin Tavern for beer, conversation, and commiseration. Suspicions, or at least questions, began to dawn on me about meddling in the races. Maybe Barney wasn't so off base after all. Something had distracted the imp jockeys and disrupted the nightmares running in full heat. Those jockeys were professionals, and so were the demon horses.

For Saturday night, the tavern crowds had returned. A table of boisterous off-duty Igors had turned on the trivia machine and were shouting answers to the questions. Four slinky female vampires occupied an adjacent table, and with their titters of laughter and occasionally running long-nailed fingers down the Igors' sleeves, they seemed to be on the prowl, though the intended victims were oblivious to the flirting.

McGoo was on his usual stool holding a beer with one waiting for me, but they were both dark brown stouts, not at all our traditional pint. Puzzled, I looked around the bar.

Francine was woefully distracted. She wandered behind the bar wiping the surfaces with rags, stacking glasses, turning the booze bottles one way and then another. She stopped and stared at the jar of pickled eyeballs, as if she had lost her train of thought.

I looked at the dark, murky beer with a deep question. McGoo shrugged. "Broaden your horizons, Shamble."

I took a sip, and was glad my tastebuds were dulled. The heavy bitterness made me think of Rhonda. "I like to try new things, McGoo, as long as they're the same as I've always had."

He had only finished a quarter of his own pint. "Francine isn't herself tonight."

"She sure isn't paying much attention," I said.

She stood at the beer tap after a German werewolf had ordered a large stein. She stared at the far wall as foam curled up and over the lip of the bucket-sized stein, and she kept pouring without noticing.

"Hey Francine!" I called, and that startled her awake.

She looked at the beer in horror, shut off the tap, and blew some of the extra foam off the top. She handed it to the werewolf, embarrassed. He slurped at the copious foam, which got all over his facial fur.

A sudden light came to Francine's eyes, and she hurried over to me. "Shamble, I was hoping you'd come in!"

"I'm always here. That's not unusual." I glanced at my pint. "This beer, though, is unusual."

"Glad you like it. Sorry ... I wasn't paying attention." Her demeanor was sagging and sad.

The trivia screen asked the most popular blood types among vampires of different ethnicities, and the Igors surprisingly got the answers right, and the vampire queens fawned all over them. "Ohhh, you know what we like," said one in a seductive voice.

"Our jobs require us to know random, useless facts," said

one of the Igors. "I can recite the average temperature range of the largest rainforest on every continent."

"So can I," said another Igor.

"And I can do the deserts, too!" said a third, proud of his prowess. The vampire queens struggled valiantly to feign interest.

Francine flicked her eyes, clearly worried about something—probably her relationship difficulties with old One Fang. Their cautious budding romance had warmed my heart. César had fawned over her, giving the old, weathered woman the attention she deserved.

Often in the past, Francine had unloaded on us about her disappointing romantic escapades, and there were plenty of them. César Marici seemed different, though. Both he and Francine were old enough not to jump into a giddy fling, though at their age it wasn't a good idea to waste time. A teenage kid with a puppy-love crush had the constitution to ride a steep rollercoaster of emotions driven by hormones and bad decisions. Francine had enough innate caution and barricaded emotions that she wouldn't let herself go overboard.

She'd been annoyed with One Fang's ill-advised showoff gesture with the banshee singing telegram, but after talking with him on the bus-stop bench, I knew how badly he wanted to make up. If Francine was so miserable without him now, she could easily take him back. César would be so excited and relieved that he might even commission a second banshee singing telegram. I hoped we could intercept him before he did that.

McGoo twirled his pint glass without daring another sip. "What's the matter, Francine? You can tell us all about it."

My BHF had never been emotionally perceptive. "We'll be your reverse bartender. You tell Shamble and me about your problems, while we have a drink."

Distracted, Francine poured me another beer, the right kind this time. McGoo was surprised at her generosity, so I slid him my stout. "You can finish this one for me."

"I need to talk to you in private, Shamble." Francine's rough and raspy voice smelled of cigarette smoke.

"That's appropriate, since I'm a private detective."

McGoo leaned closer. "We're listening, Francine."

She frowned at him. "This is personal. I need a detective."

McGoo looked at his two dark beers, wondering what to do with them.

I slid to a different stool at an empty section of the bar—One Fang's usual seat—and Francine leaned her bony elbows in front of me. "I'm worried about my boyfriend."

"I thought you two broke up, after the shattered glass and that whole singing banshee thing."

"Oh, that was just a spat. Been through enough of those. I needed to give him a cold shoulder, so he understands how annoyed I am."

"I know he feels real bad, Francine."

Her expression grew even more troubled. "César's been around the block enough times, and so have I. We both know how this works. When I get cross with him, he's supposed to get me a nice apology gift. Then we kiss and make up."

I did not let my thoughts go farther. "I hope you do that last part on your own time. There are sensitive patrons here at the tavern."

"He's vanished!" Francine blurted out. "Just gone!"

That was troubling. "I knew he was upset but ... do you think he would just head out of the Quarter without saying goodbye?"

She shook her head. "He's lived here for years, and he had a long-established dentistry practice. He just stopped showing up to see me."

"You did kick him out of the tavern," I pointed out.

"But he was always loitering outside, and he knew that I saw him. He wouldn't just run away from me."

"So ..." I scratched around the bullet hole in my forehead. "You think something's happened to him? He isn't just cooling off for a few days?"

"It's already been a few days, and I haven't heard a peep! At first he left me so many pathetic but sweet messages. But now—silence. His apartment is empty, but not packed up. Just ... abandoned. He didn't come home. Shamble, he might have been kidnapped, or got hit on the head and can't remember who he is. He does forget things, now and then."

Now I understood what she was looking for. "You want to hire me as a private investigator to find out what happened to him?"

"Yes," she said. "Sometimes men can be so dense."

"Sheyenne and Robin remind me of that often enough."

Alvina had made a bond with the old vampire, too, and she would be deeply disturbed to hear the news. "I'll need some more information, and then I'll start checking things out. Chambeaux and Deyer at your service." I pulled my fedora closer to me, since it was part of my detective's arsenal. "We'll find your boyfriend, dead or alive."

"He's already undead," Francine said.

"Then we'll just find him."

CHAPTER 17

The next day, Alvina hummed around the office, encouraging Sheyenne to hum along with her. The two were a pretty good duet. Given the dreary Unnatural Quarter, it was nice to have a little music in our lives again.

I knew it must be time for choir practice again.

McGoo showed up, grinning and full of himself, as always. "I'll walk you to the cathedral today, Al. Somebody's got to escort you through the mean streets and keep you safe."

"Aww, nobody messes with me," Alvina said.

He gave me an offhand nod. "And while I'm there, I'll poke around again about Sally Allan."

Before I could point out that I had already talked with Russell, Robin stepped up to us. "If you're going to talk to the gargoyle again, I should accompany you."

McGoo was surprised. "Are there legal ramifications?"

"Deafness ramifications." Robin held up her hands, splayed her fingers, and made a flurry of motions like a birthday-party magician trying to make playing cards disappear. "Remember, I'm fluent in GSL. Russell might open up to me."

"I really do want to know what happened to my choir director," Alvina said.

I put a hand on her shoulder. "It's important to us too, kid. I'll come along."

After meeting Sally's family, I could understand why the troll might have been depressed. Maybe suicide was a possibility after all. Who knows what goes on inside an unnatural's head?

Leaving Sheyenne to manage the office—she was glad to avoid seeing Ivory—we all headed out. Alvina skipped along in front of us.

"I look forward to hearing what the gargoyle has to say," Robin said, "or seeing what he has to sign." She was both attractive and businesslike, which could put a person at ease or in mortal terror, depending on which side of the case they were on. "Facing a lawyer tends to sharpen one's mind."

"Or sometimes it just inspires amnesia. Let's hope Russell has nothing to hide," I said.

McGoo grumbled. "I'm not looking forward to this."

Robin glanced at him, curious. "You're worried about interrogating the witness?"

"No, about climbing all those stairs again."

When we reached the cathedral, a peppy dance beat was coming from inside. The members of the Banshee Tabernacle Choir were lined up against the stone wall, dressed in their shrouds and relaxed. On the tiled floor, the Eldritch Dancers moved in formation, flailing their ribbons and streamers. The salamander troupe leader's boom box blared out tinny beats.

The slimy tentacle dancers tangled their appendages into braids and pretzels, then squirmed on top of one another, interlocking themselves into a serpent-like mound that resembled an overturned bowl of spaghetti studded with cupcake sprinkles and a dash of food coloring. They were twitchy and uneasy, still shaken from what had happened during their last recital.

But the troupe instructor was like a drill sergeant, hissing orders, getting them into line (or into squiggles). Finally, when the song ended, the flailing tentacle dancers broke apart, flew into the air, and landed on the tile floor like an exploded can of Silly String.

Alvina joined her fellow choir members in cheering and clapping. As the Eldritch Dancers slithered away, guided by the tough maternal salamander, Ivory strolled around in a royal pose, marshaling her choir members. She clapped her hands with resounding booms. "All right, little sugars. Are you ready to sing?"

Alvina and the choir members yelped out a resounding "Yes!"

Sure, Ivory was problematic, and she'd been too aggressively seductive for my tastes (and definitely for Sheyenne's), not to mention that she'd been a suspect in my own murder, but I'd gotten over it. Though Sheyenne still bore a grudge, it was mostly from their rivalry at the Basilisk Nightclub, not jealousy over me, because Sheyenne knew she didn't have anything to worry about.

When practice began, McGoo and I led Robin toward the belfry stairs. As we plodded upward, Robin pulled ahead of us by the first landing, even though she wore heels. Behind us, Ivory blew a note from a pitch pipe, then demonstrated the scales for her students in her powerful voice. When the student choir members did their own scales, though, some of them sounded like a group of geese being strangled.

McGoo winced, and I used the excuse to pause on the steps. "I think Alvina has a fine solo career in her future."

Reaching the open belfry, Robin was all business as she looked around. The bronze bell loomed high above the gallery like an enormous bomb to be dropped. I glanced at my watch. We'd heard the bell ring just as we arrived, so we had about half an hour before the clamor started again.

The gargoyle had chosen a different ledge this time, and when he saw us, the sad, stony expression on his face shifted into a smile. Since he didn't know Robin, he flashed his jagged front teeth in a friendly welcome.

"More questions?" he rasped. "Or have you solved the case? Did you find out what happened to poor Sally?"

"Still working on it, Russell, though we have a few leads," I said, but he just gave me a blank stare, since he couldn't hear me.

Robin set down her briefcase and spun through swift hand gestures while keeping eye contact with the hearing-impaired gargoyle. For our benefit, she said, "I'm telling him that I know GSL and that we can communicate that way."

Russell was startled, but pleased. With clawed fingers he responded with a sequence of similar gestures that neither McGoo nor I understood, but Robin's brown eyes sparkled. "This is excellent and useful. I don't get much chance to practice." She and Russell engaged in a back-and-forth finger conversation.

I indicated McGoo's notepad. "Are you taking all this down?"

"I'll fill in the highlights later."

Robin translated, "We're going through conversational pleasantries. He says he doesn't know many other hearing-impaired unnaturals." She frowned. "He says he's a loner, likes to be by himself in the belfry. He enjoys the view, and the bells, and the singing."

As if on cue, the choir down below went through a practice chorus of "Spooky," which set me on edge—not because their rendition was bad, but because that was Sheyenne's special song for me, and Ivory knew it. She was crossing a line by making her students sing that one.

Next to him on the ledge, Russell had a paper sandwich bag with the top rolled tight. A buzzing, humming sound emanated from inside the sack. As Robin continued her silent chat, the gargoyle responded with one hand while unrolling the paper bag with the other.

Suddenly, as if an old lady had put out a saucer of milk for feral cats, bats swooped in, cheeping in their high-pitched voices. The creatures swirled around him as if fighting for Russell's attention. The gargoyle spread his serrated dark wings and held up the sack as more bats arrived.

"Excuse me," he said aloud and reached into the bag. With clawed fingers, he pulled out a handful of stunned and twitching houseflies. He tossed the flies into the air like confetti, and the bats swooped in to gobble them before they could fly away. The bats chittered and swooped back for more free lunch.

Russell chuckled as he threw another handful of flies. "My little babies always come for their treats." The tamer ones landed on his shoulders or the pointed tips of his wings; two even perched on his smooth green head.

Again I noticed that some bats had tiny metal adornments, like circuits stuck to their throats, to their chests. "Why do your bats have bling?"

Robin forwarded the question in GSL, and Russell answered out loud. "I didn't do it, but some of these bats are domesticated. Pet owners like to pamper their little babies."

Before I could get a closer look, the creatures swirled off into the air. "Pets? Where do they come from?"

McGoo frowned. "Do a lot of people keep pet bats?"

"Some." I remembered that BatGN kept his own "battery" on the rooftop.

Russell upended the brown paper bag and dumped the last of the flies out. The whirling bats fought over the remaining insect morsels. When they realized no more food would be in the offing, the stray bats squeaked away into the sky. Only a few remained in the belfry, hanging upside down in the eaves.

Down below we heard the overlapping voices singing "Soul on Fire."

I glanced at my watch, eager to ask Russell more questions so we could be gone before the next loud *BONG* struck the tower. "Ask him what he knows about Sally."

Robin asked the question with GSL, and Russell responded with loose arms and flexible fingers. It was clearly a casual conversation. "He says the choir director would come up here, and that she was often sad. She had troubles at home, didn't feel accepted by her own family."

McGoo and I nodded. I said, "Sally's parents wanted her to get into bridge work."

Robin asked more questions and conveyed the answers. "He says Sally would ask his opinion about the choir practice."

"That's a stretch," McGoo said. "He couldn't hear any of it."

Robin shrugged. "The troll was lonely. She probably wanted the conversation more than an honest opinion, or constructive criticism."

The gargoyle became more animated as he explained further, making gestures that even Robin could barely keep up with. "He says they would talk about life, and she was often depressed."

I leaned closer to Russell. "How did you talk about life, if you couldn't hear her?"

Robin conveyed the question, and I could see the gargoyle was getting more emotional. He kept tapping his hearing aids, but to no avail. Finally, he spoke aloud, "Oh, we didn't *listen* to each other—we just talked. Each of us saying what we needed to say. It helps sometimes."

Troubled, McGoo held his notepad. "If she was downcast, do you think it's possible Sally came up here to throw herself from the belfry in the middle of a performance?"

Russell shook his head vigorously. "No, not that! She loved the choir. Sally had perfect pitch, and she could hear music in a way that nobody else could." He tapped his hearing aids again. "I'm sorry I didn't notice her that day. I might have saved her." He hung his demonic head. "I tend to be oblivious."

I saw we didn't have much time before the bell struck again, and then we'd all be as deaf as the gargoyle. After thanking him, we hurried down the stairs to the end of the choir practice, just as the loud peals rang out.

CHAPTER 18

To better understand the mind of a troll, I decided to use my connections, taking advantage of all the times I rubbed elbows with other unnaturals, passed out business cards, kept them on my holiday-card list.

Business cards made me think of Edgar Allan the troll, the Quarter's most persistent real-estate agent. Normally when I encountered Edgar—with his wide simian grin, his angular reptilian face, and his constant marketing efforts—I would immediately look for a way to extract myself from the conversation. This time, I went to his offices in the Greenlawn Cemetery on purpose.

The graveyard walkways had been freshly swept by zombie caretakers. Public benches sat in the shade of weeping willows, and fountains pumped refreshing spray into the air. Four rough-looking monthly werewolves sat on a blanket near an unoccupied grave, enjoying a picnic. A pair of orcs on the greenway played catch with a sharp-edged boulder.

It was a bright afternoon, and new homeowners would be out considering options. Around the cemetery, signs were staked into the sod next to empty plots and rundown crypts. *Offered by Edgar Allan Realty, Plots for All Occasions.* Each sign featured a black-and-white photo of the grinning troll. A plastic tube held rolled-up flyers and comp listings.

"Get away from there!" a gruff voice yelled. "Damn kids!"

A burly troll, much taller than Sally, bounded across the lawn, spooking two foolish human teenagers who were trying to tag their initials on the back of a tombstone with a can of spray paint. The terrified teenagers must have double-dared each other to do the stupid deed, and now they fled screaming. The big gray troll could have caught the hooligans and crushed them to a pulp, but he was satisfied with making them fill their trousers as they ran away.

The big troll ground to a halt next to me, barely panting. I gave him a nod. "Hey, Burt. Busy enforcing order in Greenlawn?"

"It's always kids, Shamble. Each one dumber than the last. Hard to keep a cemetery nice these days." Edgar Allan's evictions specialist usually didn't say much. It was his job to patrol the Greenlawn Cemetery and look intimidating. "Come to consider some properties? If you're in the market, Edgar has a whole binder."

"I do want to talk to Edgar." I had concocted a surefire excuse. "I'm running out of his business cards."

Burt brightened. "He'll be happy to hear that! Follow me." The big troll strode along the pathway, pausing to adjust a bouquet of plastic flowers. We passed a duplex plot where a pair of headstones had recently been relocated after the husband and wife ghosts decided to move closer to the heart of the city.

Edgar Allan's real-estate office was in a refurbished showcase crypt that had once belonged to a famous kitsch artist. Edgar Allan and Burt had been caught as squatters in the artist's crypt, and before matters could turn uglier than the trolls themselves, Robin and I had negotiated a deal for them to keep the unwanted graveyard real estate. We had owed each other favors ever since. It was a good working relationship.

Balloons and flag streamers festooned the office crypt. The chalkboard sign advertised free coffee and cookies for potential clients.

"Edgar!" Burt shouted.

In the blink of an eye, the shorter troll burst out of the door clutching brochures in one gnarled hand. He recognized me instantly. "Dan Shamble, private investigator! Ready to upgrade your offices at last?" He fanned the brochures like a Vegas poker dealer. "We have many desirable properties."

"Says he needs more business cards," Burt said.

"Oh, I always have plenty," said Edgar Allan. "Do you need a box of five hundred, or a thousand?"

"Just a small stack." I made a gap of about an inch between my thumb and forefinger. "I'm very selective where I hand them out."

"Don't be." The real-estate troll insisted on handing me a pile of cards that barely fit in his palm. The better part of valor was not to argue, so I stuffed them in the pocket of my sports jacket.

With the pleasantries over, I got down to business. "I hope you can help me on a case, Edgar."

"A case! Do you need Burt for security?"

The burly troll squared his shoulders, ready to leap into action if I snapped my fingers, but I'm not very good at snapping my fingers. Ever since my death, they've been too numb to make much noise.

"Not on this one," I said.

The troll's rubbery grin stretched out to reveal even more pointy teeth. "Are there bodies involved?"

"One body," I said. "A troll—a choir director."

Edgar hung his head, and his gray, scaly brow drew into deep furrows. "You mean Sally—my cousin, Sally Allan."

"Your cousin?"

He shrugged. "All trolls are related."

Burt added, "Inbreeding."

Edgar said, "I was sorry to hear she fell from the belfry. Do you suspect foul play?"

"At the moment, the only thing we suspect is gravity, but I'm keeping an open mind. Can you tell me about Sally? Did you know her well?"

"A very sweet troll. Liked to sing, liked to listen to music, but she had to use headphones, because her family wasn't supportive of her aspirations."

"I gathered that much," I said.

"Her father insisted, and Sally got a job working construction and deconstruction. Always liked to sing when she was under bridges, enjoyed the way her voice resonated."

"It sounds like being a choir director was her true calling."

Edgar nodded. "Oh, Sally was proud of that job, although she wasn't too happy with Sheila, her predecessor. The banshee left the cathedral's acoustics a mess, she said."

"Crumbling stone and shattered windows," I agreed. "Do you think Sally was depressed? Did she feel there was nothing to live for?"

Edgar's eyes widened. "Are you asking if she jumped from the belfry?"

"I was trying to be more subtle, but ... yes."

The troll shook his head. "I doubt it. She loved hearing the unnatural kids sing, and if she was going to kill herself, Sally would have waited until the end of the recital, just to hear the music one last time." His yellow eyes glowed. "But she wasn't a very graceful person. She had to work *under* bridges because she wasn't coordinated enough to hang from the suspension cables." He clucked his tongue against his pointed teeth. "Considering that she had big feet, she could have just tripped and fallen."

I made mental notes. "Anything else you can tell me?"

Edgar scratched one of his jagged ears. "Sally's family was disappointed in her, but not murderous. I can sympathize, since my own family didn't like my career choices either. I was a real rebel of a troll when I went into real estate." He fanned out the brochures again. "Just take one of these, have a look when you get a chance." He shoved a brochure into my gray hands. It was easier just to take it.

Burt stood tall, looking off into the distance. The words rumbled in his throat. "I miss bridges."

I WAS ALSO DETERMINED TO LOCATE THE MISSING vampire dentist. I liked having more than one case at a time.

Once Francine gave me the basic information, I compiled everything that was publicly known about César Marici: his years in dentistry, how an accidental bite during an orthodontic procedure had turned him into a vampire. I had his address and phone number, and even one of his credit card numbers, but no charges had been made since the time he disappeared.

I put out word among the trolls, including Edgar Allan, in case they found a miserable old vampire camping under a bridge somewhere. I would get out my favorite spade and keep digging.

Meanwhile, after the debacle of Saturday's Ucky Derby, I set to work investigating the other disrupted races at the Underground Downs. According to racetrack logs, the nightmares had gone out of control in eleven races. Demon horses that were favored to win grew incomprehensibly unruly in the home stretch. They would careen out of their lane, or their jockeys would flail at something near their heads. Explanatory notes were vague, though, as if the track didn't want the details shown.

Fortunately, Alvina was an excellent P.I. assistant and she used her internet abilities to search the GrueTube. She found videos shot by spectators in the stands. With so many unnaturals crowding the bleachers, cheering the nightmares on, everybody with a phone had filmed the races. Once word got around about how often the black horses crashed, even more people filmed them and posted their videos. Some even added dance music on Sick-Tok.

"Here's one of the jumping races." Alvina turned her laptop around and started the video.

The racetrack was studded with obstacles, low fences and higher spiked barriers. The animals bounded along; some of them were black nightmares, while others were demonic horned beasts, even a lavender pegasus. The horses surged forward, tearing up the turf with their hooves, and when they reached the first obstacle, they all sprang into the air and crashed down on the other side. Jockeys crouched in the saddles and shouted into the mounts' ears.

The next obstacle had spear points, and one nightmare stumbled and barely saved itself from being gutted. A horned feline demon ran ahead, swiping at the air with lion-like paws. At the final jump, the pegasus leaped high, but the jockey suddenly swatted at his cap. The winged horse shook its head back and forth, and one wing flapped out of rhythm. Before landing, the pegasus bumped into the lion demon, and they crashed and tumbled into the dirt. The unexpected entanglement let one of the trailing nightmares push past the competition to win the race. The pegasus limped off the field, holding its feathery wing tight against its back.

"Poor horsey," Alvina said. "Here's another video."

This time she showed a traditional race with seven nightmares galloping around the oval track. The video was grainy, but I saw black specks in the air—the ubiquitous bats at the Underground Downs. As the racehorses rounded the last curve and into the homestretch, a similar pileup happened. One of the jockeys thrashed, and the nightmare snorted and neighed, then lost its stride. Other black horses rushed past.

Too much of a coincidence. "Are they all like this, kid?"

"Some races are just fine, but I can show you other accidents. I've watched hundreds of them."

"I don't need that much evidence," I said.

The vampire girl ran the video back to just before things had gone wrong. I saw more bats flitting around.

"Do you want to watch Venus flytrap videos next?" Alvina asked.

"Go ahead and find the best ones," I said. "We can watch them together at dinnertime."

CHAPTER 19

After watching Alvina's disturbing wipeout videos, I couldn't jockey my thoughts into any other subject. Trying to figure out what sort of underhanded, and underhoofed, cheating might be going on, I decided to go to the source of the possible problem.

Time for another talk with BatGN. What if the mutant bookie really was rigging the Ucky Derby, stacking the odds and pocketing the winnings?

That night I strode down the familiar streets, hoping my other cases would solve themselves. I kept my alert detective eyes open, wishing I would blunder into the right solution. It happens sometimes.

So far, no one had seen César, which meant Francine was distracted and jittery in the Goblin Tavern. Maybe a miracle would happen, and her dapper vampire boyfriend would just show up and beg forgiveness. That resolution wouldn't result in many billable hours, but it would be for the best.

Unfortunately, the retired dentist didn't have much of a social life, frequented no nighttime men's clubs, had no other known acquaintances. His only hangout was the tavern, and McGoo was keeping a lookout there. (He said it was work-related.)

Passing a kabob café, I heard the sizzle of meat skewers,

and the Persian spices were strong enough that I could actually smell them. The kabob shop was owned by a real genie, and a big sign on the window promised Under New Management.

The family recipes were marvelous, but the previous genie owner—a lecherous, round-bellied man with a curled beard—had gotten in trouble for leering at women customers and suggesting with a salacious cackle that they, "Rub my lamp!" After that scandal, business was slowly returning, and the new genie proprietor catered to his customers by offering raw lumps of meat on a stick for werewolves, and non-wooden skewers out of consideration for vampire diners.

I continued along the boulevard, mulling over the incisive questions I would ask BatGN. That's when I bumped into my first headless zombie of the night.

I didn't actually bump into him, because I dodged out of the way, but the broad-shouldered guy was lurching from side to side. He wore a tattered shirt and pants, with cleanly severed vertebrae showing on his neck stump.

I mumbled, "Excuse me," and walked around him.

The headless figure curled his thumb and forefinger in an "OK" sign as he kept striding along. I turned back to look at him, wondering how he had been decapitated, where he had come from, and where he intended to go. Just another mystery in the Unnatural Quarter.

Not far away, two other headless figures ambled along and collided with a newspaper stand. One struck a lamppost with her shoulder. A fourth headless zombie came from the opposite direction and slammed into a werewolf hot dog vendor's cart. He caromed off as the proprietor clenched a hairy fist and growled insults at him. The first guy stumbled into a bicycle rack and sprawled face first on the sidewalk (if he'd had a face).

Annoyed pedestrians snapped, "Watch where you're going!"

I helped one headless man to his feet. "Can I help you, sir? Or at least point you in the right direction?"

The figure brushed off his already tattered shirt and kept slouching along.

Headless zombies wandered down the opposite side of the street as well. I had no idea where they were all coming from.

The boulevard was busy at this time of night, and cars rolled past. Monster delinquents often went cruising to show off their souped-up vehicles as they drove around the Quarter. Tonight, two gleaming Thunderbirds with chrome exhaust pipes and jacked-up frames were driven by dusty old mummies, who had freshened up their gauze for the evening in an effort to pick up chicks.

As the Thunderbirds prowled, my headless guy lurched toward the corner. Across the boulevard, another headless figure bumped into a pedestrian, spun a half turn, and wandered right out into the flow of traffic. Loud horns honked.

Seeing the danger, I shambled at top speed into the street, grabbed the decapitated man, and yanked him away just as a tan sedan screeched to a halt in front of us. The driver blared the horn as I pulled the confused, headless figure back to the sidewalk.

The leather-upholstered Dermi Taxi had nearly flattened the headless zombie. Eric, the skeleton cabbie, honked his horn again for good measure and held up a bony hand, extending a middle digit.

After I got the disoriented zombie to safety, the cabbie rolled down the window and turned his empty eye sockets toward me. "Hey, Dan Shamble! You want a ride? Where you going?"

"No thanks, I'll walk," I said, adding the mystery of the abbreviated zombies to the stew of my preoccupied thoughts.

CHAPTER 20

I t was full dark by the time I reached BatGN's ramshackle office building and climbed the creaking steps. The place seemed abandoned, like a specter of an old office park. The other locked businesses didn't look as if they'd been opened in years—videotape rental shops, a record store, an adding machine/calculator repair shop, a microfiche storage specialist.

BatGN didn't advertise his services as a "gambling profitability specialist," but his clients knew where to find him. According to Barney, the man-bat didn't have a great reputation, but there weren't many bookies to choose from, especially not certified unnatural ones—and the mutant was decidedly unnatural.

I had researched some old cases and discovered that a few competing bookies had met mysterious ends. It would not be good to bet on a bookie's odds of survival in the Quarter.

According to rumor, BatGN had an under-the-table relationship with the rich racetrack owner Vincent Galdi. I wondered if the entrepreneur himself was throwing the races —but why would he want to cast suspicion on the rejuvenated Underground Downs? Maybe I should have a talk with him as well. Ivory apparently had a romantic relationship with the guy, so maybe the vamp singer would be a way for me to get my foot in the door.

Tonight, though, I wanted to see if BatGN could explain the too-frequent stumbles of professional monster horses and their superstar imp jockeys.

The bookie's office door was open, and the light was on. When I poked my head in the door, I saw BatGN's empty desk and chair. His green visor rested on top of his ledger.

"Hello? Zombie detective here to ask a few questions."

No answer, and the bookie's office was too small to provide any hiding places. The potted artificial plant looked freshly watered. The black rocking horse glared at me. A coat rack on the far wall had only empty hangers. With his large leathery wings, I doubted BatGN had much use for a sweater or an overcoat.

I called out again, loud enough to wake the dead from a hangover.

Hearing no answer, I took the opportunity to snoop around, paying close attention to the photos on the walls. The first was a fiery portrait of a proud nightmare, Knife in the Back, with a list of racing cups and ribbons under its name, next to a smaller photo of an imp rider in a red jersey, Itch the jockey.

The next picture showed a photo finish of three raging nightmares crossing the finish line simultaneously: White Widow, Marley, and Beetlebaum. On a low shelf beneath the framed pictures rested an ostentatious silver cup shaped to hold the ashes of a jockey and his horse, Tornado Bait, UQ Derby Champion.

BatGN must have been involved in nightmare racing for some time. I was looking at a set of blue ribbons for a horse named Eye Socket when I heard a flurry of noises up on the roof. Glancing at the water-stained ceiling tiles, I remembered the "battery" on the rooftop.

I found roof-access stairs at the end of the hall, and when I emerged into the starry night, the big batlike figure was standing under a bright mercury light on the rooftop. The dazzling light had attracted a cloud of moths and mosquitoes in a suicidal game of tag.

Wearing his vest, BatGN opened the trapdoor roof of a rickety plywood coop walled with chicken wire. The bookie raised his heavy wings to release dozens of bats from the rooftop cage. "There, my pretties! I turned the light on for you. Have a feast! My bugs are better than anyone else's." The bats squeaked and swirled into freedom, flitting around the mutant bookie's funnel-like ears. He cackled. "You don't need to go anywhere else. Stay here with me!"

The bats dive-bombed into the glare from the mercury light, gulping bugs. BatGN stretched his own wings to make a big silhouette against the glow.

"So, do you have individual names for your bats?" I asked.

The startled bookie whirled. I was surprised he hadn't heard me with those giant ears. He let out a high-pitched shriek, as if trying to echolocate me, when I was standing right in front of him.

I held up my hands to calm him. "I came to have a chat, but you weren't in your office."

"I'm here with my pretties." With a gnarled hand, he rapped the chicken-wire wall of the coop. "Best battery in the Quarter, and they all know it."

In the bright light, the flying bats flashed glints of

reflective metals. Maybe some of these creatures also had the odd bling I had seen with Russell up in the belfry. BatGN certainly seemed the sort of guy to adorn his pets.

"I bet I know why you're here, Dan Chambeaux." He reached into one pocket of his vest and pulled out a deck of playing cards. "Pick a card, any card, and I'll read your future."

I did as instructed, just to make him feel comfortable. "Apparently my future is the six of clubs."

"It's all about probabilities." He glanced up as his bats continued to devour night insects. "I bet you're here to ask questions about horse racing and gambling."

"You have an amazing grasp of probabilities."

From his other vest pocket, BatGN withdrew his twenty-sided die, squatted down, and rolled it on the rooftop. "Ha, seventeen! I think you're here to ask questions about what happened last Saturday, when the nightmares crashed." He rolled the die again and nodded. "And it's about that sore-loser imp."

I pretended to be astonished. "Right again!"

The mutant bookie rose to his full height, pocketed the cards and the die. "There's nothing to tell, Mr. Chambeaux. Everything in life is a chance. Every decision you make sets up another chain of alternatives. What are the odds of this, and what are the odds of that?"

"I try to make the right decisions in the first place and live with the consequences," I said.

"But uncertainty is what makes life interesting! We don't want to know exactly who's going to win a race or what's going to happen when we take a chance. Then it wouldn't be *living*. It would be like watching a rerun."

"I like reruns," I said. "But when somebody places a bet on a horse race, they expect it to be a fair race, and may the best nightmare win."

"It's still a gamble. Every time you cross a street, it's a gamble."

I remembered the headless zombies causing a traffic hazard.

The bookie found a switch and turned off the dazzling mercury light, which left the remaining insects lost and confused. Disappointed that dinner was over, the pet bats fluttered back into the chicken-wire coop.

"I'm a bookie. I love to play the odds," BatGN said, "but I like to think the odds are in my favor."

"Doesn't everybody?" I asked.

The fierce-looking mutant man-bat gave a solemn nod. "Barney certainly does, but he's wrong."

CHAPTER 21

Late mornings were dead at the Goblin Tavern, a perfect time to meet with Francine and try to make headway in the case of the missing old vampire. I gathered all my notes about César Marici, so I could unearth his whereabouts. I hoped that didn't mean literally.

Alvina insisted on going along. "You need a detective's assistant, and I want to help find my friend César."

I hesitated. "I'm just going to ask questions, kid."

"Oh, I can ask questions. Lots of them! Don't you want me to ask questions? I'm good at asking questions."

"You certainly are. Come on."

Any day now we expected to receive Dr. Schrank's written psychological assessment for Alvina to go to Nosferatu Academy, but for now the kid was still being homeschooled. She had finished her Egyptian diorama and already raced three months ahead in her class workbooks.

"I'll give you extra credit if we solve the case," I said. She took my hand and skipped along, knowing the way to the tavern by heart.

Though the bar was closed, the door had been propped open with a thick wooden stake. I called out Francine's name as Alvina bounded inside.

The Goblin Tavern looked like a ghost town rather than a ghost's drinking establishment. The barstools and chairs were upended on the tables so Francine could clean the floors. A mop leaned against the wall in a bucket that smelled of pine solvent. Or Zom-B-Fresh.

With a rattle of bottles, the bartender emerged from the back storeroom carrying a heavy box. "Glad you could make it over, Shamble. I'll be ready in a minute." She set the case on top of the bar.

Alvina ran over to help, pulling out bottles of expensive liquor, lining them up on the bar and comparing the classy labels. Francine's top-shelf booze would be full again.

The bartender looked even more haggard than usual, as if she wasn't getting her regular three hours of sleep a night. Her eyes were red from crying, or maybe an allergic reaction to something.

I reassured her, "We'll find him, Francine."

"I miss him. I hope he's not hurt."

"I once had a puppy with a locator chip in his ear," Alvina said. "Maybe we should have done that with César."

Francine gave her a wan smile. "Good suggestion, squirt." She reached up to place the expensive booze in empty slots on the top shelf, but didn't pay much attention to the arrangement.

I placed my notepad on the bar. "Here's what I found so far, Francine, but I need your help to fill in the blanks."

I went over César's vital data, and Francine confirmed it. She shook her head. "That's all just facts and figures, though. We should go to his apartment to look around. Hands-on experience. Maybe you'll notice something I missed."

"How are we going to get inside?" I asked.

"César gave me a key." Francine raised her eyebrows.

"Where did you think I spend most of my mornings when we're not open for business?"

Apparently, this relationship had progressed farther than just flirting across the bar.

"You two must be best friends!" Alvina said.

The cheery words hit Francine hard. Leaving the empty liquor case on the bar and the mop against the wall, she grabbed her purse. "Let's go."

César Marici's apartment was only a couple of blocks away, which would have facilitated their trysts. The hall carpet on the building's first floor had been tracked by countless scuffing footsteps. Francine paused in front of the door to Apartment 7 and squared her shoulders, as if gathering her courage, then knocked. Maybe she hoped he would answer the door.

After a long hesitation, she used the key in the lock. "César, baby, are you here?" She flicked on the overhead light, since all the shades were drawn. The air smelled musty and sad, like an old man's place, with a persistent undertone of a mothball-scented air freshener.

Alvina skipped ahead. "Hello, César? Are you here? It's Alvina."

Francine hesitated just inside the door, as if she couldn't find any words.

The kitchen had a dining nook with a Formica-topped dinette table and two chairs. I noticed there were no dirty dishes in the sink (highly suspicious). The cushions on the sitting room sofa were covered with plastic protectors. Down a short hallway were the bedroom and bathroom.

I flipped through a stack of unopened envelopes on the table. A week's worth of newspapers filled one of the dinette chairs. "If he disappeared, how did all this get inside the apartment?"

Francine looked embarrassed. "Oh, I've been coming here to pick up his mail. I want his place all nice and tidy for when he comes back. I even did the dishes."

Francine might have erased clues, but I didn't scold her for it. She meant well. "When was the last time you saw him here?"

"The night before ... before the singing telegram."

The refrigerator was mostly empty, as a bachelor's refrigerator should be—just two bottles of blood, both past the Sell By date.

"He didn't send you a message or leave any note?" I asked. She shook her head. "When you cleaned up the apartment, were there signs of a struggle?"

"Struggle? Like if he was forcibly abducted?"

I realized that was a long shot. "He probably didn't have much pep left in him to fight back."

Francine's eyes had a strange glint. "César had plenty of pep, once I got his motor running."

She led me through the living room and down the hall. I poked my head into the bathroom, which had no mirror above the vanity. I saw two toothbrushes and two containers of floss by the sink.

"Look what I found!" Alvina called from the bedroom.

She had opened the lid of a residential coffin, swinging it up and down. "Nice hinges. No squeak." She dug around inside, ran her fingers along the silk lining, and straightened the wadded sheets. "But it's messy. He didn't make his own coffin, like I always do."

Francine put her hands on her hips, wearing a wistful

smile. "That might look like a one-person coffin, but César and I had some wild times snuggled up all nice and cozy."

"A sleepover sounds like fun!" Alvina said.

"Just close the lid on the coffin, kid," I told her.

"I wish he'd come back," Alvina said with a sad sigh. "We had a real connection."

"So did we," Francine said. "He wouldn't just up and leave me, Shamble. César was a compassionate man, a gentle soul for a vampire ... and a dentist."

One Fang had tacked old Thank You cards and crayon drawings from past patients on the wall. A framed watercolor painting showed a smiling César shaking hands with another dapper vampire who oozed elegance and wealth. They both stood under the sign for the Underground Downs racetrack. The painting was signed, "With Greatest Gratitude—Your Friend and Patient Vincent Galdi."

I looked closer at the painting. Under normal circumstances, this would have been a proudly famed celebrity photograph, but since César and Galdi were both vampires, no camera could take their picture. "Wait, your César knew Vincent Galdi?" It was a surprise to think an old retired dentist hung out with the wealthy and powerful.

Francine sighed. "Galdi was the reason César could afford to retire from his dentistry practice. That rich vamp gave him a big payoff for something, and César's lived on it ever since. That's one of the reasons he could buy me fancy things."

"Maybe that's how he paid for the banshee singing telegram!" Alvina said.

She pulled open the drawers of his dresser and nightstand, finding old socks, undershirts, and neatly folded white briefs, but she was much more interested in the next drawer. "Look, free toothbrushes!" She pulled out a wrapped sample.

"Those were for his patients," Francine said. "Go ahead and take one, squirt. Always remember to brush."

"And floss." Alvina snatched a sample floss roll, too.

CHAPTER 22

When we got back to the office, Alvina was on a mission. She spent an hour on her laptop designing a flyer, *Lost Old Vampire*.

Since there were no photos of One Fang, Sheyenne found records from when César Marici had been a living dentist. Since turning into a vampire, his appearance hadn't changed much, so they were good enough for our purposes. In the old photos he was smiling, wearing scrubs, showing his latex gloves as if preparing for brain surgery instead of root canals. He looked all too eager to dive into a patient's mouth.

Alvina used the photos on her flyer. *Responds to the name César. If found, please call* _____. She put down our office number.

"Good work, honey," Sheyenne said.

The kid was determined. "I'll post it on the Nextdoor Neighborhood Watch chat groups, and add it on all the Unnatural Quarter social media."

I wanted to help, too. "Print up a stack of the flyers, and we can put them up on lampposts and vacant lot fences."

"Printing? On paper?" Alvina looked puzzled. "I suppose we could try that, too."

I reminded her that many people in the Quarter were still old school.

She considered. "Should we file a missing old vampire report with my other half-daddy? The police should be helping, too."

As if summoned by a secret spell, McGoo pushed open the door. "I'm here to take you to choir practice, Al."

"We can go as soon as I post this." Alvina finished typing, closed the browser window, and slid down from her seat. "I'll race you."

Sheyenne glowed. "Enjoy your lessons while you can, honey. Once you start school, you might not have time for extracurricular activities."

"I'll keep my grades up! I promise!"

After she and McGoo headed off, I said, "Someday the kid might have a singing voice as beautiful as yours."

Sheyenne looked wistfully at me. "All that talk about singing makes me want to go back to the Basilisk Nightclub, Beaux. I do miss it."

That brightened a regular gloomy day. "We haven't been there since Fletcher and his partner reopened it. Want to go tonight?"

"I'd love to!"

After dark, I brushed the wrinkles and lint from my stitched-up sport jacket and dusted off my fedora. Sheyenne and I walked arm in arm to the nightclub. The sign on the door said, "Now Revamped."

Looking at the place, she let out a sigh. "So many memories, both good ones and bad."

I knew I had a doofus grin on my face. "It's where I met you, Spooky, so that cancels out all the bad memories."

Fletcher Knowles, the owner of Basilisk, had originally

hired Sheyenne as a cocktail waitress, but she filled in as a singer on the all-too-frequent evenings when Ivory behaved like a diva, as she usually did. After being poisoned and coming back as a ghost, Sheyenne hadn't returned to singing on stage, though I knew she had enjoyed it. We still went to the nightclub together on special occasions, and I'd even been there on the night a tentacle creature crushed Fletcher in an alley out back. Later, his ghost had hired us to help him with some legal difficulties. It was long past time for us to visit again.

We arrived just as Basilisk opened for the evening. I smiled as we looked around. The interior still had red leather booths, a long wooden bar with leather-upholstered stools, a gaudy ceiling that reminded me of a boudoir rather than an upscale nightclub.

Sheyenne's attention was drawn to the piano, which would be played by a lounge lizard later in the evening, and the intimate singing stage where Ivory vamped whenever she showed up.

A new section had been added to the bar, where polished chrome and stainless steel encircled a coffee station and blood bar. With an espresso machine alongside an aerator and dialysis machine, the barista could offer fresh and frothy drinks. A teenage kid was wiping down the apparatus and setting out the cups for the evening customers. He pretended to ignore the low but heated argument taking place between the owner and a familiar necromancer.

Fletcher's ghostly expression showed consternation. "This is a nice place, Mr. Alterro. We're not in the market to sell silly tchotchkes."

With a huff, Alterro held open his display case to show six of the loquacious zombie shrunken heads packed in tissue paper. "But they're a crowd pleaser! With a high profit margin." He waved his hashtag-tattooed hand. "Hours of entertainment. Your customers will be delighted. People come into Basilisk to get a piece of tail. Now they can get a head, too."

Fletcher's ghost frowned at the display case. The living shrunken heads puckered up. Some grimaced, some frowned, one even tried to spit at him, but the decapitated head was short on saliva. Another one gave Fletcher a raspberry.

"They don't seem very pleasant," he said.

"Eff you!" one of the heads snarled.

"I've taught them not to use bad language," Alterro said with a grin.

Sheyenne and I wandered over, and the obsequious necromancer turned to us. "What do you think, my dear friends? You must be in the market for one of my delightful shrunken heads."

"That's a hard pass," I said. "We didn't want one the first time we saw you at your table on the street."

"We don't want you, either!" One of the heads scowled at me—or maybe it was at the necromancer.

"Sorry, Mr. Alterro. We're just not interested in featuring them at Basilisk," Fletcher said. "Now, please leave. We have a lot of prep work before the evening rush."

"It would be a bigger rush if you sold shrunken heads." He sounded more desperate than ever as he closed his display case. I could still hear the heads muttering and grumbling inside. With an indignant swirl, Alterro barged out the door.

Fletcher looked at us, relieved. "He's very pushy. Sorry you had to see that."

Sheyenne was more interested in the stage. I could tell she was distracted.

Looking at Fletcher, I said, "I like what you've done with the place. The blood bar is a nice addition."

"Harry insisted on it. We're going to put satellite blood bars inside popular, high-class locations."

"Don't people mainly come to Basilisk for the singing?" Sheyenne asked.

Fletcher snorted. "It used to bring in a good crowd, but Ivory is too unreliable, and I got tired of disappointed customers." He gave Sheyenne a puppy-dog look. "Why don't you come back? Just for guest appearances—say, only ... three nights a week?"

"I've been pretty busy since I died." She snuggled closer to me. "I manage the offices of Chambeaux and Deyer, and I need to keep my relationship solid."

I nodded toward the stage, though. "I do love it when you sing, Spooky."

"Maybe once in a while ..." Sheyenne said, "for special occasions."

Fletcher was hopeful. "I'd love to hire another full-time singer, maybe two. But how are they going to upstage Ivory?"

"Easy ... all they have to do is show up when they're supposed to," I said. "Did you know that Ivory took a job as director for the Banshee Tabernacle Choir? She must have needed the extra money."

That was obviously news to Fletcher. "If she doesn't

sing, she doesn't get paid. No wonder she needs money. And she's been spending a lot of time at the racetrack, too, with her new boyfriend."

"Vincent Galdi," I said.

"Goldfanger," Fletcher said. "Her priority just isn't Basilisk anymore. I'm afraid Ivory's cold, black heart isn't in it anymore. She was a star here, and she could have been much bigger."

"Her ego was already big enough," Sheyenne said. "If I came back as a guest singer, Ivory would probably barge on stage just to spite me."

The espresso machine hissed out a burst of steam. The teenage human barista placed a cup of Americano in front of me. "Here you are, Mr. Chambeaux. Fletcher says you like coffee."

I thought of the sludge I consumed at the office, as well as the black oily substance that Esther served at the Ghoul's Diner. "What I drink may not actually qualify as coffee."

"This one's on the house, Shamble," Fletcher said. "You've done a lot for me, and Joey needs the practice."

I took a sip, finding it remarkably good. "You're going to spoil me."

"You won't spoil," Sheyenne said. "You're the best-preserved zombie in the Quarter."

Fletcher got back to the matter at hand. "I really would like to have you sing, Sheyenne ... and Ivory, and anyone else with talent. I could feature several new acts." He brightened as an idea came to mind. "The Unnatural Quarter has talent —hey, that's catchy! A talent show. I could open up the stage, advertise that we're looking for a replacement full-time singer, and invite contestants. We could have a sing off!

Bring in performers from all over the place and let them show off their skills."

Sheyenne warmed to the idea. "Hmmm, I wasn't anxious to sing on the Basilisk stage again, but the idea of beating Ivory in a singing contest—now that sounds interesting. Sign me up!"

CHAPTER 23

The right sort of person, dead or undead, can find romance anywhere. It's a matter of attitude and squinting through rose-colored glasses, and Sheyenne always put me in a positive mood. She gave me warm fuzzies faster than a litter of newborn werewolf cubs.

Leaving Basilisk, she drifted along, shining brighter than before. The idea of an Unnatural Quarter singing contest made her sparkle with possibilities. "It'll be good to sing again, Beaux."

We walked along, dead hand in incorporeal hand, and Sheyenne hummed a lilting melody. Getting into the mood, I whistled along with her. I wasn't adept enough to match my ghost girlfriend's musical skill, but the night breeze whistled through the bullet hole in my forehead as a counterpoint. I'm mostly tone deaf, but we made beautiful music together.

A miasmic mist rolled along the ground, and the full moon rose bright enough for a lycanthrope's bachelor party. Growls came from behind dark buildings, and screams echoed in the distance. Squeaking bats fluttered about, sensing the romantic tension and the pheromones. One bat even landed on my shoulder, folded its wings, and bobbed its ugly head close to my neck. When Sheyenne tried to pet it with her spectral hand, the bat flew off again. Love was in the air.

The Big Uneasy had turned the world on its head, bringing monsters and legendary creatures back into a new normal. Even after more than a dozen years, some had trouble accepting a new universe filled with different sorts of people with unusual appearances, strange cultures, and nonhuman feeding habits. The unnaturals had a tough time adapting, just as the upended humans did.

For the most part, monsters were goodhearted people, just as humans were, although there were many hateful exceptions on both sides. Unnaturals had no monopoly on being monsters. But at least the topsy-turvy world provided job security for a zombie detective.

Near the swamp pond, we sat on an empty park bench on the greenway, from which we could gaze across the scum-covered pond. Toads (or maybe tadpoles from homeless frog demons) let out raucous thrumming, while a nest of mutated crickets on the muddy shore played a rival tune among the reeds. A spotted frog sat on a lily pad, croaking and happy in its limited existence. It was a night for music.

"You're the best thing that's ever happened to me, Spooky," I said, snuggling close to her on the bench.

She gave me a strange look. "You can still say that after I was poisoned, and I died in your arms, and then you were shot?" She frowned. "And all we had was one night together."

"It was a good night," I said. "And we're still here. Look at everything we've got." I gestured toward the swamp pond and the thick mist crawling along the grass. In the background, dark and sinister buildings lined the Quarter.

A crocodile rose up from the pond and gulped down the frog and the lily pad in one bite. The crickets and the other frogs fell silent in mourning, then struck up the soundtrack again.

"I like it when you sing for me." I smiled. "Do 'Spooky' again? You don't need the lounge lizard and the piano."

She drifted in front of me like a performer flirting with the audience. "I have everything I need." Her poltergeist form took on a pale shimmer. She hummed a few notes to get rolling, then moved into the first verse of "Spooky" from the Classics IV.

It was our special song. I almost felt my heart start beating again.

Then, a second voice joined in, adding harmony to the chorus. At first, I barely heard it over the crickets and the frogs, but the singing grew louder and closer. Sheyenne looked over my shoulder, but didn't stop singing. She was deep into the music, focused on me, and I was riveted by her.

But I recognized the little girl's voice. Alvina emerged from the darkness to the park bench and didn't drop a note. Sheyenne went back to the first verse, as if "Spooky" could go on and on like a deep track from a 1970s progressive rock album.

I was surprised my little vamp was out so late, alone in one of the seedy and dangerous parts of the Quarter. But Alvina was a night creature, and we had given up on normal bedtime hours for her.

Both of them were smiling as they sang, but Alvina changed it up by weaving in the chorus of the "Hokey Pokey" as a mashup with "Spooky." The two intertwined songs rolled toward a grand finale, and Sheyenne and Alvina ended on a high note, then took a bow for me. I applauded hard enough to feel my dead hands smacking together.

Sheyenne adored the kid. "That's Dan's favorite song. Where did you learn it?"

The kid was about to blurt out an answer, but I cut her off. "She's been practicing." I didn't want to spoil the evening by explaining what Ivory was teaching the Banshee Tabernacle Choir. I put a hand on the kid's shoulder. "You should be in your cardboard air conditioner box for the night."

"I snuck out." Alvina giggled. "I saw you two and followed. Are you on a date?"

"Every day is a date with Sheyenne."

"Awww, Beaux, that's sweet." Then she turned to Alvina. "Once you start going to Nosferatu Academy, you'll have to get a good day's sleep."

"I'm not in school yet, so I may as well enjoy my last nights of freedom." Alvina's pigtails jiggled as she nodded. "But I can't wait to get some fun homework, too, and meet my teachers and make new friends. I wonder if Nosferatu Academy has a playground."

I wrenched myself up from the park bench as the crickets and frogs began their full-throated symphony again.

Sheyenne said, "Tomorrow I'll call Dr. Schrank about Alvina's assessment."

"I hope the school is ready for a kid like her," I said.

CHAPTER 24

Holding the telephone message slip between thumb and forefinger, Robin gave us her best courtroom victory smile, like the cat that ate the prosecutor. "We have the paperwork to prove that our Alvina is completely sane, adjusted to her life, and fully grounded."

"And don't forget cute as a button," I said as we all walked into the office.

Alvina grabbed the slip and read the phone message. "It's from Dr. Schrank!"

Sheyenne and I were still aglow from our romantic night, and this only made things better. I was surprised the shrink would make a business call so late at night, but an unnatural therapist had to be on call at all hours.

Robin said, "She's written a thorough report that is ready to be delivered to Nosferatu Academy. It even has footnotes."

"Footnotes?" I said. "Wow, she was really thorough."

"You can pick it up at Dr. Schrank's office any time. She'll sign and seal it." Robin looked at me. "Then Alvina can be fully enrolled."

Robin had been pulling an all-nighter, since her legal workload had been heavy in the past week. The lagoon creatures had received permits for their specialty pond and landscaping service, and the engraver had agreed to make restitution for the embarrassing typo on Earl Thrombins's gravestone. Tomorrow, Robin was due in court to argue on behalf of the lava-creature family suing the neighbors over their excessive and hazardous sprinkler system.

Even though we'd just arrived, I took my cue and turned back to the door. I hadn't even had time to remove my fedora. "I know my priorities. I'll fetch it right away."

Sheyenne ushered Alvina along. "Come on, honey, let's get you ready for bed upstairs. I want you sound asleep before sunup."

"Can I read a little bit first?" Alvina pleaded. "I'm just getting to the exciting part."

Mavis and Alma Wannovich from Howard Phillips Publishing had given her the children's illustrated version of the *Necronomicon*, and she'd been reading it every night before curling up in her cardboard box to sleep. She enjoyed the story and wanted to finish before the sequel was published.

"Don't forget to brush your teeth," I called. "Use one of the toothbrushes you got from César's apartment."

"And floss, too!" said Alvina.

"Never forget to floss," I agreed, although I often forgot to floss.

I pulled open the door, eager to read about all the psychological goodness the shrink had found inside the kid's brain.

WALKING WITHOUT SHEYENNE MADE THE STREETS FEEL more gloomy. This time I didn't bump into any disoriented headless figures, at least, but I saw zombies slumped on benches, at bus stops, leaning against brick walls. Some were engaged in light, slurred banter, while others just stared ahead, caught up in their thoughts, or lack thereof. They seemed sad, as if they had nothing to be undead for. Dr. Eva Schrank had her work cut out for her.

Do you have a screw loose? We have the psychological toolkit to help.

Most of the lights were off in the medical office building when I arrived. The optometrist was closed, but the unnatural dermatologist's office showed signs of life, though the door was shut and the shade drawn. As I walked past, I could hear a sinister bubbling and burbling, as if lotions had taken over the office and were plotting a well-moisturized overthrow.

On the third floor, Dr. Schrank was open for business.

I took the stairs rather than the elevator up to the third floor. Seeing the sad and unkempt zombies out on the streets reminded me to keep myself well-preserved. Besides, after shuffling up to the belfry tower, I could handle a few stairs.

As I walked down the quiet hall, a group of zombies emerged from the therapist's office ahead. They moved with slow, even footsteps and swung their arms with the rhythm of their gait. Unlike the downtrodden walkers I had seen on the street, these shamblers seemed light and cheery. Their backs were straight, their shoulders squared, their spoiled-meat lips turned up in smiles.

"We're in this together," one said, sounding encouraged.

"No slurring," said another. "Be happy."

They nodded a greeting to me as they passed. I said,

"You all look happy and content. Did the doctor help you out?"

"We're well centered," said one zombie. "Got our priorities in life."

"No slurring, be happy," said another in a singsong voice.

One shambling woman said, "Dr. Schrank teaches us to think about our hearts." She rubbed the center of her chest. "Not just brains."

I was pleased to see the therapist's obvious success. These zombies didn't seem to have a care in the world.

Inside the office, Dr. Schrank sat at her main desk, filling out reports to shrink her workload. She wore her usual bib overalls and, seeing me enter, she self-consciously adjusted the shawl that covered her shoulders and the front of her chest. "Mr. Chambeaux! I didn't expect you to arrive so quickly."

"Zombies can be lightning fast if we have incentive," I said. "And I'm very happy to pick up Alvina's report."

The therapist smiled. "As I said in my phone message, that girl is exceptionally well-adjusted, flexible, and adaptable. She has a great spirit and a great personality. She'll fit right in at Nosferatu Academy."

I was glad to hear that. "I hope the other monster students have the same attitude."

Dr. Schrank pressed a hand against her bib overalls, as if she had heartburn. "No, but Alvina will help bring up the average scores." She rummaged through the folders stacked on her desk. "Here's my brief summary. I've certified each page, added sealing wax, and ribbons at the appropriate places."

I flipped through what looked like award certifications

and county-fair diplomas. The therapist took the folder back from me.

"One last step for the cover letter." She jabbed her thumb with a letter opener. When blood welled up, she squished it on the cover letter to leave a crimson fingerprint. She blew gently on the document to dry the blood. "There, that should be everything the school needs."

The paperwork had solved itself. I wished all cases could be like that.

I looked more closely at the photos tacked on a cork bulletin board on the wall behind Dr. Schrank's desk. Some of the polaroids were blank, likely well-adjusted vampire patients or invisible men. There were freckle-faced human kids, furry-faced werewolf kids, and scaly-faced trolls of all ages—including one who looked familiar.

"Those are some of my satisfied patients," the shrink explained. "Posted with their permission, of course. Therapy is nothing to be ashamed of."

I leaned closer. "Is that one Sally Allan, the choir director?"

"Oh yes, from the Banshee Tabernacle Choir. It's unusual for a troll to love to sing." Her eyes twinkled. "I'm sure you can guess what part of the song she liked best."

I didn't realize she was making a joke. "What part?"

"The bridge!" She chuckled, and I rolled my eyes. McGoo would probably have found it funny.

This discovery opened new possibilities. "Sally fell from the belfry under mysterious circumstances. We don't know if she was pushed, or stumbled, or did it on purpose. Since she was in therapy ..." I let the question hang, but Dr. Schrank simply looked at me with an unreadable expression.

I continued, "I know Sally had family troubles, felt dissatisfied with their expectations. Do you think her psychological problems were serious enough that she might have considered jumping?"

"Not in my professional opinion." Dr. Schrank pressed her palms to her bib overalls. "Sally was very sad about how her family treated her, but with my training, she had the proper emotional and unnatural toolkit to handle her problems."

"So, not suicidal then?" I asked. The opinion seemed to be unanimous.

"I'm confident I shrank away all those darker feelings." The therapist pulled out a pair of pliers from the toolkit on the opposite side of her desk. "We all have problems, Mr. Chambeaux. You just need to know how to fix your problems, how to adjust your weak points, tighten any screws that are loose." She clacked the pliers together.

"I saw some of your zombie patients walking down the hall," I said. "They seemed very happy."

"More of my success stories. And what about you, Mr. Chambeaux? You must have traumas in your past, disappointments, sad feelings, emotional turmoil. You could use some therapy." She clacked the pliers together again. "Everyone can benefit from it."

I started backing toward the door. "Thanks, but I'll keep my worries to myself."

"You don't have to bear the burden all alone." Schrank rose from her desk. "I can lighten your load, turn that frown upside down."

"Was I frowning?"

She handed me a card. "I host a community group

therapy that meets every Wednesday night. Patients of all kinds, unnaturals of all kinds. Sharing is caring, and we help one another out. Unload your problems, whatever they are."

I slipped the card into my jacket pocket next to the thick stack of Edgar Allan's real-estate cards and gave her my insincere reassurance that I would consider it.

CHAPTER 25

Everything in life was a gamble, according to the wisdom of BatGN, and the risks were finally getting through my thick skull (possibly via the bullet hole in my forehead).

The expiration date of our office insurance policy was near, and Robin reminded me that we didn't dare let it lapse. She had always been more astute about facts and figures, risks and rewards. I didn't need to be convinced.

Two days after I had picked up Dr. Schrank's report, Robin took the time to review our full insurance policy, using a ruler to make sure she read every single line and analyzed the fine print. With a red pen, she flagged objectionable clauses or points for renegotiation, then presented me with the document as if she expected me to read the whole thing and make more notations.

"I agree with all your comments," I said.

"Good, then come with me to the insurance office. We need to present a united front for the Boogeyman."

I looked helplessly around the office but found no convenient excuse that would prevent me from going. "But ... the cases don't solve themselves."

"Insurance doesn't renew itself either." She tapped her fingers on the policy papers. "We're within the renewal window, and we have some leverage because we're long-standing clients."

"And because we helped Boo out with his scary, crazy aunts," I added. I was never going to forget that case. "Sure, I'll come along. The policy does list both of our names."

Carrying her briefcase, she grabbed the car keys. "I'll drive."

Sheyenne and Alvina were filling out school paperwork online, now that we had the therapist's report. The kid was busily choosing her favorite classes.

The Pro Bono Mobile's engine rumbled, and the chassis rattled as Robin started the car. I buckled my seatbelt in the passenger seat. I may already be undead, but I could still suffer physical damage, and I didn't want to use the Wannovich sisters' repair spell any more often than necessary.

On the drive, Robin chatted about her victory in court the previous day on behalf of the lava monster family; the neighbors would have to remove their sprinkler system and use decorative rock instead of flammable foliage in their landscaping. She also told me that the new gravestone for Earl (instead of Ear L.) Thrombins would be installed in Greenlawn Cemetery by Saturday. It was a good week for her.

Before long, we reached the strip mall that housed the Boogeyman's Life and Afterlife insurance office, next to a tanning parlor, a restaurant, and an art gallery.

"Park at the far end of the lot," I suggested. "If Boo sees the condition of the Pro Bono Mobile, he might revoke our auto insurance policy."

Robin patted the steering wheel of her beloved old car.

"We're fully covered, Dan, and ever since Wrex installed all his repairs, the car runs like a charm."

I thought that "evil hex" sounded more appropriate than "charm," especially since we still didn't know all of the modifications the gremlin mechanics had slipped into the old Ford. But Robin had owned the vehicle since her early college days, and with our cash flow, Chambeaux & Deyer Investigations wouldn't be purchasing a new company car anytime soon.

Professional and determined, Robin took her briefcase and headed toward the strip mall office. I walked briskly beside her, sure that the two of us looked like tax auditors.

A year ago, the Boogeyman—or "Boo" to his friends—had engaged our services, desperate for relief from his even-more-terrifying aunts. I had resolved the family conflict by proving that the scary aunties each had their own soft spot, and Boo could go back to his more casual terror and paranoia.

When we entered the tiny office, Boo was with a pair of clients, who wanted full coverage for everything. One was a big golem with rounded gray features, a blunt nose, rubbery smile, and eye indentations that looked like someone had pushed their thumbs deep into a ball of modeling clay.

In the chair next to him sat a fidgety fiftyish man with a crew cut and florid face. He held a gray, black-billed cap in his lap. Both he and the golem wore gray rent-a-cop security uniforms from the Temporary Security Agency.

I had met the security guards Urg and Bill before, most recently after a blood heist by Ma Hemoglobin and her boys. The Temporary Security Agency's name could be interpreted in several different ways. Did the Temporary

Security Agency provide security that was only short term, or did the company offer short employment gigs for security guards who wanted the experience for their résumés? Or did the term "Temporary" emphasize the fact that the survival rate of security guards in the Quarter was so low that most jobs were brief?

The gaunt Boogeyman looked up at us from his small desk. "I'll be with you in a moment." He was bald, with pale skin and sunken eyes above hollow cheeks.

Boo turned his full horrifying attention back to the clients. He had a real talent for making people uneasy and inspiring irrational fears, which made him a natural insurance salesman. Any client who came in just wanting peace of mind, soon became so disturbed that they purchased riders for every imaginable apocalyptic event before leaving.

In the chair, Bill fidgeted with his cap, swallowing hard. Perspiration beads stood out on his forehead. Urg looked glum.

The Boogeyman was as somber as an executioner. "Gentlemen, I'm afraid it's not possible to cover both of you with standard life and casualty insurance. I may be able to make an exception for the golem, because there are numerous repair spells available. If Urg should happen to be squashed flat as part of his job duties, for instance, his innate sturdiness would be a mitigating factor."

He turned his ghastly face toward the human security guard, who nearly jumped out of his seat. "But Bill, surely you are aware that a human security guard working amongst monsters is an extremely high-risk profession."

Bill's face was downcast. "I know the statistics. It's even worse than deep-sea crab fishermen."

Boo reached out a gray hand to give the man a reassuring pat. The touch of his cold, gray fingers made Bill jump.

"We'll figure something out, though it may cost you. My agency can provide a high-risk policy that covers death and dismemberment, but not incidental mangling. Exceptions for teeth and claws, but not tentacles or poisonous stings. That sort of thing."

"Thank you," Bill said.

The golem turned a serious gaze on his human partner. "Don't worry, Bill. I promise to protect you."

"That helps, Urg." Bill stood from the chair and settled the gray cap on his head. He was ready to run away.

Boo gave them a hideous and friendly smile as they turned to leave. "I'll get you a quote with different scenarios, then we can have another conversation."

After they were gone, Robin and I took the chairs across the tiny desk from the Boogeyman. Since Bill's chair was moist from his anxiety, I wiped it down with a tissue so Robin's pantsuit wouldn't get dirty. I sat in the golem's chair, even though it still had a few clay smears.

Boo said in his hollow, icy voice, "Mr. Chambeaux, Ms. Deyer, I'm always delighted to see you." His mouth hung open as if in mid-scream, which was apparently his expression of delight.

"How are the aunties?" I asked.

He sulked. "Still horrific. I join them for lunch every Sunday, as promised. It's a curse."

"Glad to hear that." Robin pulled out the document from

her briefcase. "It's time to renew our policy, and we'd like to renegotiate a few clauses."

Her comment seemed to unsettle Boo. "That's an unpleasant prospect." Robin could be quite frightening when she went into legal mode.

"There are many uncertainties in life," I said, remembering my conversation with BatGN. "We have unnatural, violent, and often confusing clients, and many of the clauses in our contract are vague when it comes to unnatural situations." I put my fedora in my lap, just as Bill had fingered his security guard cap. "I need to make sure my business and my family are covered, in case anything happens to me." I paused. "Again. And our current policy is exceptionally restrictive."

Robin extended the marked-up policy. "This shouldn't take long. I've already flagged all the necessary changes to negotiate. I consider them to be nonnegotiable."

The Boogeyman reviewed the markings, and the two got into a heated debate. Though I sat next to Robin for moral support, I didn't quite follow the dialogue, since I don't speak insurance-ese. She tapped a finger on the contract language, intimidating Boo until he agreed to make all the changes requested.

Robin closed her briefcase, satisfied. "Dan and I are very happy to be your loyal client. Now we don't have to worry about any disasters."

"It is very good coverage," Boo insisted, relieved that the ordeal was over.

As we left, I opened the door for Robin. She wore a victorious smile. "I consider that an hour well spent, even though it wasn't billable."

We exited just as a sallow-faced woman entered. Her expression appeared miserable, and her hair was tangled and damp from sea mist. At first I thought she might be Boo's girlfriend, because she appeared to be his gloomy type. Then I recognized the banshee Sheila.

She nodded a glum greeting to me as the Boogeyman rose from his desk. Sheila said in a mortified singsong voice, "Do you cover broken windows? Or can you help me write a waiver, in case something goes wrong when I perform?"

Robin slipped the banshee one of our business cards. "I can help write up that waiver, if and when you're ready."

My partner's smile was even wider as we walked to the Pro Bono Mobile at the back of the lot. "As I said, Dan, an hour well spent."

CHAPTER 26

Robin went to the Quarter's zoning office to resolve the last permitting issues for the lagoon creatures. As for me, I had to go back to Barney & Clyde's Grocery.

That Saturday would be another running of the Ucky Derby, and Barney was sure to be watching. I had no real proof that the man-bat bookie was cheating (and if so, how?), or that Vincent Galdi was somehow throwing the races.

In front of the main entrance to the grocery, a display table held Styrofoam wig stands and severed mannequin heads. *"Special $5. Marked down for quick and easy recapitation!"* Clyde was busy stacking the random assortment of heads, arranging them to face the same direction. He looked up at me. "I want to encourage headless zombie customers to buy these instead of ransacking the lettuce and cabbage from the produce section."

I nodded. "Small businesses have to adapt to meet the needs of their local customers."

Clyde fit one more mannequin head on the display. "Those headless people aren't bad, but they're awfully clumsy. We're seeing more and more neck stumps lately, and Barney and Clyde Grocers has to stay a 'head' of the competition." The imp snickered at his own joke.

Where was McGoo when I needed him?

"Is your brother in? I wanted to give him an update about his case."

"About his *bookie*, you mean." Clyde frowned in disapproval. "Barney won't stop betting, convinced that the next one is a sure thing, but it's always a sure loser. First it was poker, then golem boxing, and now the nightmare races. I wish he'd stop gambling!" The imp was so angry he knocked a mannequin head to the ground. I bent stiffly to pick it up.

"Can't you just cut him off?" I asked.

Clyde shook his head. "He's co-owner of the grocery, exactly fifty percent, and neither of us can make a binding decision without the other. But our store operates on a shoestring, and our profits are going right out the window!" He indicated all the drastic sales. Mystery Meat had been marked down yet again. "It's all I can do to keep the customers coming in. We were a landmark in the neighborhood, and now a giant supermarket is going up outside of town. That'll drain away our shoppers!"

I had heard of it. "Unsafeway?"

Clyde nodded. "And what little profit we make, my brother gambles away. He insists that one big win would put us on Easy Street for life—but that's not the store address!" The imp raised his hands in frustration. "This is Division Street."

Division Street sounded appropriate for the two quarreling brothers. "Can't you reason with him? He knows what it's costing you both—not just financially, but in your fraternal relationship."

"We've had worse imp family feuds. You should've seen the last family picnic at the park. Even the weather wizards were taken by surprise and called it a 'significant weather event.'" Finished with his display, he went back into the store. I shambled after him.

As the automatic doors whooshed shut behind us, he paused to look at me. "Gambling is a sickness, and Barney needs help. Even if you managed to prove that the races were rigged and there was no chance of winning, my brother would just gamble on something else."

I tilted back my fedora as an idea formed in my head. "I have a suggestion, if he'll listen."

"I wouldn't bet on it, but then I don't have a gambling problem. Be my guest." He gestured toward the back of the store where Barney had hauled a pair of white plastic buckets to the Live Bait and Entrails section. One foul-smelling tub held "Chitlins—Great for Southern cooking."

Wearing a blood-and-slime-stained apron, he threw handfuls of earthworms into a mulch-filled terrarium, and they wriggled into their new home. He poured chopped entrails into an adjacent tank with live piranhas. The third bin held bulk hard candy.

I approached, catching him up to his elbows in guts. Barney brightened. "Mr. Shamble!" He flung more entrails to the hungry piranhas. "Gotta fatten them up. It's fish fry night on Friday. Did you expose that bastard yet?"

"I'm waiting for him to expose himself," I said, then got down to business. "Look, Barney, I was skeptical when you first presented your case. Bookies aren't honest to start with. Being sketchy is a natural part of their profession."

"BatGN's a cheat, and he's throwing the races! He rigs the bets to make sure I always lose."

"But why would he want *you* to lose, Barney?"

The imp blinked at me as if I was stupid. "So he can keep all the money."

"And how does he throw the races, or know which horse is going to disrupt the running? He just sits up in the bleachers with everybody else."

"He knows the odds better than anyone. Have you seen his twenty-sided die?"

"If that's the secret, why don't you buy your own twenty-sided die? There's a gaming shop right around the corner. In fact, they have dice of all shapes and sizes. Buy a handful."

"That would be cheating," Barney pouted, "and I won't stoop to BatGN's level."

"Maybe ..." I hesitated to bring the idea up, but I remembered how upset Clyde was. "Maybe you should take a break from gambling until we figure all this out."

"What? And miss the Ucky Derby on Saturday? It only happens once every week!"

I tried to sound stern, yet paternal. "It's come to my attention that your gambling losses are harming your grocery store business."

"I'll fix it all with one big win!"

"Gambling is nothing to take chances on, Barney. Could you at least consider that it might be an addiction for you?"

"You don't understand, Mr. Shamble...." He picked up the now-empty buckets of slop, and I followed him through the swinging doors to the storeroom in the back.

I had made up my mind. I reached into my jacket pocket, fumbled among the thick stack of Edgar Allan's business cards, and pulled out the one I was looking for.

"I know a therapist, Dr. Eva Schrank. She holds a group session for unnaturals on Wednesday nights where everybody can talk things through, whatever their problems are. Why don't we go? I'll join you. I might get a few things off my chest myself."

The little imp was skeptical. "I don't need a shrink. I'm already just a little guy."

"If you were slightly smaller, wouldn't you qualify to be a jockey? Wasn't that your dream?" I asked.

That made him reconsider. "Maybe it wouldn't be entirely bad...." He set the empty bloodstained buckets on the floor. "And you promise you'll go with me?"

"You won't be alone, Barney. Group therapy with monsters—I can't think of a better way to spend an evening."

Though he was obviously doubtful, the imp agreed to join me.

CHAPTER 27

The smell behind the Ghoul's Diner was even worse than the smells wafting from the kitchen.

Heading back from the grocery store, I passed by the diner—a favorite, if unfortunate, hangout of mine, a place for bad food and bad service. I went to the diner more often than was healthy for me, and I'm already dead.

I heard a shuffling of boxes and banging of metal from behind the building. Curious, as a detective should be, I went through a dingy alley to the back delivery door where Albert received shipments of uncooked slop and where he dumped out the remnants of cooked slop.

Albert would take breaks out here on the stoop, habitually smoking a cigarette as he remembered his more living and less rotting days. But when it was too much of an inconvenience, he smoked the occasional cigarette right in the kitchen, because any ashes in the food only improved the taste.

Behind the diner, a dumpster was overloaded with decaying food, smashed boxes, empty metal cans, and maybe a discarded body or two. With a low buzz, countless flies circled the garbage feast.

A dark, gray-green figure hunched over the treasure trove in the dumpster. His demonic wings were spread open, shading his body, twitching and flapping as he rustled about.

The backs of the leathery wings bore bright signboard letters in fresh orange paint: *Eat at Ghoul's Diner.*

It was Russell. The gargoyle had swung open the dumpster lid and was digging through the debris and offal, stirring up decomposing rubbish.

Since I'd only seen him high up in the open belfry, I hadn't pegged him as a dumpster diver, or a dumpster dweller. He swirled an open brown paper sack back and forth in the air.

"Russell, what are you doing?" I called before remembering that the gargoyle could barely hear even the loud tolling bells. I raised my voice. "Russell!"

He flinched away with a guilty expression, then flapped his *Eat at Ghoul's Diner* wings as if he might take flight. But when he recognized me, his shoulders slumped with relief. "Oh, Dan Shamble!" He flailed the brown paper bag in the air over the garbage. "I'll save some of them for you."

I stepped closer. "Some of what?"

The gargoyle kept darting and circling with the sack. "Flies—fresh, fat, and juicy." He shifted something rotten in the dumpster bed, which stirred up the buzzing insects, and he pounced, swooshing the paper bag through the cloud of flies, then expertly closed the top of the bag and rolled the edges tight. "The best ones are locally sourced."

Flies were a renewable resource in the Quarter, but I didn't know what the resource was good for.

He grinned with his pointed teeth. "For my pets," he explained, and I recalled Russell tossing flies like breadcrumbs to the bats in the belfry. "That's why they keep coming back to me."

The diner's back door opened, and Esther flounced out

carrying a sack of garbage. The harpy waitress's oily dark plumage was ruffled, and when she spotted us, her sharp face became a straight razor of fury. "What are you doing back here? Leave our garbage alone!"

The harpy's shriek penetrated even the gargoyle's hearing, and he cringed. In order to defuse the situation, I put up a hand to calm Esther, knowing she would recognize me and expect a bigger tip next time.

But Russell clutched his sack of flies and turned around to show her his spread wings. He looked over his shoulder to make sure she could see the orange letters. "I have permission—ad swap with Albert."

Esther tossed the bulging garbage bag on the mound in the dumpster. "I don't know anything about that!" She put her hands on her hips, adjusted her waitress apron. "How does Albert think that's going to get any more customers if you're lurking here in a back alley? Idiot!" She stalked back into the diner. She hadn't even bothered to acknowledge my presence, much to my relief.

Now, it suddenly occurred to me that I'd actually been communicating with the hearing-impaired gargoyle. "Hey, how come you can understand me, Russell? I thought your hearing aids didn't work."

He tapped at the earbud deep inside his pointed ear. "Works better far from the belfry for some reason." He plucked out the device and looked at it. I could no longer hear the thin, whining feedback. "Maybe it's because I'm away from the bats. Their echolocation interferes with my hearing aids."

Glad to be able to talk with him more naturally, I

gestured for him to follow me. "Come on inside the diner. I'll buy you a cup of coffee."

I didn't know what the gargoyle did for a living, other than renting out his wings as advertising space, and I was sorry to see him digging through back-alley dumpsters just to catch flies.

Russell was glad for the invitation, and we went around to the front of the diner. The welcome, or warning, bell jingled as I held the door open wide. He tucked his wings tight against his shoulders so he could fit through.

The waitress glowered at us. "Who said you two could use the front door?"

"The Welcome sign did," I said. It was best not to engage in a debate with Esther, although everyone wanted to—at least once.

Back in the kitchen, Albert slouched over the pots on his stove. The big dishwasher sat idle, and I was disappointed not to see our four-armed former client Mary Celeste working today, but recently she had been getting more jobs as a professional hand model, which was her true life's dream.

I found empty stools for us at the counter. "Two cups of coffee, please."

Russell took a seat, curling his barbed tail around front so that other customers wouldn't trip on it. "Cream and sugar for me."

Esther was insulted by the order. "Just coffee? No lunch?" She grabbed the coffeepot as if it were a kidnapping victim. "I'm billing you for lunch, since you're taking up space and breathing our air."

"I don't breathe much air, Esther. Just when I need to talk."

"Then stop talking so much. I've got other customers to worry about."

The gargoyle twitched his wings at her tone, but I agreed to Esther's coercion. She poured coffee into two dirty mugs—apparently, Albert had decided he didn't need a dishwasher after all—and set them in front of us. "Get your own damn cream and sugar." She gestured to a lone set of condiments at the far end of the counter.

I reassured Russell. "It's nothing personal. Esther treats everyone that way."

"I know. I often stop in for lunch after I harvest flies."

I fetched the condiments for him, and he poured cream and a large helping of sugar into his mug. "Did you find out what happened to Sally yet?" he asked. "I sure miss her leading choir practice."

"No answers yet. You were the only witness, and you didn't witness anything."

Eyes downcast, he slurped his coffee. "I'm usually isolated in my own world."

I studied his demonic features, large eyes, pointed ears, sharp teeth. "But you seem to hear a lot better at street level."

He tapped the earbuds. "Still a little hard, but I get the gist."

"Why don't you move down here, spend more time with other unnaturals? Take part in society. Wouldn't you be less lonely?"

Russell held the coffee mug in two clawed hands. "I don't really want conversation. Too much chatter, with nothing to say."

"I hear that," I said, by way of making conversation.

"I like the quiet, just me and the bells, and the bats, and the view." He hung his head. "Don't like the murders, though ... or whatever happened to Sally."

"UQPD is doing a full investigation," I said. "You'll have your peace back soon enough."

The gargoyle drained the dregs of his mug, which mostly consisted of undissolved sugar. "Thanks for the coffee, Mr. Shamble. I better get back to the belfry, though, while these flies are still fresh."

I raised my mug in a salute as Russell left the diner. I dropped a twenty-dollar bill on the countertop next to the coffee mugs just as Albert placed steaming piles of his lunch special under the heat lamp. I hurried out before he could attempt to serve me.

CHAPTER 28

Sheyenne personally delivered Dr. Schrank's psychological report to Nosferatu Academy and confirmed that Alvina could start classes the following Monday.

"Yay!" The kid clapped her hands and acted like a ten-year-old girl again, even if she was more than twelve. I wasn't going to tell her to change her ways. I thought she was adorable.

Robin came out of her office, satisfied. "Good thing. If they hadn't accepted her, I would have filed a discrimination lawsuit."

"I can't wait to meet my new friends," Alvina said, "and maybe even make a few enemies."

Sheyenne's spectral brow furrowed. "Why would you want enemies, honey?"

"To crush them into submission."

Sheyenne flashed me a disappointed look. I shrugged. "I didn't teach her that! Must have been McGoo."

Robin took heart in the kid's attitude, though. "You might be cut out to become a prosecuting attorney, Alvina. You must be way ahead of all the other students in your class."

Although we'd passed the first hurdle of educational

bureaucracy, we had another important requirement before her first day at school: she needed new clothes, a new backpack, and school supplies. Budget conscious, Sheyenne suggested we try shopping at the Unnatural Quarter Flea Market.

Robin cocked her eyebrows. "I'll go along, too. I enjoy seeing the exotic vendors with exotic items. Besides, you might need legal advice."

The flea market was a sprawling collection of tables, booths, and tents spread across the cracked asphalt of a drive-in movie theater parking lot. It reminded me of an Arabian bazaar run by monsters, sorcerers, and craftspeople hawking their wares.

The peeling movie-projection screen at the back of the parking lot had been painted over with a tall mural of a giant mutated flea with a round body, tiny eyes, and a sharp proboscis.

Lester's Flea Market
Every Monday-Wednesday-Friday

Lester, the enormous hard-bodied insect, had created a vending area for unnatural craftsmen, potion sellers, soothsayers, and crocheting spiders. His flea market had been a tremendous success, as much a social gathering as it was a place to buy unusual items.

It was a sad story behind the scenes, though. Wealth and fame had proved too much for Lester the flea. The fast, rich lifestyle had gone to his tiny head, and he had blown his fortune on high-priced blood and mating females. Lester flaunted his riches until one night, bathing in a vat of fresh blood, he had gorged himself, drinking and drinking until he simply *popped*. Although that was the end of Lester the giant flea, his flea market endured.

As we walked through the gate, the colors, smells, and noises thrilled Alvina. A skeleton banjo player picked out lively tunes as he clattered among the customers, passing around a top hat for donations. Not to be outdone, the Phantom of the Opera sat in his best going-out-in-public tux and ceramic mask, playing ominous dirges on a portable Wurlitzer.

The front section was a farmers' market where local gardeners, herbalists, and wood witches set up tables with leafy vegetables, corn by the bushel, elderberries, graveyard fungus, Spanish moss, mandrake root, unnamed writhing tubers marked "on special," and carrots. Middle-aged human women sold jars of jellies and jams. An enterprising zombie couple sold jars of a lumpy, slimy substance labeled "James and Gabby Johnson's Gray Matter."

A fire demon was selling hot sauce in asbestos bottles, offering free samples on crackers, but Robin warned us not to try any, because she was worried about the harmful effects of asbestos.

Lester's Flea Market had no listing of vendors, so we just wandered and looked. Long-haired hippy liches offered bright, tie-dyed shrouds. Edgar Allan the troll and burly Burt worked the crowd, handing out business cards, but I turned Alvina down a different aisle before they could see us.

Frieda, the spider-lady reference librarian, sat behind

her table, a flurry of jointed and pointed limbs as she wove custom tapestries. Vultures circled overhead, as if looking for bargains.

"Look, backpacks!" Alvina raced to a table where a spotted frog demon displayed pink, lavender, and peach-colored backpacks with appliqued cartoon figures—superheroes, large-eyed unicorns, and little werewolf scamps.

Robin clucked her tongue. "Those must be unlicensed. That's trademark infringement."

The frog demon flicked out a forked tongue and blinked his huge eyes. "Ayup."

"When I have a student ID card, that's like a license," Alvina said. "Can I get one? Pleeeease?" She adored a pastel unicorn on a pink backpack, and how could we resist?

A wizard and a mad scientist shared a table, selling lab notebooks and spell scrolls. I picked up one of the notepads. "Are any of these blank for classwork?"

The mad scientist squinted through very thick glasses. "Some have notations written in invisible ink, so they might as well be blank."

"It'll be good for school," said Alvina.

"We'll take one," I said.

Using her poltergeist powers, Sheyenne looked through the spell tomes, perusing the written incantations and diagrams. "Here's an old textbook, but your school probably uses something newer."

"It's college level," said the wizard. "Our elementary-school spellbooks sold out at the beginning of the semester."

I put my hand on Alvina's shoulder. "She's a late entry,

but she reads way above her grade level. She'll advance to college-level courses very soon now."

The mad scientist indicated a blasted area behind their table, which had been burned and singed. "We have place in back if you want to try any of them out."

We declined the offer, but we did purchase two of the invisible-ink notebooks.

At the next table, a familiar figure stood behind an array of discolored and disgruntled shrunken heads. "Go away!" yelled one of the heads.

"What do you want to buy us for?" said another.

"Die! Die! You'll all die!" said another.

"Welcome!" Alterro rubbed his hands together and flashed us a wide, unappetizing grin beneath his handlebar mustache. "Mr. Chambeaux, you brought your friends and family. Can I interest you in a little head?"

"No!" the shrunken heads all said in unison.

The necromancer chuckled. "See how much fun they are! I'm going to sell out soon, but I'll make more."

"We're just here to get school supplies for Alvina, Mr. Alterro," I said. "Still not in the market for any shrunken heads."

"You know, shrunken heads can be useful in school," Alterro said in a wheedling voice. "Your little vampire girl could keep the head beside her as she studies at home, then take it with her to class. During tests, it could whisper answers to her."

"I don't need to cheat," said Alvina. "I'm already smart."

"I'm not," said a shrunken head.

Alterro gave a scolding flick of finger to the head's brow. "Flea market special today. Each head comes with a free teeth-whitening spell." He pulled the top sheet from a stack of printed leaflets under a rock on the table. "And you can subscribe to my monthly mail-order service. Are you sure you don't need it for your work?"

"We're sure," Robin and Sheyenne said at the same time.

Alvina clutched her new unicorn backpack as she tickled one of the shrunken heads under its shrunken chin. It squinched its rubbery lips, puckered them and then tried to bite her finger. Alvina found it hilarious. "They are kind of cute."

Before I could make further excuses, a huffy woman in a business dress marched up to the shrunken-head table. "Excuse me, Mr. Alterro! I have a complaint."

She was accompanied by one of the headless zombies, a lurching disoriented figure in tattered clothes. It might have been the same one I rescued from being run over by the Dermi Taxi the other night.

"Uh, yes, ma'am?" Alterro stammered. "Always happy to ..." His voice trailed off as he recognized her. He flinched away from the headless zombie.

"I want my money back, sir. I bought one of your shrunken heads at the flea market last week." She reached into her large purse and pulled out a grimacing object. Exposed to the sunshine, the shrunken head began snarling at the headless figure next to her, "Mine! Mine! Mine!"

"My souvenir head says he belongs to this zombie right here."

"Well ... uh ... obviously not. Look at the size differential."

"Mine! Mine! Mine!" said the shrunken head.

The headless figure extended his hands out in the air, trying to locate his head.

Frowning, Robin stepped closer to the table. "Mr. Alterro, do you have free title to these shrunken heads you're selling?"

Panicked, the mail-order necromancer began to gather up the heads on display, dumping them into his tissue-lined carrying case. "Uh, very sorry about the mix-up, ma'am. I can't understand what might have happened." He fumbled in his money envelope and pulled out two twenty-dollar bills. "Here, please take this refund with my apologies."

Robin pressed the matter. "Where exactly are you getting these shrunken heads, Mr. Alterro? Do you have a permit to sell them?"

"I paid for my flea market table, free and clear." Alterro packed up in a whirlwind. "It's a novelty item, unregulated." He yanked the top spell from his stack of mail-order flyers and thrust it at the dissatisfied woman. "Here, let me offer you a free Three Wishes spell to make up for the inconvenience."

She studied the paper while the detached and minimized head kept yelling, "Mine! Mine!" It rolled dark eyes at the headless zombie.

"Where *do* you get your heads, Alterro?" I asked.

"How do I know this Three Wishes spell isn't a scam?" the woman demanded.

The necromancer finished throwing everything into his carrying case, ready to bolt. "It's Three Wishes, but please take care to read the fine print so nothing unfortunate happens."

The other shrunken heads kept mumbling in the padded

case as Alterro scuttled off. With remarkable speed, he wove his way through the numerous flea market tables.

Sheyenne shook her head, looking after him. "Good thing we didn't subscribe to his monthly services." She gestured Alvina down another aisle. "Come on, honey. Let's go find you a churro."

CHAPTER 29

I consider myself a well-adjusted zombie, but Sheyenne reminded me that the people who most vehemently object to therapy are usually the ones who need it most. Thinking it through, I decided not to push back on the idea, thus proving that I didn't need the services of Dr. Eva Schrank for any emotional or unnatural problems of my own.

But Barney could certainly use some help for his gambling addiction, and the imp was unlikely to go to a group session by himself. I try to do what the clients need, whether or not they realize it, so I arranged to be his therapy wing man. On Wednesday, I picked him up from the grocery store just as night was falling. He had removed his grocer's apron and put on a button-down shirt with a bowtie.

Clyde was refilling the bins of large moth pupae—"Great for roasting!"—and offered us an encouraging nod. He gave Barney a big hug, much to his brother's embarrassment. "I'm proud of you, bro."

"I'm just going along to support Mr. Shamble," the imp said.

Clyde and I exchanged a knowing look. "We've got each other's backs," I said.

He and I set off toward the cathedral-turned-performance-hall, where Dr. Schrank held her community sessions. At the side entrance, a sunken set of stairs led to a dungeon-level entrance to the basement fellowship rooms. The community space was used for various unnatural support meetings, Brain-anon, a sex-addict circle for succubi, the weekly gathering of the Spanish Inquisition, and other therapy sessions that were open to the general public.

Barney spotted a flyer on the cathedral's message board at the base of the stairs. "No problem is too small for Schrank to shrink." I felt reassured by that, because my problems were indeed quite small.

The imp's anxiety expressed itself as bursts of wind. The fedora blew off my head, and I barely caught it in time. "It's OK, Barney. They only want to talk out their problems, and you can just listen." I opened the door and ushered the green grocer inside. "It'll make you feel better."

"How can listening to other people's stupid problems make me feel better?"

"It'll make you realize you're part of one big miserable family."

We located the proper basement room by following the crowd noise. There were no windows underground, and the community room was lit with flickering fluorescent ceiling lights. Scuffed metal folding chairs—the same ones used for Alvina's choir recital—were arranged around a canvas director's chair, where the therapist would sit.

The smell of burnt coffee wafted from an old Mr. Coffee maker on a card table, next to a stack of Styrofoam cups, a jar of powdered creamer, and a sugar dispenser. A refrigerator held blood boxes, energy drinks, an assortment of Monster Chow protein shakes, and bottled water.

A low drone of conversation filled the room, growls and raspy voices from werewolves with patchy fur, a shifty-eyed vampire whose skin was bronzed with spray tan, an amphibious creature with mottled skin covered with thick smears of lotion. A few listless zombies stood around, and I was glad to see that they all had their heads. Several furry gremlins clustered together, chattering, while sullen goblins stood in a corner. The group therapy session had likely been imposed on them by the court.

I smiled. "See, Barney—it looks like a fun and friendly group."

"I don't see any other imps."

"That means you're special. It doesn't matter what type of unnatural you are or what type of problem you have. Dr. Schrank has the right tools to help."

"Maybe I could use a hammer ..."

The therapist, still wearing her bib overalls, stood at the cork bulletin board and group message center. She had a troubled look on her face as she yanked down a flyer. She tore it in half and tossed the pieces into the trash can.

I approached to introduce her to Barney. "So, that's not a service you endorse, Dr. Schrank?"

Startled, she pressed a palm to the center of his chest. "Sorry, I was preoccupied." She fished the torn flyer out of the wastebasket, and I saw that it advertised Alterro's Spells 'N' Such. "We definitely won't be promoting that necromancer's services anymore."

I recalled seeing Alterro scuttling away from Dr. Schrank's office when we'd come for our first appointment for Alvina. "I thought he was a former client of yours."

Schrank sniffed. "I'm not allowed to talk about my patients, although I'd certainly like to talk about this one." She looked at the torn flyer in her hands, then tore the pieces in half again. "I've canceled my office subscription to his Spell of the Month Club, and he will no longer be welcome at our public sessions."

Still jittery, Barney looked around as if he wanted to flee. "But the sign says anyone welcome."

"That necromancer's not just anyone!" She drew a breath to calm herself. "Alterro is full of himself, too profit oriented, completely self-centered."

"Some might call that the mark of a good businessman," I said.

"Not Alterro. He's unethical." Embarrassed, she apologized for her attitude. "I tried to help him, but when I expressed concerns about what he was doing, he wouldn't listen. I gave him my 'full Schrank,' and it rolled off of him like water from a slime demon." She sighed. "In all my years as a therapist, I've learned you can't help a monster who doesn't want to be helped."

She turned away from us. Glancing at the clock on the wall, the doctor snapped her fingers to get the attention of the attendees milling about. "Please take your chairs. We're ready to begin."

The unnaturals in need of therapy took their seats, while a few hurried to refill their cups or snag a blood box from the fridge. The glum goblins sat together in one section of the folding chairs, and Barney and I found seats near Dr. Schrank. The zombies, moving slower than the other attendees, settled into any chair that was left.

The therapist straightened the shawl over her shoulders and tied the ends loosely in front of the overall bib as she leaned back in the director's chair. "Good evening."

She paused for a faltering chorus of "Good evening, Dr.

Schrank" responses, then began the session by having each person introduce themselves around the circle. I wanted to tug my fedora down over my face and keep a low profile, but I participated so I could better help Barney. On the walk over to the cathedral, we had discussed his gambling habits. Clyde had also had words with his brother, but the imp still didn't admit he had a real problem.

"Now then, who would like to begin?" said the shrink.

"Brains," said one of the lackluster zombies. "Brains taste better than tofu."

The other zombies agreed, though I kept my opinion to myself. When all was said and done, I didn't much care for tofu.

"Sometimes you have to learn to eat healthier, for medical and cultural reasons, Mr. Paxinos," Dr. Schrank said.

"Ted," said the zombie.

"Hi, Ted," said the group.

"Glad we're on a first-name basis," he said. "But I still think brains taste better than tofu."

No one was eager to take the opposite side of the debate.

"Have you tried James and Gabby Johnson's Gray Matter?" another zombie suggested. "You can get it at the flea market."

"I can spread it on tofu, I guess," Ted said.

"I miss the sun," said the artificially tanned vampire, leaning forward in his chair. "I get Seasonal Affective Disorder when I have to spend too much time in my coffin."

"I recently read a paper that suggested bright solar lamps can help with that," Schrank suggested.

The vamp shook his head. "It's not the same."

Now she took a sterner posture with the brain-addict zombie and the sun-starved vampire. "It can never just be the same—we have to accept that. You're all here because you've made bad choices."

"I like being here," said the amphibious creature with the skin cream.

"I'm here to support a friend," I said when the unnatural faces turned toward me.

Barney fidgeted on the metal seat, as if gathering his courage. Finally he drew a deep breath and blurted out, "I ... I have a problem."

I was proud that he finally admitted it. I leaned closer. "Go ahead Barney, it's okay."

Ted encouraged him. "You can tell us."

The imp said with great determination, "I have a problem. I ... I gamble on the nightmare races. I do it quite often."

With everyone listening, he pressed on, "And my problem is that my bookie is cheating me!"

The audience gasped, but I was disappointed.

Barney continued, "But Mr. Shamble here is going to solve it! Pretty soon, I won't have any problems at all."

CHAPTER 30

Seeing that Barney's obsession would not be shaken, I knew I had to find absolute proof about the nightmare races, one way or another. I decided to have a look at the demon steeds themselves—and that meant going straight to the source of the hay and the manure.

The stables were adjacent to the Underground Downs, where the black animals were kept for the weekly races. Since no other track in the country would dare to host the enormous steeds, this was the only place for them.

I parked in the far lot so the roaring engine wouldn't scare the already-fierce beasts. Alvina wanted to join me so she could pet the pretty horses, but it was safest for her, and maybe for the nightmares, if I went alone.

The wide stable doors were open to let in the day's fresh gloom. Nearby, a wagon was piled high with bales of dried black weeds, thorny vines, nightshade, hemlock, and poison ivy. As thoroughbreds, the nightmares deserved the best diet.

I stepped toward the stable and was surrounded by the heady aroma of horse apples, which smelled nothing like apples at all. Nightmare manure was toxic, like steaming cannon balls, but it had intrinsic value. A wood nymph stable hand trundled past me with a wheelbarrow heaped with nightmare apples. Outside the stable, a pickup truck from a local landscaping service was loading up with dung for special plantings.

The wood nymph turned her mossy head toward me and winked. "Here to see the nightmares? They need a special treat—did you come prepared?"

I was new to this. "I didn't think that far ahead."

The wood nymph reached into the tattered brown pocket of her tree-bark skirt and pulled out a ball of glittering white crystals.

"A sugar lump?" I asked.

"Sugar laced with strychnine." She handed it to me. "Gives them that extra pep, and they'll love you for it."

I thanked the wood nymph as she pushed the wheelbarrow toward the landscaping truck.

Inside the stables, I was glad that my sense of smell had been deadened, so I got only the highlights of the stench. The nightmares were in their armored stalls—sleek, black beasts with spiky manes, flared nostrils, and scarlet eyes. They snorted smoke at me. With razor-edged hooves they pawed at the gates of their stalls. I couldn't imagine how the little imp jockeys were brave enough to climb into the saddle.

Stable hands lovingly brushed the nightmares' coats and sharpened mane spikes and hooves, even though the next running of the Ucky Derby was still two days away.

I looked at names on the stalls: Frankensteed, Cloven Hoof, Dashing Entrails, Glue Factory, and Hoof 'N' Mouth. Each animal was owned by either a wealthy patron or a consortium of investors. Vincent Galdi, the godfather of the racetrack community, owned five of them himself.

A nightmare in an unattended stall snorted and whickered. I looked into the fiery eyes and said, "Good girl.

Nice girl." I pulled out the strychnine sugar lump. "Here you go. Want a treat?"

Cautiously, I extended the sugar lump, and the beast lunged at me like a striking rattler. Startled, I tossed the crystalline lump in the air, and the steed gobbled it up, whinnying with satisfaction.

The other nightmares glowered at me, angry that I hadn't brought treats for all of them.

"What's your business here, sir?"

"No harassing the animals!"

I turned to see two familiar security guards—the gray golem Urg and the skittish Bill. Both wore gray Temporary Security Agency uniforms.

"I was just giving the sweet thing a treat," I said. "Not here to cause any trouble."

Nervous, Bill let Urg fill the space between us, but he sounded brave when he spoke from behind the clay guy. "Good, because we're private security, and we don't like it when anyone causes trouble!"

"Gives us something to do, though," Urg said.

I shifted my position so I could see Bill's sweaty expression. "I'm Dan Chambeaux, private investigator. We've crossed paths a few times, most recently at the Boogeyman's Insurance Agency."

Urg said, "Oh, yeah. And at Ma Hemoglobin's blood heist. I was really shellacked."

Bill relaxed. "So, you're only a zombie detective, not a bloodthirsty monster with a taste for security guards?"

"Not today, just investigating the nightmare races. I'm surprised to see you two here. I thought you were more cut out for shopping malls."

"Bill couldn't get insurance, so we asked for a stable job," said Urg.

Bill flushed, looking disappointed. "And they assigned us here! Stupid TSA."

I slipped into P.I. mode. "Maybe you've seen something. Are you familiar with the suspicious disruptions in recent races? Do you know BatGN, the bookie?"

The two guards looked at each other. "BatGN comes every week," Bill said.

"He likes the races," Urg said.

"He plays the odds," I said, "and my client suspects fraudulent behavior. He might have something to do with all the accidents, but I can't figure out how."

We walked down the line of stalls, stopped between Dashing Entrails and Glue Factory. "Aren't both of these animals owned by Vincent Galdi?"

Bill took a notepad from his pocket, reviewed his handwritten scrawls. "Yes, those are two of Goldfanger's horses."

"Isn't he concerned about the reputation of the nightmare races? Allegations of tampering?"

"Maybe you should ask him." Urg glanced over his shoulder toward the back of the stables. "He's in his office, up there."

The large private office took up the second floor of the stable complex. From there, Vincent Galdi would have had a great view of the track, but all the windows were blackened.

"Knock first," Bill warned. "He's with his new girlfriend."

This was an interesting lead, but I could handle Ivory.

"I'll do that, thanks." I headed toward the stairs that led up to the private office.

Mercifully, it was only one flight and far less strenuous than ascending to a belfry. In the upper hall, the office had two massive mahogany doors like the Presidential Suite in a fancy hotel. I could hear the rising and falling notes of a sultry voice crooning a sexy song.

When I knocked on the door, the singing fell silent. There was bumping around, a thump against the door. "To your left!" called a man's voice, sounding frustrated. Afterward, I heard a fumbling at the latch, and the door swung open.

I faced a broad-shouldered headless zombie dressed in a dark suit, black tie, and white shirt. Obviously security. Behind him stood two similarly dressed headless figures who wandered in circles, probably trying to find the door to respond to the knock. One of the headless goons had drawn his pistol but didn't know where to point it.

"Who is it?" called the man, but the headless bodyguards obviously couldn't see me.

I raised my voice. "Dan Chambeaux, private investigator." I took a gamble. "Ivory knows me."

I heard a squeal of delight, and the headless guards were shouldered aside. Behind them, the overconfident vamp diva grinned from fang to fang. Her ego was as large as her breasts. "Dan Chambeaux! What an honor." She glanced over her shoulder. "Goldie, it's a dear friend of mine, a strong supporter of my singing career. He has a thing for me, but now I'm yours."

"Let him in," said the male voice.

Ivory took me by the arm and pulled me into the large office. "Come in, sugar."

Her voice was as sweet as a strychnine-laced lump. "Thanks, Ivory. I'm investigating possible tampering in the nightmare races."

"Tampering?" The male voice sounded offended. "Everybody needs a little corruption, but there's nothing unusual here."

As I stepped around the headless bodyguards, I faced a tall man with slicked-back dark hair and bright eyes as sharp as ice picks. He wore a perfectly tailored tuxedo that looked like it was designed for a million-dollar funeral. When he extended a hand and smiled at me, I saw that both of his long incisors were covered with gold veneers. Now his name made sense.

"Pleased to meet you, Mr. Chambeaux. I am Vincent Galdi."

I shook his hand. "As a businessman, you've done a great deal for the Unnatural Quarter, sir."

"Indeed. The Underground Downs and the entire racing profession wouldn't exist without me. I considered it a wonderful investment."

Ivory stalked over and clung to his arm. "And I love you for it, sugar."

"You love all the gifts I shower you with," Vincent said.

"I adore them."

One of the headless bodyguards wandered out into the hall as if to check for further threats, while the others kept blundering about in the large office. Galdi had an enormous mahogany desk, several leather-upholstered executive chairs, and a glass-topped table.

The heavily tinted windows filtered out any toxic sunlight, while offering an unobstructed view of the racetrack. The track had been prepped with white chalk lines marking the lanes for practice, and it would be groomed again before the Saturday races.

Vincent grimaced at the fumbling guards. "Useless idiots. I needed to hire additional security, and I asked for a lot of muscle but no brains. Boy, I got that in spades."

Ivory grasped one guard's shoulders and turned him so that at least he faced the proper direction.

"The guys look intimidating, but they're shit for security," Vincent said. "I'm going to have to let them go."

Ivory slid up to him. "You did a good thing by employing them, sugar. It shows your compassion. You've always been generous, generous to a fault."

"To a fault," Vincent agreed. "Now, how can I help you, Mr. Chambeaux? What is this about tampering and corruption?"

I summarized my client's concerns and asked about Vincent's relationship to the mutant bookie.

"No relationship." He seemed embarrassed. "The races are big business, and you can't stop people who operate on the fringes. We offer standardized gambling stations right at the racetrack, but some people choose to use more traditional but seedier sources—then they complain when they receive unethical treatment."

"But what about the races themselves? All those unexplained accidents and disruptions when the nightmares are running."

Vincent shrugged. "It's a rough sport. The nightmares are unruly and running at top speed, like bats out of hell."

That gave me an idea. "Speaking of bats—"

Before I could ask about the little dark shapes I had seen flitting near the nightmares before they went berserk, I noticed a framed painting behind Goldfanger's desk—a painting just like the one I had seen in One Fang's deserted apartment. "That's César Marici, the dentist. He's another ... client of mine."

Vincent gave me a smile to show off his gilded fangs, then tapped one with a well-manicured fingernail. "César was an excellent dentist, came highly recommended. He created the most distinctive part of my personal branding."

Now the pieces began to fall into place. "Oh! You must be the patient who accidentally bit him and turned him into a vampire."

Vincent brushed at the lapel of his tuxedo, removing imaginary lint. "I'm rather chagrined by that unfortunate incident. Laughing gas doesn't usually affect me like that."

"So, you turned him," I said. "He was old and ready to retire."

"Life's a gamble," Vincent said, sounding defensive. "And I made it worth his while. After what happened, I gave him a huge conciliatory bonus. César was able to retire, and now he lives a pampered life doing whatever he pleases. We're good."

"How is he involved with your case, sugar?" Ivory asked.

"César disappeared without a trace, and I'm looking for him," I said. "Have you seen him?"

Vincent scoffed. "We parted as dear friends, but we move in different circles."

I thought of the racetrack. "Or ovals."

Ivory's short attention span had reached its limit. "Mr.

Chambeaux, I need to get back to exercising my voice." She draped herself on Goldfanger's arm. "Fletcher at the Basilisk had the gall to announce a singing competition, looking for a replacement for me. For me! I am going to prepare for it, and I am going to win. I'll sing my heart out, and I'll make their ears bleed."

I wondered if that was really the best way to win the competition.

"My dear Ivory is right." Vincent gestured me toward the door. "If you have further questions for me, I'll make myself available if it helps keep the reputation of the Underground Downs clean and pure."

"As pure as the driven snow," Ivory said.

"Show him out," Vincent said.

The headless guards shouldered one another, trying to find the door. The one with the drawn handgun turned in circles in search of a target. I dodged the security and made my own way out. The headless guards did manage to close the door behind me.

As I walked away, I heard Ivory start to sing again.

CHAPTER 31

told the imp grocers what I had learned at the stables, and I commended Barney for going to the group therapy session. He hadn't made any breakthroughs, but progress was made in baby steps. Nevertheless, Clyde was so pleased that I had gotten his brother to the session that he gifted me two piranhas in a water-filled plastic bag. I knew Alvina would enjoy having little bloodthirsty pets.

When I returned to the office, Sheyenne helped the kid put her piranhas in a makeshift fishbowl on the kitchen counter near the loquacious and potty-mouthed black mold. The fish circled around, glowering at the dark fungus. Sheyenne must have intended it as a threat, but the mold did not seem cowed. It formed words on the wall: HERE FISHY, FISHY, FISHY. Alvina dunked her finger into the fishbowl, playing with the piranhas.

Back in my office, I mulled over cases, but after staring at my notes for an hour, I felt restless and decided to try my usual routine. I slid the .38 into the pocket of my sport jacket and donned my fedora. "Going for a walk," I said to Sheyenne.

"Going to the Goblin Tavern, you mean," she teased.

"Eventually, but first I want to clear my head." I tapped the bullet hole above my eyebrow as I headed out the door.

Studies show that the human thought process is

improved by moving about instead of sitting still. Remember that old statue by Rodin, *The Thinker*? Naked guy bent over in an awkward position with chin in hand? He could have gotten more thinking done if he'd wandered around.

I ambled from block to block thinking about Goldfanger and Ivory, who had become director of the Banshee Tabernacle Choir after Sally fell to her death. Was Ivory involved with that? Could she have wanted the position so badly that she would murder for it? Did she need a second income because Fletcher had cut her pay at Basilisk, since she rarely bothered to take the stage? But if Vincent Gardi was her sugar daddy, why would she go to such lengths to do that? And how was Galdi's connection to César Marici relevant? Yet another way the wealthy owner of Underground Downs was connected to my cases ... and I didn't like coincidences.

Then there was BatGN with his private battery up on the roof, and Russell feeding treats to his beloved bats in the cathedral belfry. And Eva Schrank, the unnatural shrink, had treated Sally for troll depression.

No wonder I needed to walk around and clear my head. The cases were tangled like Silly String in my thoughts, and every time I pulled on one, something else unraveled.

So, with all that, I wasn't thinking at all about the mail-order necromancer and his convoluted schemes—when I saw him in his embroidered robes, handlebar mustache, and big personality. He sauntered along a shadowy side street, leading a group of zombies like the Pied Piper on a day that rat prices had gone up.

Alterro had always struck me as a loud and seedy sort who made flashy used-car salesmen seem like pillars of the community. The necromancer considered himself an imaginative entrepreneur, which was just a fancy way of saying con man. He was full of big ideas and little implementation, and others paid the price when the surefire schemes fell through.

When he first introduced his Spells 'N' Such subscription service, he'd sent mailers to every denizen of the Unnatural Quarter in hopes of enticing them into more expensive premium plans, including limited-edition spells and "surprise charms" for elite subscribers. I knew now that Dr. Schrank had broken ties with him, and I expected his novelty shrunken heads would peter out sooner or later.

"Right this way," Alterro said to his undead followers in a loud stage whisper. "Keep in the shadows so no one sees you." The zombies shambled after him. "Free brain ice cream!"

"Two scoops," said one of the zombies. I thought I recognized Ted Paxinos, from the group therapy session.

"You can have two scoops, if you want," Alterro agreed. "This way." He danced along, and the zombies followed him.

Brain ice cream? Everything about Alterro seemed to be furtive. I remembered the dissatisfied woman with the shrunken head at Lester's Flea Market. How was Alterro trying to scam these zombies now? Determined to see what he was up to, I followed them at a safe distance. If he glanced back, maybe he would think I was just part of the gang.

Alterro guided them toward an industrial warehouse and storage unit district. I wondered what he intended to do with them there.

Then the phone in my pocket rang. The "Marimba" ringtone cut through the hushed silence, startling the zombies ahead of me. They turned around. "Brain ice cream?" Ted asked.

Alterro heard the disturbance and stopped, but I ducked into a dark doorway as I answered the phone. Caller ID said it was the Goblin Tavern.

Her raspy voice said, "Shamble, it's Francine! I need you here."

"I was planning to stop by in the next hour or so."

"Now! I just got a call from César. It's a clue."

I'd been without a clue for quite a while, so now she had my attention. "Be right there." I glanced back, still suspicious about what the necromancer was doing, but Alterro and his zombie followers had already ducked around a corner.

I was at least ten blocks from the tavern, and I started shambling as fast as I could. Fortunately, as soon as I reached the busier streets, a flesh-colored car screeched to a halt beside me. "Hey buddy, need a ride?" Eric leaned out the window. "Hop in. I'll get you where you're going."

I yanked open the back door and jumped in. "Good timing. To the Goblin Tavern, and make it snappy!"

"You got it, buddy." He stomped on the accelerator. "Only a few more minutes left in happy hour, but we'll make it."

It was a sickening blur of a trip, but the Dermi Taxi got me there in five minutes flat. After paying the skeleton, I rushed inside.

A handful of customers sat at the barstools or cocktail tables. McGoo wasn't in his usual place.

Francine looked up with her usual haggard expression, and I could tell she was alarmed. "What is it, Francine? What's the clue?"

She pulled out her phone. "I got a text from an unknown number, and all it said was 'My head hurts!'" She showed me the words on the screen. "I'm sure it's from César!"

I tried to understand. "But you don't recognize the number?"

"I'd recognize César's voice anywhere!"

"It's just a text."

"Still, I know it's him."

"My head hurts ..." I mused. "But from an unknown number."

Francine said, "He's in trouble, Shamble. I know it. Look at that!" She tapped the phone screen. "His head hurts."

This seemed more serious than just a vampire hangover. I copied down the number. "I'll see what I can find out, I promise."

CHAPTER 32

Even as a ghost, Sheyenne liked singing in the shower. She used my dingy apartment shower, complete with a drip and a rust stain around the drain; most importantly, the acoustics were perfect. Sheyenne sang as she practiced for the talent competition at Basilisk, which Fletcher had advertised as "Cursed Idol."

"You're ready, Spooky," I reassured her. "And you're going to win tonight."

She played coy, though she shimmered from the compliment. "It doesn't matter if I win, Beaux—so long as I beat Ivory."

As we got ready for the big night, McGoo showed up, breathless from running. "Wouldn't miss it for anything! Even brought my own earplugs for the other performances."

Technically, Alvina wasn't old enough to enter a nightclub, but McGoo and I both gave our permission, and Fletcher agreed to look the other way, especially since the kid was an integral part of the performance.

In not too many years, we were going to have to get the kid an official ID card. And it would pose challenges, because Alvina would always look like a ten-year-old girl, and because vampires didn't show up even on bad DMV photos.

Though we arrived an hour early, Basilisk was packed.

Unnaturals and a few curious humans filled the bar and the booths. Vampires, zombies, and ghouls engaged in small talk over their drinks. Reporters and photographers were there to provide media coverage.

I looked around the nightclub. "I didn't realize a singing contest would be such a big event." Fortunately, one of the round tables in front of the stage had been reserved for our party, so we had the best seats in the house.

"It's the Quarter's first-ever Cursed Idol Competition," Robin said. "People are curious."

"And a little nervous," McGoo added as he pulled out a chair for Robin.

Warming up the audience, the lounge lizard tinkled his nimble scaly fingers across the piano keys. On stage stood a green stone figure of an elder god with a cuttlefish head, bulky body, and dragon wings—the actual cursed idol for which the competition had been named.

As Sheyenne headed backstage to get ready, I gave her an air kiss. "Good luck, Spooky. You'll knock 'em deader than they already are."

Alvina skipped along at her side as they both ducked behind the curtains.

Good thing Ivory had her own special dressing room with a double-wide coffin where she slept all day long. Fletcher wanted to prevent any fireworks from Ivory accidentally bumping into Sheyenne before the show started.

Now Fletcher was helping out behind the busy bar. I went to get beers for me and McGoo and a club soda for Robin, but when I saw the teenaged barista working his arcane machinery, I decided on a cup of good coffee instead.

As I waited for my Americano, Fletcher poured Robin's club soda and McGoo's beer in red plastic cups, which seemed odd for such an upscale place.

When he set the plastic cups in front of me, I asked, "Are you ready for this, Fletcher? I feel sort of responsible for the whole thing."

The ghost was obviously excited by the crowd. "Responsible, Shamble? You were the inspiration for the contest. It's good to bring in some fresh blood, and no matter what happens, Ivory will know she has competition."

The barista handed me my Americano in a Styrofoam cup, and Fletcher nudged the other two drinks closer to me. "On the house."

The lounge lizard played a peppy circus tune, then some dramatic pounding that sounded like the song from that *Carmina Burana* movie.

"What's with the plastic cups?" I asked.

Fletcher leaned an ectoplasmic elbow on the bar, looking toward the angry idol on the otherwise empty stage. "Not taking any chances with the other contestants. All the bottles are wrapped up and insulated, and we're using only plastic or Styrofoam cups. The audience has signed damage waivers. It's going to be great!"

I thanked him and went back to our table, handing the drinks to Robin and McGoo. I was pretty sure I had a goofy smile on my face.

Each table in the nightclub had a small bowl with individually wrapped breath mints and ear plugs. McGoo had brought his own plugs, but I made sure he took a breath mint.

At last, the lights flickered down and back up, and the cursed idol's artificial eyes glowed behind the tentacle face.

Fletcher drifted onto the stage as emcee, raising his translucent hands for the audience's attention. "Welcome to the very first Cursed Idol Competition. We have a really big show and a lot of singers, so ... let's get started." He looked at a piece of paper that floated in the air in front of him.

"Our first contestant is well-known in the Quarter, star of the big stage. Highbrow audience members might have heard him perform at the Phantom's Opera House. Let's have a hand for ... Stentor!"

The back curtains were thrust open by a huge hand and almost torn down from the hanging bar as a hulking figure lurched out to stand before us. The ogre's head was as big as a suitcase, his thick lips hanging open. Hair, or fur, or wires stuck out from his chin and head.

I smiled, pleasantly surprised. Robin clapped harder.

"Thank you, thank you!" Stentor said, then glanced over at the lounge lizard. "I'll need no accompaniment."

The piano player lifted his scaly fingers off the keys and leaned back on the bench to watch.

The ogre was a former client of ours, a renowned opera singer whose voice had been stolen, and he'd come to Chambeaux & Deyer to get it back. After I solved his case, he'd continued his well-respected operatic career. The ogre was best known for his dramatic performance in *Don Giovanni*, though his most popular run had been a revival of *Cats*.

Stentor cleared his throat. "You all know this one." He drew in a breath large enough to inflate a hot-air balloon and then sang "Memories," the biggest hit from *Cats*. He clasped his hands behind his back, closed his eyes, and thrust out the words like a battering ram.

Stentor was proud of his "three window performances," which shattered even the wire-reinforced frames at the opera house. Fortunately, Basilisk had no glass to break, but the ogre's voice was powerful enough to knock the cocktail tables and chairs a few inches farther from the stage.

Robin, McGoo, and I held on and endured the performance, and we applauded heartily when Stentor was finished. After giving a deep bow to the audience, the ogre stalked off stage left.

Next on the program was a barbershop quartet of zombies, which seemed unusual, but I was curious. When the four marched in an uneven and unruly shuffle onto the stage, however, I saw they were all headless zombies. The lounge lizard played a lively tune, "In the Good Old Summertime."

The decapitated figures managed to stand together in a line, but did nothing else, since they had no mouths to sing. They swayed a little. When the piano player finished the tune, the silent headless zombies bowed before shuffling off the stage.

The third contestant was Sheila, who turned her mournful face toward Fletcher. "For the record, sir, you do have the proper insurance for my performance?"

After he reassured her, the banshee gave a quick plug for her singing telegram service, and advised us to all put our earplugs in place. Robin and I each tore open a packet from the bowl and followed instructions, while McGoo took out his personal set. I jammed the foam wads into my ears just in time for Sheila to unleash a shrieking and moaning rendition of "Happy Birthday to You," Marilyn Monroe fashion, as a sample of her telegram service.

At the bar, the news reporters jotted down notes. One foolishly used a digital recorder to capture the performance, and it melted into a black plastic lump.

After the banshee left, Ivory came out for her big number, and the audience fell into a hush. The vamp diva glided forward in a feathery pearlescent dress that set off her ebony skin, her red lipstick, and her bleached white fangs.

"Thank you all for coming to hear me tonight—and every night." Her voice was sultry as molasses, or tar. She swept her gaze across the crowd, ignoring me. "Let's give a round of applause to the other contestants. It's so sweet that they actually try."

She clapped politely, which inspired a patter of applause in the nightclub.

Robin's nostrils flared, and I ground my teeth together—and Ivory hadn't even started to sing yet. McGoo looked flustered.

The vamp gestured to the lounge lizard with her lacquered nails. "Go ahead, sugar. Just like we rehearsed."

As soon as the first few notes came out of the piano, my nostrils flared, too. I would have recognized that melody anywhere.

"She picked that song on purpose, Dan!" Robin hissed.

"I know she did."

Ivory swayed as she sang a slow and sexy rendition of "Spooky," Sheyenne's signature song. When my ghost girlfriend sang it to me, I felt uplifted and sparkly inside. Now, hearing the lyrics from Ivory made my skin crawl.

The rest of the crowd, knowing nothing of our history

with that tune, clapped with delight, the most enthusiastic response to any of the performances so far. Robin and I sat straight-backed, our hands flat on the table. Glowering, McGoo crossed his arms over his chest. None of us was going to clap for that!

Ivory winked directly at me before she sashayed off the stage.

Fletcher's ghost reappeared in the limelight next to the cursed idol. "Our final contestant tonight is a real favorite here at Basilisk, though we haven't heard her in a long time. Miss Sheyenne Carey!"

The crowd whistled in anticipation, and the beautiful blonde ghost shimmered right though the stage curtains without even rustling them. Her ectoplasmic expression was troubled and uncertain, but when she saw me, along with Robin and McGoo right up front, she was buoyed up. I put a hand over my heart for her.

Sheyenne brightened like a manifestation of a torch song. "This song may sound a little familiar to you," she said to the audience, as sweet as a girl next door. "But this version has a very personal meaning for me."

She flashed an accusatory glance at the lounge lizard, who just shrugged his narrow shoulders. She gave him an impatient wave. "All right then. Here goes."

The lizard's fingers tinkled the keys as he played the same song we had just heard Ivory sing. Sheyenne began singing "Spooky," but instead of the husky, lewd tones from the busty vamp, Sheyenne's version was filled with deep emotion and yearning. Sweet and sparkling, she instantly had the audience wrapped around her ghostly finger.

But she wasn't done yet. When she reached the first

chorus, the stage curtains parted, and Alvina skipped out to join her, turning the song into a duet. Their voices overlapped perfectly. If anything, it was even better than the private performance they'd given me by the park bench.

If I'd had any zombie tears, I would have been bawling like a baby. As it was, a few drops of embalming fluid leaked out of the corner of my eye. McGoo was whistling and cheering.

Stentor and Sheila were sonic powerhouses that could cause structural damage, but Sheyenne and the little vampire girl brought down the house in their own way. When they finished, the applause went on and on. Even the cursed idol glowed with pleasure.

Miffed, Ivory pulled the curtains back and glared out at the stage, directing her ire especially toward Alvina. "I taught that vampire kid everything she knows!" With a huff, she swirled back behind the curtains.

No one was surprised when Sheyenne and Alvina took home the Cursed Idol trophy. They were already winners in my heart.

CHAPTER 33

The Cursed Idol winner's trophy looked impressive on the shelf above Sheyenne's desk. We made sure to place it where new clients would notice when they entered our offices.

McGoo arrived, still on a proud high from the competition the night before, but he hadn't come for a social visit. He waved a scrap of paper at me. "Shamble, I tracked down that unknown number from One Fang's text."

"We're not positive it was him," I said. "Anyone could have sent a text that his head hurts."

"We know whose *phone* sent it," McGoo said. "The number belongs to a necromancer named Alterro."

"Alterro? What does he have to do with César Marici?" Of all the case entanglements, I hadn't seen any connection between those two.

"Maybe they were on a family plan from the cell carrier service," Sheyenne suggested.

"Unfortunately, there's no address connected to the account. You'll have to find Alterro some other way." McGoo frowned.

"We bump into him all the time, usually when we don't want to," I said. "Maybe we'll get lucky now."

McGoo was agitated. "If that guy knows anything about César's whereabouts, you've got to find him, Shamble.

Francine's a wreck—and she keeps messing up the drink orders."

"César's my vampire friend!" Alvina added with a pleading tone. "He might be in trouble."

I said, "Thanks for the lead, McGoo. I'll look into it right away."

He grinned in appreciation at the Cursed Idol trophy before he headed off to walk his daily beat in the Quarter.

Time to take a different approach. Alterro's involvement put a new spin on César's disappearance. I was still creeped out from what I had seen a couple of nights ago, the necromancer of ill repute leading zombies with the promise of brain ice cream. Now the incident seemed more nefarious.

Sheyenne rummaged through her file drawers and pulled out an old Spells 'N' Such flyer, searching for an address, but it listed only a post office box. Next, she called up business licenses from the UQ Chamber of Commerce, but without success.

"I've got another idea," I said. "Dr. Schrank had some unpleasant business dealings with Alterro. She might have more direct details on him."

Sheyenne agreed. "It's time for you to go to the therapist, Beaux."

"Say hi to her for me!" Alvina said. "I start school on Monday."

It was Saturday morning, and I hoped Dr. Schrank would be in her office. I grabbed my fedora and set off to pry open the shrink's toolkit.

At the medical office building, the dermatology clinic was open for a weekend special. Just inside the clinic doors, a skeleton sat in the waiting area. I wondered what dermatology services he could possibly need, but pushed the thought out of my mind, because it's not polite to dig into other people's medical problems.

Taking the elevator to floor three, I emerged into the quiet hall, where the office doors were closed up tight like morgue refrigerators—including Dr. Schrank's office. My heart sank. Maybe the therapist took weekends off.

Not giving up easily, I tried the door and was surprised to find it unlocked—a positive sign. One thing I had learned about therapy was that it helps to keep a positive attitude. Anxious to find Alterro, and hopefully César, I pushed the door open. "Excuse me, Dr. Schrank?"

Sometimes, even when you glimpse things for only a flash of a second, the image burns itself into your memory and you can never unsee it.

Dr. Schrank was standing behind her desk with her back to me. I'd caught her in the middle of changing clothes. Her lacy shawl lay on the desktop, and she'd unclipped her overall straps and pulled down the front bib.

What startled me was not the unexpected flash of her boobs when she spun around. Much more riveting was the gaping hole in the center of her chest, right where her heart should have been. It looked as if someone had taken a sternum-sized paper punch and made a giant peephole straight through her torso. I could see the wall on the other side of her desk, and I even noted the picture of the troll choir director.

With a gasp, Dr. Schrank yanked up the bib on her overalls, aghast.

I was aghast as well. "Sorry, ma'am! The door was

unlocked, and I ... I had a few questions. And, uh, now I have even more questions."

She finished pulling up the overall straps on her shoulders. "That was something you weren't supposed to see!"

I decided the obvious approach was best. "What happened to your heart?"

"A birth defect. I don't have a heart." She adjusted her overalls and primly tucked the shawl into place as she gathered her dignity. "I'm a big emotional vacuum, but that makes me a good therapist. I found my heart's true calling."

"I don't understand," I said.

"Understanding takes many sessions of therapy, Mr. Chambeaux. Don't expect a breakthrough right away."

"I don't need a breakthrough, just an explanation. I'm a zombie private investigator, and I like to have all the answers."

"You have a hole in your head. I have a hole in my chest," she said. "It's perfectly unnatural."

I tapped my brow. "At least I know where my bullet hole came from."

Dr. Schrank sank into the chair behind her desk. "It's nothing to be ashamed of. I'm happy with who I am, and I've used my handicap to help people. A good therapist should never become too attached to her patients, and a heartless therapist never has that problem."

I took a seat in the chair across from her desk. Hoping to make her more comfortable, I picked up one of her notepads and grabbed a pen. "It's all right. Tell me all about it."

She sat back. "The only time I feel anything is when I shrink away the problems of other unnaturals. It makes my figurative heart swell." Her eyes had an odd green sparkle, and I felt giddy, as if burdens had been lifted from my shoulders. "There's nothing to worry about."

I could tell she was working some sort of spell on me. "Stop that! I like worrying." I remembered her deliriously happy zombie patients who seemed to be walking on air as they left their session. "There should be a warning about too much happiness and contentment."

She rolled her chair back. "Very well, I won't give you the full Schrank, but I've had many satisfied customers. I take away their miserable emotions."

"The Quarter must be like an all-you-can-eat buffet for you."

"I try to consume in moderation. Taking away other people's problems fills me up while I shrink theirs. That's why I'm a shrink. I don't mind that nickname. I've done a lot of good." She sounded defensive.

Though I was still wrestling to understand, I raised a hand to reassure her. "Who am I to judge personal weirdness? If you're helping people, I doubt even my lawyer partner would file a grievance, unless somebody complained."

"Nobody complains, Mr. Chambeaux," the therapist said. "They're happy and satisfied."

I set the notepad aside and concentrated on the important part. "Ma'am, I'm not here to discuss your condition. I'm working on a missing-persons case. I have a tip that Alterro the necromancer is involved, and possibly in other shady activity as well."

The therapist's expression darkened. "Of course he's involved in shady activity! I regret that I signed up for Spells

'N' Such. I paid for the premium platinum plan because I had a very specific need. In order to help with my 'problem-reduction work,' I requested a powerful shrinking spell. He claimed it was a special order, and he charged me extra.

"But when I tried it, the spell did not shrink away problems or moods, as I expected. It simply reduced the size of my client!" She lowered her voice. "One of my former patients, a big burly orc, now has to pass himself off as a little goblin! I demanded satisfaction, but Alterro insisted that he makes no guarantees with his spells. He refused to give me my money back, and he wouldn't return the orc to regular orc size." She pounded on her desk. "He even had the nerve to put up flyers in my group therapy room! If I ever see him at one of my sessions again"—she raised her fist—"I'll give him some *physical* therapy."

I glanced at the metal toolbox on her desk. "Always use the right tool for the right job." Then an idea occurred to me, another unexpected connection. "Wait, if Alterro hangs around by the cathedral for the public meetings, do you think he might have ..." I glanced at the framed picture of the smiling troll choir director. "Might he have had anything to do with Sally's death?"

The therapist considered. "Sally said she often heard high-pitched noises that ruined her enjoyment of the choir performance. It was out of the range of human hearing, but she insisted it was there. How could Alterro be connected with that?"

I remembered the whining feedback from Russell's hearing aids, but I shook my head. "I'll ask him when I find him. I also need to question him about a missing vampire dentist. Can you help me track him down? It's urgent."

Dr. Schrank dug in her files, but shook her head. "Just a mail drop. No known physical location."

Now I liked the shady mail-order necromancer even less, but it was Saturday morning, and I had the whole day ahead of me. "I'm going to poke around the belfry some more. If you think of anything else, please let me know."

The therapist placed both hands over the center of her chest as additional coverage for the hole where her heart should have been. "Would you like me to give you a warm fuzzy before you go? It might help."

"No thanks." I turned back to the door. "I want to keep my wits about me."

CHAPTER 34

When investigating cases, it's best not to do everything solo. Sheyenne has chided me for going commando at inappropriate times, even if it's only for brief intervals.

So, as I headed to the cathedral, I called McGoo to let him know where I was going, as a precaution. I told him which wild goose I was chasing on a Saturday.

"You are one dedicated zombie detective!" he said. "Climbing all those stairs …"

"The cases don't solve themselves. Fighting crime and solving mysteries is always an uphill battle."

I knew that Alterro schmoozed some of the unnatural self-help groups that met at the cathedral, trying to sell his spells and shrunken heads. Maybe he had encountered Sally Allan? No one had ever asked Russell about seeing the necromancer.

Knowing the exertion that awaited me on the stairs, I decided to drive over in the Pro Bono Mobile. When I attempted to change the radio station back to the classic rock I preferred, I discovered another surprise feature that Wrex and his repair gremlins had installed: with a blatt and a puff, gray-black smoke gushed out of the exhaust pipes—not due to a bad carburetor or broken head gasket, but as an actual deployed smokescreen. I switched back to Alvina's modern pop station, and the smoke dissipated.

Now that was a problem I'd have to fix.

On this bright Saturday morning, I found a parking spot right around the corner. I poked around the lower entrance and found the community rooms locked, hosting no unnatural therapy sessions, succubus support groups, or Silver Singles Club.

I went out front to the main entrance, and the big old cathedral seemed as empty as a tomb. Inside the big gallery, tall stone columns rose to the vaulted ceiling. Several hunchbacks and lab Igors sat together in the front pews, whispering, and I realized they were just here to listen to the imminent cacophony of the noon bells.

My destination was up in the belfry itself. As I climbed the interminable stairs, I hoped Russell was in his usual place. Otherwise, it would be a lot of wasted effort. I reached the open belfry and felt the warm breeze and sunshine on my gray skin. The bell hung mercifully silent at the top of the tower. For now.

"Russell!" I called out, knowing he wasn't likely to hear me. I marched across the big tower in search of the gargoyle. Around me, bats fluttered and chirped, then darted away.

At one of the arched window openings, the gargoyle sat with his legs dangling over the dropoff, looking out at the city. His angular wings were spread enough to display *Eat at Ghoul's Diner*. If Russell spent the whole day hiding up in the belfry, Albert wasn't getting much benefit from the paid ad space.

He held another bag of fresh flies, and the adoring bats

swirled around him. As he flung out a handful of buzzing insects, bats looped in the air, doing tricks for their treats.

Russell was clearly at ease, and he chuckled as he tossed more flies into the air. Several bats alighted on his shoulders.

"Yes, my babies," the gargoyle said. "Russell has the best treats."

I entered his peripheral vision, and he turned. "Hello, Mr. Shamble."

"It's a nice Saturday morning," I replied, but I might as well have just been moving my lips. "I have another idea about Sally's death."

"What's that you say?" Russell tapped a finger against his ears. Mixed with the squeaking and cheeping bats was a high-pitched feedback whine. I just gave him a dumb smile and waved.

More bats settled on his shoulders, and one perched on his head. All of them sported unusual metallic bling, little circuitry chips or digital squares. I raised my voice, "Do you know what that is on all the bats?"

Russell listened hard. He furrowed his brow and considered deeply. "Seventeen I think."

Hearing the pervasive flutter and squeak of the flying rodents, I wondered if this noise was what the ultrasensitive troll choir director had heard. Much of the chirping was out of the range of human or unnatural hearing, but Sally had noticed it during the choir performance, making her indignant enough to climb the belfry stairs so she could confront ... what? Russell had been on his usual perch at the time, but he claimed not to have seen or noticed anything.

Had the necromancer been up here waiting for her?

In any good mystery, the old deaf gargoyle would have

been the obvious suspect. But I had read the fictionalized versions of our Shamble & Die cases, and I knew full well that they were not good mysteries.

Taking the notepad from my pocket, I scribbled down notes and a question. "Have you seen a necromancer up here? Alterro? He probably tried to sell you something."

Russell considered. "No, no necromancers."

"Any shrunken heads?"

"Just normal-sized heads."

I wrote a brief explanation about Alterro and his suspicious activities, but the gargoyle still shook his head. Thinking about the annoying tone the choir director had heard, I asked him about interference from the bats and even asked him if he knew about the battery that the bookie kept on his roof.

Russell scrutinized the words, moved his lips as he read, as if that might help him decipher my handwriting. His pets remained close, even though his paper sack was empty. "I know BatGN has a battery, but bats shouldn't be kept in cages." He rustled the sack. "I treat them kindly, know each animal as an individual." He crumpled the paper bag and tossed it out into the open air. "No matter what bling that other owner uses, the bats keep coming back to me."

Russell twitched his leathery wings, animating the *Eat at Ghoul's Diner* signboard.

"You sure you don't know anything about Alterro the necromancer?" I pointed to the name written on the pad.

Russell shook his head. "Never heard of him."

That lead had gone cold, but it was a long shot, odds that even Barney wouldn't have taken. I gave the gargoyle a thumbs up and left him to ponder the view as I walked back around the belfry. Glancing at my watch, I saw that it was nearly noon, and I didn't want to be here when the bell rang out the hour twelve times.

When I was halfway around the tower, a monstrous form loomed in front of me, a mutant half-man/half-bat wearing a vest, a green accountant's visor, and a murderous expression. He held a control device in one hand, and his bat ears flared larger when he confronted me. "You ask too many questions, Dan Shamble."

"How many questions?" I asked. "Which ones?"

"No more of your meddling. I came to retrieve my bats! I need them this afternoon—they have work to do."

"What sort of work does a bat do?"

"Not just any bats—*trained* bats!" the bookie said.

"How do you train them? Do they do tricks? What do you keep them for? Is there a secret in your battery?"

"See what I mean about all those questions!"

"I am a zombie detective," I said. "Occupational hazard."

He sneered toward where Russell sat gazing obliviously out at the city. "That gargoyle keeps luring my special bats here! I try to keep them in my battery, but I have to turn them loose to stretch their wings. Today, however, I've got a lot of money riding on the nightmare races."

"What do the bats have to do with the nightmare races?"

"Is that another question?"

"Was that a question?" I cleverly countered.

Gloating, he revealed his diabolical plot, because unnatural villains are quite predictable. Unfortunately, when evil-doers explain their schemes, they usually intend to kill you shortly thereafter.

BatGN raised the odd control box in his clawed hand. "I

transmit signals and drive the bats into a frenzy using the receivers implanted on their bodies. I program the specific horses I want the bats to target, and I send instructions and amplifications. They swoop closer. With their squeaks, they disrupt the imp jockeys, and the sound drives the nightmares nuts. I can make any of them crash, so that my own chosen steed wins the race."

"But that's cheating!"

"It's technology! Increasing the odds, like weighting the dice." With his other hand he plucked out the well-worn twenty-sided die from his vest pocket. He tossed it on the floor, looked at the number, and snatched it back up. "You lose, Dan Shamble."

I had just had to line up the colored squares on the sides of the Rubik's cube—and that was no easy feat. "So, you transmit disruptive messages to your trained bats to change the results of the Ucky Derby. And that device in your hand"—I nodded toward the controls—"that's your Bat-Signal?"

"It's my *BatGN-Signal*—proprietary tech!"

Now the Rubik's cube was snapping into place. "And the choir director ... did she discover your scheme?"

"Yes, that nosy troll could hear my signals because that damn gargoyle was feeding my bats again! She came up here to investigate and ended up seeing too much."

"So, you pushed her from the high belfry," I speculated.

"Exactly!" The mutant bookie lurched toward me, intimidating. He was a very large, strong, and furry creature. "Let me demonstrate."

He seized the front of my sport jacket and lifted me up. My feet dangled off the ground, while I fumbled in my pocket to pull out the .38. I was close to the inner railing and the yawning drop to the stone floor of the cathedral.

Now I knew what Sally the troll had experienced.

Just then, the clock struck noon, and the enormous bell rang out with a crash of sound. The physical wave made even BatGN stagger.

I tried to squirm loose, but as the bell struck a second and third time, the bookie lifted me up over the rail. I swatted at him, trying to break free as the fourth *BONG!* rang out.

BatGN gave an extra shove and tossed me out into the open. I fell into empty space as the bell continued ringing.

IN FICTION, THIS IS THE POINT WHERE THE AUTHOR would begin some rambling pointless diversion, a discussion about the meaning of life or the hazardous coincidences that occur every day, all to draw out the cliffhanger suspense.

Here, I could have reviewed and reiterated the novel's theme, about the risks one takes in life, how every action is a vagary of chances. I could have left the reader hanging at the story's most intensely tense moment as they wondered what had happened to their beloved main character, the intrepid zombie private investigator who'd gotten himself into such a dire predicament.

But I won't do that now, because it's a cheap shot. I won't distract the reader or delay the story at all, but instead will continue immediately with the hair-raising crisis. Anything else would annoy the audience.

I fell out into the open air, plummeting toward the floor far below the belfry. I dropped head-first, which gave me the perfect view of where I would splatter, just like Sally. In fact, I could still make out the faint chalk outline where the choir director's body had struck in the middle of the recent recital.

I yelled at the top of my lungs, but the bronze bell was so loud that no one could even hear me scream. The floor was coming up so damn fast.

I saw a flutter of movement, and before I knew it, a dark green figure swooped in. Russell snatched me out of the air and backflapped his wings. He slowed us enough for a gentle landing in the middle of the cathedral floor.

"You had a nasty fall there, Mr. Shamble! Lucky I saw you out of the corner of my eye."

My knees were so weak, I could barely stand, but Russell supported me as I swayed.

The bells finally stopped ringing.

The cathedral's front door swung open, and McGoo rushed in, breathing hard. "Couldn't find a parking spot," he said, then did a double take. "What happened to you, Shamble? You look like you fell from a great height."

Officer Toby McGoohan was very perceptive.

We needed to grab the culprit. "It's BatGN! He's the one who threw Sally Allen from the belfry—like he just threw me."

McGoo eyed me up and down. "Good to see you unsplattered."

"Russell caught me in time."

Smiling, the gargoyle bobbed his head, though he probably hadn't heard anything we said.

"We've got to stop him, McGoo." I hurried back to the belfry stairs. "Barney was right! That bookie *has* been using his pet bats with implants and sonic technology to disrupt the nightmare races. You've got to arrest him, McGoo. BatGN is still up there. Run!"

"Run?" he asked in dismay. "Up the stairs?"

"He's a murderer and a cheat. We need to stop the Bat-Signal."

We huffed and puffed from one landing to the next. Climbing to the top of the belfry took a lot longer than falling from it. I was charged with enough adrenaline to reach the open tower with McGoo only three steps behind me. Russell flew up to meet us there.

But the belfry was empty. I looked out across the city. "Maybe he flew away."

The mutant bookie had escaped—taking all his sonic controlled bats with him.

CHAPTER 35

The Saturday afternoon nightmare races were ready to start at the Underground Downs, and McGoo and I had to get there before BatGN disrupted the Ucky Derby again.

McGoo wiped sweat from his forehead as we hurried to the Pro Bono Mobile. "Is this thing safe?"

"As safe as anything in the Unnatural Quarter."

I started the engine with a roar, and we drove off at high speed toward the racetrack. Since McGoo was in uniform, he flashed his badge and got us a free parking spot in the front lot.

We rushed together into the Downs, him flashing his cop badge, me raising my private investigator license. "Coming through!" Neither of us had had such a workout in some time, but the situation demanded it. Being thrown from a high belfry gave me a new and urgent perspective on existence.

Thankfully, the day's first race hadn't yet begun, and a few nervous humans placed bets in the computerized machines outside the stands. Two furtive rat creatures peeped over their shoulders, pretending to be in line, but they were snooping at the bets.

By the time we pushed through the turnstiles and into

the bleachers, Ivory was on a platform above the track, crooning out "The Star-Spangled Banner."

"Let's search the stands," I said. "Hurry!"

After a smattering of applause when Ivory finished, the announcer's voice boomed over the loudspeakers, introducing the first race. Wearing a pearlescent white dress, the vamp singer started climbing the stairs toward Vincent Galdi's private box on the far side of the bleachers.

Huffing, we climbed into the stands under the black awning. As before, the seats were crowded with unnatural gamblers, nightmare fans, and families on outings.

Wrex and his gremlin mechanics leaned over the rail in the front row, waving, shouting, and cursing, as if to intimidate the demon horses and their imp jockeys. The shrunken head on Wrex's belt moved its rubbery mouth as if trying to cheer, too, but all it kept saying was, "Kris! Kris! Kris!"

I scanned the bleachers, trying to spot the mutant bookie with his Bat-Signal control. Last week, he had sat in a high, isolated corner in the deepest shadow of the awning, but those seats were already taken.

"Maybe we got here ahead of him, Shamble," McGoo said. "You really think he flew here?"

"The Pro Bono Mobile is fast, but BatGN wouldn't miss this." I kept searching up and down the bleachers. "He has a lot riding on those nightmares."

I saw Goldfanger in his fine tuxedo on the landing just outside of his private box, presumably to greet Ivory. But as the diva climbed up to him, the rich businessman was engaged in a heated conversation with BatGN! The murderous bookie had an urgent look on his hideous face, and his thick bat wings draped behind him like wilted sleeping bags. Ivory looked annoyed as she joined them, no doubt because her sugar daddy was ignoring her.

McGoo saw the bookie at the same time and shouted, "There he is!" Apparently, he decided to dispense with the element of surprise.

The crowd noise rose to a crescendo as the buzzer rang to start the first nightmare race. The gates flew open, and a storm of thoroughbred black steeds surged out.

BatGN's enormous ears managed to hear McGoo shout above all the chaos. He whirled and spread his wings, astonished to see a zombie detective come back from the dead.

"Stop right there!" I yelled, then added, "Cheater!"

As the demon horses raced along the first leg of the run, nobody was paying attention to the panicked bookie. People called out names, encouraging their horses and cursing their rivals. The imp jockeys hunched in their saddles, clutching the reins and bouncing along.

Seeing me rushing toward them, Ivory didn't seem to know whether to flirt or sneer. Goldfanger looked cool and formal, but he was clearly angry at BatGN. He gave the mutant bookie a dismissive wave.

With our quarry in sight, McGoo and I charged up the bleacher steps to Goldfanger's private box.

BatGN turned to flee. Flapping his heavy wings to create a tailwind, he bolted down the steps toward the front of the racetrack. Holding the Bat-Signal controls, he stabbed buttons with a clawed finger.

Suddenly, like a cloud of mosquitoes on a muggy summer night, his enhanced bats emerged from the shadows of the dark awning and swooped around him. They reminded me of flies attracted to a fresh dog turd.

The announcer rattled off nonstop rapid-fire commentary as the horses pounded around the curve, neck and neck. With their electronic instructions, the bats whipped away from the bleachers and out toward the running horses.

I didn't have sensitive ears, but the fury of squeaking and squealing would have been within the range of imp or nightmare hearing.

As he fled through the stands, the mutant bookie shoved a mummy who was heading back to his seat with a tray of hot dogs and soft drinks. The mummy stumbled, spilling his food and unraveling his gauze. BatGN's clawed foot got tangled in one of the bandages, and he hopped around until he tore the cloth free. He continued toward the front row of seats.

McGoo and I yelled after him, hoping someone else might make a citizen's arrest, but the spectators only cared about their nightmares.

On the way, McGoo accidentally bumped into a cheering orc, who snarled then shoved an elbow in his gut, making him double over. I pulled him onward.

"You won't get away, BatGN!" I yelled, because defiance is often the best policy.

When he reached the front row at the edge of the track, the mutant bookie suddenly came to a halt, blocked by a livid, diminutive imp in a grocer's apron. Barney was so furious that angry breezes gusted into BatGN's face. "I know what you're doing. I've been to a group therapy session! You're cheating."

Though we were still many rows away, I called, "Barney

—the Bat-Signal in his hand! That's how he's controlling the bats."

BatGN tried to shove the imp aside, but Barney got in his way again. Wind rippled like a raspberry blown in the bookie's face. "You're rigging the horses. You're throwing the races! I want my gambling money."

"I bet you do," growled the bookie.

The announcer kept rattling off the progress of the race as the nightmares pounded around the final curve and into the home stretch. Glue Factory pulled ahead of Eye Socket, running hard, but Beetlebaum was still in the lead. Marley fell behind, clearly their worst nightmare.

I could see the trained bats homing in on the horses, squeaking out of the range of human hearing, but enough to drive imp jockeys and nightmares into a frenzy.

Barney swatted the control box in BatGN's hand, smashing the buttons. With a surge of imp energy, he shorted out the controls.

Out above the track, the trained bats went wild, diving in front of the demon horses, harrying the jockeys.

With a grunt and a push, BatGN knocked the imp aside and ran along the front row of seats by the railing above the track, trying to reach the exit.

McGoo and I closed in as an outraged Barney scrambled after the bookie. As BatGN fled recklessly, he bumped into a big orc in the front row who was engrossed in the race, cheering his horse on. Annoyed, the orc elbowed BatGN so hard it knocked him into the rail and sent him tumbling over the barrier.

The bookie flapped his big wings in an attempt to take

flight, but his wingspan-to-body-mass ratio ruined the aerodynamic possibilities of lifting off from ground level.

As the nightmares pounded into the home stretch, the uncontrolled bats drove the black beasts wild. The imp jockeys flailed about as if they had suddenly passed through a cloud of hornets. The nightmares ran completely amuck, knocking two jockeys out of the saddle, and the dazed imps landed in the churned dirt, while the nightmares thundered past like a snorting avalanche.

In my head, I heard the grand operatic chorus of *Carmina Burana*.

BatGN spread his wide wings to drive off the oncoming horses, but it was like waving a red flag in front of a maddened bull. His panicked squeal rose in pitch until it went mercifully beyond the range of human hearing.

The nightmares trampled him into a furry red splatter in the turf and surged toward the finish line. A second later, Marley brought up the rear, adding his mark to the red mess.

In the stands, the spectators kept cheering. Wrex and his gremlin companions were prancing with excitement. "Good race! Nightmare pileup!"

Finally catching up with Barney, McGoo and I looked down at the muddy stain trampled into the racetrack. "I'm glad I didn't bet on BatGN," said the imp.

Down at my feet, I found an irregular geometric object. In his frantic flight, the bookie had dropped his twenty-sided die. It had come up with a one.

"I didn't like his odds," I said.

CHAPTER 36

Eventually, the rampaging nightmares were rounded up by fearless stable gremlins. Over the loudspeakers, the announcer managed to keep a bright and cheery tone. "You can never bet on what might happen at the Ucky Derby—but you can bet on the races! We're going to take a short break to groom the track again and remove a few unsightly stains. Take this opportunity to purchase our reasonably priced refreshments at the concession stand."

Of all the bizarre things we had been through, the concession prices were still among the most unreasonable. Still, many of the unnaturals took the announcer's suggestion and drifted toward the refreshment stand.

Wrex and his giggly companions kept slapping their paws in high fives. The shrunken head at Wrex's side continued his monotonous shout of, "Kris, Kris, Kris!" over and over.

The cloud of bats had dispersed into the open sky, no doubt heading back to the cathedral in hopes that Russell might have new snacks for them.

The remaining monsters in the bleachers were restless, grumbling about the race and bickering over which nightmare had actually won, since the results had not yet been posted.

I looked down at the trampled red mess, all that remained of the man-bat bookie. "What are the odds?"

I would have felt more sympathy if he hadn't thrown me off the belfry.

"The odds are posted somewhere around here." McGoo glanced up at the board.

After all the drama and disruption, Vincent Galdi made his way down from the private observation box with Ivory on his arm. He was accompanied by his four business-suited bodyguards, who looked intimidating, though headless. They tried to guard their boss, but they had trouble gauging the separation of the bleacher steps.

Looking cool and dapper in his tux with Ivory clinging to his elbow, the wealthy businessman approached me and McGoo.

"Just another day at the races," I said to him.

Galdi seemed disappointed. "That bookie always left a bad taste in my mouth, never willing to take a chance on a real wager—misses the whole point of the sport." He sniffed.

"You shouldn't have been in business with him, sugar. I don't know what you saw in that ugly, fuzzy thing."

Goldfanger was embarrassed. "It's a long tradition that vampires and bats go together."

Ivory stroked his black tux jacket. "Now you have me."

When he smiled, his gold incisors gleamed in the hazy afternoon sunlight.

Barney, who had been incensed and vengeful, now seemed frantic, wringing his little green hands. "BatGN got what he deserved for cheating his clients ... but now what am I going to do? He was my bookie—how am I going to win a million dollars and pay our grocery bills?"

Galdi gave him a cool look. "The Underground Downs has legal gambling machines at every entrance. You could place your bet in a perfectly official and regulated manner."

"I don't want to pay the high service fee!" the imp groaned.

"That's a chance you'll have to take."

As Barney pouted, Goldfanger turned to me. "Thank you for your assistance in resolving our unfortunate disruptions at the track, Mr. Chambeaux. The police must be involved, of course, but I would pay you for a full summary report once you wrap up the case. From now on, the races will be much cleaner." The vampire turned to see the bleachers filling up again as unnaturals came back with trays of overpriced food and drink. "Our patrons will appreciate it."

"And so will the nightmares," I said.

With Ivory following, Galdi turned away, then hesitated. "On a more personal note, have you found my missing dentist friend? I'm rather worried about César. He was a good fellow."

"Still looking for connections," I said. "Part of my investigation took me to the races and exposed BatGN, but I'm not sure that has anything to do with his disappearance."

The erudite businessman tapped a well-manicured finger against his left fang. "Ivory reminded me that I did receive a note from him not long ago. He was smitten with a sweet young lady he wanted to impress."

"That's Francine," I said.

"A sweet young thing," McGoo added, struggling to keep a straight face.

"He mentioned that they were having a bit of a lover's

spat, and he wanted to make it up to her by getting a very special gift."

"He was pretty miserable," I admitted.

Galdi continued, "He asked to borrow money from me, and of course I gave it to him out of friendship. He intended to buy a perfect keepsake for his sweetheart ... a special novelty shrunken head."

As the headless business-suited zombies clustered around Goldfanger, Wrex and his gremlin friends pushed past Barney, in a hurry to get another round of refreshments before the next race began.

Dangling from the gremlin's belt, Wrex's shrunken head became more animated, pulling his lips back. He attempted to shout, though with very little lung capacity. "Mine, mine, mine!" He rolled his eyes and focused on one of the business-suited bodyguards.

The headless figure responded to the voice, turning his shoulders as he looked for the source.

"Mine!" the shrunken head yelled again, and the guard lurched closer. "My body!"

"That is peculiar," said Galdi.

I looked at the desperate head, then at the responsive body, putting two and two together. The leathery face of the shrunken head was discolored and distorted, not unlike some of the rotting zombies I had met on the street.

Kris ...?

Then I remembered a kindly neighbor zombie I had met in the doppelgangered neighborhood of Hairy Harry. I had chatted with him once as he shuffled down to his mailbox.

"Mr. Hamilton?" I asked. "Kris Hamilton, is that you?"

"Mine!" the shrunken head said. "Kris."

McGoo glanced from the headless body to the head, and the answer was so obvious that even he made the logical leap. "How did that little head come from that big body?"

"There must have been an intermediary step," I said.

McGoo stepped up to the gremlin mechanic and spoke with the full authority of the UQPD. "Sir, we're going to have to confiscate that shrunken head. It's evidence in a crime."

Incensed, Wrex grabbed the shrunken head's hair. "Mine!" To which the shrunken head responded, "Mine!" as he looked at the guard's headless body.

With cool confidence, Goldfanger reached into his tuxedo pocket and pulled out a wad of bills. "Let me make things right. I trust you'll consider this worth your time?" He peeled off three hundred dollars and extended them to the gremlin.

Wrex unclipped the shrunken head as he grabbed the bills. "Yours!"

Winkin, Blinkin, and Todd clustered around him, chattering. "Now we can afford *two* hot dogs!"

"And a beer!" said Todd. "To share." The gremlins scurried off with their unexpected fortune.

I took Mr. Hamilton's head and settled it on Mr. Hamilton's shoulders, trying to align the spinal column on the neck stump. It was like trying to put a plucked apple back onto a tree, and the headless body kept fidgeting. Eventually the pieces matched, and the head was back where it belonged, although the sizes were oddly mismatched.

He raised his big hands and held them to either side of his head, making sure it didn't fall off again. Now he spoke normally. "Much better."

"Maybe we can shrink the body to match," McGoo suggested.

Now I remembered Eva Schrank telling me how Alterro's flaky spell had reduced an orc to the size of a goblin. That necromancer again ...

"I just made the connection, McGoo! We have to find Alterro!"

Kris Hamilton said, "I can show you where it happened —lots of other zombies were there. And that bad man with the bad mustache made my head so tiny!" He shook his miniature head on his broad shoulders. "And he promised brain ice cream."

The other three headless bodyguards bumped shoulders, agitated. One turned completely the opposite direction. Another guard drew his gun and pointed it at spectators in the bleachers.

Vincent Galdi was annoyed at the situation. "Are you saying these novelty shrunken heads came from kidnapped zombies? And my friend César is mixed up in it somehow?"

The business-suited bodyguards kept wandering in agitation as if they wanted to rush off and do something.

Ivory stroked Galdi's arm. "Why don't you let them take care of themselves, sugar?"

"Agreed. These men want to go get their heads back." He nodded to them. "I release you all from your employment contracts and give you a month's pay." He glanced at me and McGoo. "I'll call it an ... unseverance package."

In a high-pitched voice, Mr. Hamilton's tiny head told us where to find Alterro's secret hideout and business offices. It was the same area where I had seen the shady necromancer leading his group of duped zombies.

"Let's get over there right away, McGoo," I said. "Maybe he's holding César prisoner—or worse."

"Francine won't like it if he has a miniaturized head," McGoo said, "though she does seem pretty infatuated with the guy."

As we rushed out of the Underground Downs to the parking lot, Mr. Hamilton followed, while the other three cumbersome headless zombies did their best to keep up. It would be good to have extra muscle if we were going to close in on the villain, though I'd have liked to have extra brains and eyes as well.

When we reached the rusty Ford Maverick in the front lot, McGoo asked the most important question. "How are we all going to fit inside the car?"

"You and me in front. Mr. Hamilton in back." I looked at the burly trio of headless guards struggling to catch up. "Hmmm, if only we had—"

Just then the skin-upholstered cab rolled up to us, and Eric leaned out the driver window, pulling down his cap with a bony finger. "Need a ride, guys?"

I indicated the three headless guards. "They do." I gave the cabby the address as our reinforcements piled into his back seat. "Make it snappy!"

McGoo and Mr. Hamilton had already taken their seats in the Pro Bono Mobile. The Maverick seemed to sense my urgency, and it started up with the sound of a Saturn V.

Behind us, Eric roared the taxi's engine, spraying gravel into the other parked vehicles.

We were off to find where Alterro manufactured his conversation-piece little heads.

CHAPTER 37

We reached the rundown-looking business park late on Saturday afternoon—truly the deadest time in the Unnatural Quarter. From the back seat of the car, Mr. Hamilton's tiny head shouted, "There! That's the doorway!"

The only marked business was a dispensary for arcane herbs, called Head Shop. That was our first clue. The Head Shop door said CLOSED, and I suspected the shop was only a front for Alterro's other head business.

The eager zombie in the back seat climbed out the moment I shut off the loud engine. The Dermi Taxi pulled up behind us and sat idling while the headless bodyguards clambered out.

"I'll pay the taxi, Shamble," McGoo said. "You check the door."

I was surprised by his generosity—maybe some of Goldfanger's philanthropy had rubbed off on him? McGoo extracted a wallet from the suit jacket of a headless guard, from which he took out two twenty-dollar bills to keep the skeleton cabby happy.

Mr. Hamilton pointed to an unmarked steel door instead of the Head Shop entrance. "No, this one."

Alterro probably used the side office as his true evil lair. I checked the door and found it unlocked.

McGoo and I pulled out our pistols. After a little coaching, the headless bodyguards drew their weapons as well. Mr. Hamilton reached under his pinstripe jacket to a holster and produced a revolver.

McGoo looked at me before heading inside to investigate. "What more do we need?"

"A bit of luck," I said. "But let's gamble—the odds are on our side." I still had BatGN's twenty-sided die in my trouser pocket, but I decided not to roll.

I pushed the door open to reveal an expansive but dimly lit laboratory or workroom. In the quiet gloom, I heard figures stirring, then a rattle of cage bars. Leaned against the wall just inside the door was a brightly painted sign with a smiling clown. *Zombie Special—Free Brain Ice Cream!*

McGoo looked at the cheery clown. "It's horrifying."

We crept deeper into the workspace. On a long wooden bench inside the dim main room, six zombies were manacled by the ankles to the bench. Their wrists were cuffed behind their backs, with another chain strung through their arms.

All of the zombies had very tiny heads, no bigger than a grapefruit. Seeing us, the tiny-headed zombies broke out in a chorus of pleas that sound like a whining fly's voice. "Helllppp mmmeeee! Helllppp mmmeee!"

Mr. Hamilton groaned. "They've been prepped, but not harvested yet."

A shrunken-head-sized plastic bin sat beside each chained zombie, and I realized what I was looking at. "You mean Alterro works his shrinking spell and then just ... snips them off?"

"Like rosebuds," said Mr. Hamilton.

"I'd like to prune something off him," McGoo grumbled.

A plaintive voice spoke up. "Excuse me? Could I please get a hand over here?"

In the shadows on the far side of the room was a silver-barred cage large enough to hold a bear. In this instance, the cage held only a dapper old vampire, whom I recognized at once. One Fang seemed miserable, but I was glad to see that the former dentist's head was the proper size. Francine would appreciate that.

"César!" I said. "I hoped we'd find you here."

"I didn't realize anyone was looking for me." The old vampire grasped the silver bars. I heard a sizzling sound, and then One Fang yanked his hands back and scowled at his smoking palms.

"Francine hired me to find you. Sorry it took so long—this was a complicated case."

The headless bodyguards turned slowly around with their guns extended, though they couldn't see or hear anything. I flinched out of the way when one of them pointed the pistol toward me.

"Is Alterro here?" I asked, ready for a fight. "We know he's the one behind all this."

"He stepped out for lunch," César explained. "He usually goes to the taco truck two blocks away. They've got fast service—he won't be gone long."

I hurried to the silver cage. I didn't have a key, but any good zombie P.I. had a personal set of lockpicks. I pulled the tools from my pocket and set to work.

Mr. Hamilton went to comfort the tiny-headed zombies chained to the bench, but he would have to wait his turn for the lock picks.

César waited at the back of the cage as I worked. "I was

just trying to buy Francine a shrunken head. After that mess with the banshee singing telegram, I needed to get her something memorable, so she would forgive me."

"She forgave you right away," I reassured him. "But it would have been nice if you'd helped clean up the mess you caused."

One Fang hung his head. "I'll remember that next time."

"Next time? I'd suggest that you not commission another banshee singing telegram."

"I kept seeing those shrunken heads around, but when I wanted to actually buy one, of course they were nowhere to be found. I tried the flea market, then went to the usual vendor alleys, but no luck. I finally tracked Alterro down at the Head Shop, determined to make my special purchase—but I accidentally saw too much!

"I tried to run, but he had a whole stack of different spells printed on flyers. He grabbed one designed to stop vampires in their tracks, and I was helpless! I've been stuck here in this cage for days."

"Francine misses you," I said, and that seemed to make him feel better.

McGoo stepped up to the bars. "But why did Alterro keep you prisoner at all? What did he intend to do with you?"

I finally cracked the lock, and César burst out, shaking with relief. "He was experimenting on me! He wanted to make a vampire shrunken head, but when he worked the charm on me, it fizzled. The shrinking spell specifically only works on zombies. Ohhh, did it give me a headache! Worst migraine I've ever experienced." The old vamp pressed his hands to his temples. "I just want to see Francine."

Now I understood what his mysterious text meant.

"We'll take you back to Francine as soon as we free these other victims." I hurried to the long bench where Mr. Hamilton was rattling the chain that bound the tiny-headed zombies.

The zombie victims turned to me with small hopeful expressions on their tiny faces as I set to work with the lockpicks.

Before I could finish, Alterro strode into the warehouse, whistling to himself. He carried a cardboard to-go box. When he saw us, he dropped his tacos on the floor.

Anger welled up in me. "Alterro, we're putting an end to your scheme!"

One of the headless bodyguards swung his arm up and fired his gun, but at the wrong wall. The ricochet whined.

The necromancer grabbed the top sheet from a stack of flyers on a table. "Dan Shamble! You've always been too much trouble, and never a good customer." He held up the paper and started reading aloud from the spell.

César yelled, "Stop him! That's the zombie head-shrinking spell!"

Alterro's handlebar mustache wobbled as he rolled off the magic words at a fast clip. I staggered back as the magic boiled toward me.

Thinking fast, McGoo threw himself in front of me, waving his arms to block the spell. When Alterro finished his brief incantation, McGoo groaned, holding the top of his skull. "Oh, what a headache!"

I was glad to find my corpus intact, but now I was even angrier. In just one day I'd been thrown from a belfry and nearly had my head miniaturized. Talk about a string of bad luck!

Alterro tossed aside the useless flyer. "Wrong spell! That's the zombie-specific one." His voice took on a deeper, more evil tone as he pulled out the next sheet in the stack. "I paid the spell service a premium for this more versatile, all-purpose *generic head-shrinking spell!* It's just arrived!"

As he started rattling off the darkly powerful words, he glowered at McGoo. His voice grew louder as he boomed out the incantation.

McGoo was on his hands and knees, crawling away. He winced from the agony in his skull. Now I knew I couldn't dodge the magic. We were both wide open.

But before the necromancer finished his recitation, César snatched the spell flyer right out of his hands and whipped it around so that it faced the other direction. As the puffed-up necromancer recited the last potent words, the magic rippled out—but not toward me.

Instead, the ultra-potent generic head-shrinking spell slammed into Alterro himself. "No, no, no!" he cried, and his voice grew thinner, going up octave after octave as his head and his handlebar mustache miniaturized down and down until it was as small as the other shrunken heads.

And the magic kept going, until the incredible shrinking necromancer's head became the size of a plum, then a grape, then a pea, and finally disappeared with a *pop!* His body flailed, and his hands twitched, but his head was gone.

Before he could collapse to the floor, one of the business-suited bodyguards swung his pistol and opened fire three times, shooting Alterro in the chest. It put an unnecessary, but reassuring, period at the end of the sentence.

As the gunshot echoes faded, we stood around in shock, and then the chained shrunken-headed zombies began to cheer.

I bent down next to the dead mail-order necromancer and found even more good news. "Look, here's his set of keys."

CHAPTER 38

Alas, Alterro did not keep his keychain organized or labeled, and the fact that the keys were now bloodstained made them all the more difficult to use.

McGoo took the set from me, insisting that he was more nimble. He fumbled with the padlock and chain for so long, I was sure I could have freed them faster with the lockpicks anyway. He blamed it on his splitting headache. But at last the zombies were unleashed.

McGoo called in UQPD reinforcements and also summoned an ambulance. Before long, the Head Shop business park became a racket of sirens and flashing lights. It was all comforting to me in a way, but it did not help my BHF's migraine.

Meanwhile, a contrite César borrowed my phone to call Francine, and I knew she would be thrilled to hear from him. I was happy to close another one of my cases.

The headless, business-suited guards stood with guns drawn, ready for some kind of counterattack, but I gently disarmed them. They could look intimidating without any more risk of blind gunfire.

Although the bodyguards had been released from Vincent Galdi's employment, they still did not have their heads. Even a thorough search of Alterro's workspace did not locate their missing pieces. I guessed they were among the shrunken heads the necromancer had already sold to unsuspecting customers like Wrex.

Emergency Mortician Techs checked over One Fang and the tiny-headed zombies, pronouncing them undead but healthy. They could not make the same assessment of the blood-soaked and equally headless body of the mail-order necromancer on the floor.

Our most pressing priority was to take care of the tiny-headed zombie prisoners who had been freed from their chains. They functioned well enough, because zombies are accustomed to very small brains, but their disproportionate body parts were a problem.

Mr. Hamilton climbed into the back of the ambulance so that all the headshrunk zombies could travel to the hospital together. McGoo offered to stay and fill out the paperwork, and to bask in the glow of solving the big case, so I followed them to the hospital alone. Thanks to the invigorated engines, the Pro Bono Mobile arrived at the emergency room even faster than the ambulance with its flashing lights and screaming sirens.

On the way, I called the office to tell Sheyenne and Robin what had happened. Alvina was particularly delighted to hear that César was unharmed, other than being a bit embarrassed.

After speaking with a dusty mummy receptionist, I found the hospital examination room where the tiny-headed patients had been taken. I had to sit in the waiting room and page through year-old unnatural celebrity magazines before I was allowed to go in.

Dr. Zonda Nefarious, the hospital's highest-ranking

witch doctor, tended the miserable zombies, pacing around them with her clipboard. Although her stethoscope hung on her chest, she didn't bother to use it since none of the zombies had heartbeats. She clucked her tongue as she tallied the symptoms and filled out a separate sheet for each patient.

She looked up as I entered. "Mr. Chambeaux, this is a very intriguing case you've brought us." The witch doctor walked among the disproportioned zombies, narrowing her eyes as she made more notes. "It appears that each one of these victims has a shrunken head."

"I concur with the diagnosis." I pulled Alterro's dangerous flyers from my pocket, both the generic and the zombie-specific incantations. "Here are the spells that were used to shrink their heads."

She took the papers and studied them. "Interesting. I'm more used to shrunken heads done the old-school way."

"Helllppp mmmeee!" the zombies said in a chorus.

"Yes, yes, we're getting to that." First, the witch doctor focused on Mr. Hamilton, since he was the most articulate. She poked at his thin neck and studied the scar line where his head had reattached itself.

The privacy curtains rustled, and a large sow pushed her way into the examination room, followed by a witch in a voluminous black dress. I smiled in surprise and relief. "Mavis! Alma! What are you doing here?" The two witches had helped me out on many cases before.

Dr. Nefarious turned, still holding her clipboard. "Oh, I asked the Wannoviches here for a second opinion. Mr. Chambeaux, show them the spell."

Alma, who had been transformed into a sow due to a

hazardous misspelling, raised her flat snout and snuffled the flyer. Mavis stepped up next to her. "A spell? You already have the spell?"

"Yes, I brought it with me." As they looked at the paper, I briefed them on the mail-order necromancer's insidious novelty-item scheme.

Mavis studied both spells. "Interesting. I've seen something like this before." She bent down to show it to the sow. Alma snuffled, squinted her small eyes, and grunted a comment.

"I agree," Mavis said. "In order to resize all these heads, we must develop a counterspell. Dr. Nefarious, I suggest we bring in the entire Pointy Hat Society."

"Yes, all hats on deck. As a research team we can solve this tiny problem." The witch doctor poked Mr. Hamilton's neck with a sharp finger.

I took my leave, reassuring all the miserable patients, "Your heads are in good hands."

But my work as a private investigator was not done. The bodyguards still needed to be reunited with their own heads.

A DIFFERENT REUNION TOOK PLACE AT THE GOBLIN Tavern, and it was even more heartwarming than reattaching Mr. Hamilton's head to his body.

César entered the bar and took his seat, grinning sheepishly. He had changed clothes to make himself presentable, and he looked even more dapper than ever, far too suave to be a retired dentist (but vampires always had a glamour ability about them).

Francine lit up like an ignited emergency flare. "I was so worried about you César! You just disappeared."

Because of the momentous occasion, I had brought Alvina along, and she squirmed and wiggled on the barstool next to me, slurping her Shirley Jugular. "I'm so glad you're okay, César! When you disappeared, that really sucked— even though I did get a new toothbrush and floss."

Francine leaned over the bar and planted a kiss in the middle of César's forehead. "Don't ever do that to me again!"

If he hadn't been a vampire, he would have flushed bright red. "I didn't do it on purpose." He seemed unsure about the situation, guilty about his botched romantic gesture. "I'm sorry. I just meant to do something special for you, but the singing telegram didn't turn out well."

"It was a nice thought," Francine admitted, "but disastrous. Whatever made you think I would want a banshee singing telegram?"

César spread his hands, as if the answer were obvious. "The same thing that convinced me you'd want a novelty talking shrunken head."

Francine planted her hands on her narrow hips. "And why would you look at me and think I'd want a shriveled-up talking zombie head?"

He looked away. "Because it was exotic and unusual ... and I think *you're* exotic and unusual. A singing telegram seemed like a romantic gesture. Francine, I love your quirky sense of humor and your strange interests. We get along so well. I wanted to write you a love letter, but dentists aren't very poetic."

Francine pulled out her phone. "So you sent me a text

instead? This isn't even sexting. 'My head hurts.' What's that supposed to mean?"

"Wait, I didn't know you would want me to send a sext!" Now he did manage a brief flush of his cheeks. "I was trapped in a cage. But one time, Alterro left his cellphone on the table barely within reach. I burned myself pretty bad on the silver bars, but I managed to grab the phone while he went out to lunch. I only had time to send a very brief message before he came back."

"If you only had time for a brief message," I pointed out, "an *address* might have been more effective than 'My head hurts.'"

"I realize that now. But I was miserable without you, Francine, and I wasn't thinking straight. Can you please forgive me?"

She poured herself a tall bourbon from the best bottle on the top shelf, took a long sip, and said, "Of course I forgive you. You're my sweetie. I just hope you learned your lesson. Banshee singing telegrams? Shrunken zombie heads? Maybe next time just send flowers and take me to a nice dinner."

CHAPTER 39

Being thrown from a high belfry had left me scuffed up and worse for wear. Even the soft landing, thanks to Russell's heroic rescue, had rumpled my sport jacket and dented my fedora. Both needed a good cleaning and pressing, and Sheyenne whisked them off to the dry cleaner.

Sitting in my office, though, I felt naked without my usual garb. What kind of private investigator would be seen without his jacket and fedora?

My physical body was not in tip-top condition either, and if I let myself deteriorate further, I could no longer claim to be a well-preserved zombie. (Repeatedly climbing all those stairs had gotten my thighs in pretty good shape, though.)

Luckily, I was due for my monthly maintenance spell, which Mavis and Alma Wannovich provided in exchange for the inside scoop on some of my cases and adventures. Their ghost writer, Linda Bullwer, used the details as inspiration for the lowbrow and cornball Shamble & Die Mysteries.

Mavis and Alma came to the Chambeaux & Deyer offices accompanied by the frumpy vampire ghost writer. "We decided to make an office call," Mavis said. "That way Sheyenne can give us the background material for the next novel in the series."

Alvina scurried out of the kitchen, emitting a squeal of delight. "Piggy, piggy!" The big sow made a similar sound as the kid gave her a big hug.

Robin emerged from her office. "All client names and specifics need to be changed, as you're well aware. Privacy reasons."

"Of course, dear," said Mavis.

Linda Bullwer interjected, "So far I've managed to convey a compelling and urgent sense of realism without crossing any infringement boundaries."

Since Alvina was starting school the following day, we had moved her Ancient Egypt diorama from the conference table to the side credenza so that Chambeaux & Deyer could get back to our regular business.

As we gathered in the conference room, Robin asked, "Would you like a cup of coffee, or maybe some green tea?"

Sheyenne glanced toward the kitchenette and the malicious black mold. "Maybe we should just stick to conversation today …" Our guests took their seats, while Alvina ran to get herself a blood box.

Linda Bullwer placed a manila folder and a notepad on the table. She spread out newspaper clippings, highlighted notes, and chapter outlines. "The eighth novel in the series will be about the doppelgänger invasion and the evil, formerly virgin librarian Stella Artois."

"That was a good case," I said. "Be sure you get Hairy Harry in there, otherwise he'll growl at you."

Linda scribbled a note on her pad. "It's a challenge to depict the rogue werewolf cop in a realistic yet sympathetic manner. He's so gruff."

Alvina returned to the conference room, slurping through the straw in her blood box. "I'm his agent."

Robin took out her yellow legal pad and the self-scribing pencil. "We'll need to review the manuscript and suggest any changes before publication."

Alma gave an indignant snort, and Mavis frowned. "We have a First Amendment right to publish as we see fit."

"I'll mainly look at grammar and punctuation," Alvina said.

Linda Bullwer considered. "I wouldn't mind having another beta reader to help spot plot holes. Some of the adventures are rather ridiculous." She described how she intended to spice up the story of the stolen *Necronomicon*, the Old Tymers, and the disappearing neighborhoods. "It never hurts to add more sex scenes and car chases," she said.

"As long as they're realistic," Robin added.

Linda made a note of that.

I asked, "How is your other big project, Ms. Bullwer? The sequel to the *Necronomicon*?"

The ghost writer beamed. "I think it's some of my best work. Extra plot twists, greater exploration of the characters —and it's even thicker than the original! *Necronomicon II: Double Trouble* is going to be fine literature. It's in the editing stages now."

"It needs a little work," Mavis said. "We're going to release it together with the new Shamble & Die novel, which we plan to title *Double-Booked*, to maintain the binary theme. For advertising."

I admitted that I had been seeing double in most of those cases.

Mavis wasn't done yet, though. "In other good news,

Howard Phillips Publishing is preparing to do audiobooks of the entire Shamble & Die series. It's an expanding market and many unnaturals like to listen to a good story while they're working out at All-Day/All-Nite Fitness, or when they lie back in their coffins and drift off to sleep at dawn."

"Audiobooks?" I asked. "Who are you going to get to voice me?"

"We have many great possibilities," Mavis said, "and we intend to secure the most remarkable voice we can afford." She scratched the wart on her nose. "Alas, we can't afford much."

The big sow paced the conference room, snuffling out a spell pattern on the carpet. From her enormous purse, Mavis removed a black candle and a tin of magic powder. "Now then, Mr. Chambeaux, let's freshen you up."

I had been through the procedure many times before, and the Wannoviches were well practiced. Linda Bullwer assisted with the spell preparations, as needed.

When the witch sisters were finished, I could flex my limbs and even make recognizable facial expressions. I felt as good as undead, and I hoped my fedora and jacket would be just as fresh very soon.

Robin raised another matter. "You're working with Dr. Nefarious to help the rescued zombies with the shrunken heads. Have you made any progress?"

"Oh, we have the entire Pointy Hat Society comparing scrapbooks and exchanging ideas to find the right spell. We think we can restore those poor victims. Alma had a very innovative approach that shows great promise."

I was curious. "How are you going to enlarge those tiny heads?"

"We are interviewing narcissistic and egotistical celebrities who have really big heads. We may be able to incorporate that information to inflate the size of the afflicted zombie heads."

"Be sure you talk to Ivory," Sheyenne suggested.

Mavis made a note. "Oh, good idea."

Before long, the Wannovich sisters and Linda Bullwer left satisfied. When they were gone, Sheyenne looked at the clock and smiled with relief. "In a few minutes, we have another appointment, Beaux. A house call."

"A house call?" I touched my shirt. "But I don't have my jacket or my fedora back from cleaning yet. Where are we going?"

"No, a house call here in our offices. I made special arrangements. Since the patient can't come to Dr. Schrank, she will come to the patient."

Her explanation left me even more confused than before, which is not how explanations are supposed to work. But before she could offer further clarification, the heartless but empathetic therapist arrived, carrying her heavy toolbox.

Alvina sprang up to greet her. "Dr. Schrank! Are you here to see me again?"

"No, no, my dear girl. You have been perfectly therapized, a clean bill of mental health. You have the toolkit you need for life."

The shrink wore her bib overalls and she had donned a carpentry cap, probably a special outfit for making house calls. Her shawl was well-adjusted, just like Alvina.

Dr. Schrank set the toolbox on Sheyenne's desk and removed a sharp tree-trimming saw. "Just in case I need to cut some drywall. Certain patients need tough love."

Sheyenne drifted forward. "Right this way, Dr. Schrank." While Robin and I stared after her, perplexed, she led the therapist into the kitchen. "Here's the offending fungus. I certainly hope you can help us."

The therapist clucked her tongue. "My, my, just as you said. I certainly see some anger issues here, and the fungal penmanship is quite bad." She set the heavy toolkit on the kitchen counter next to the microwave and the coffeepot. "This might take several sessions. Please give me some time alone with the black mold, and I'll begin."

Sheyenne returned to the main office and gave us a hopeful shrug. "It can't hurt."

From the kitchenette, Dr. Schrank said, "Now then, tell me what you can remember about your mother."

CHAPTER 40

It was choir practice day, and Alvina was thrilled to go back to the cathedral for a fun session with her fellow shrouded singers. Ivory hogged the spotlight, projecting her voice louder than any of her protégés. That seemed to be her teaching method. Or maybe she was practicing for the next Cursed Idol Competition.

Since the kids would be singing for the next hour, I went up to chat with Russell. I felt better, now that I had my fedora and jacket back. As I climbed the belfry stairs, I could hear the beautiful harmonies of the "Hokey Pokey," which transitioned into the catchy theme from *Carmina Burana*.

Later, McGoo and I would go together to talk with Sally Allan's family. They needed to have closure, although they still might not agree with her questionable career choices. They could never bridge that family gap.

The gargoyle was up in the belfry, exactly where I expected him to be. The air was moist, and a few puddles dotted the floor and window railings. It had rained that morning, and Russell must have sat out in the drenching downpour. The heavy rain had washed much of the paint from his outstretched wings, erasing the ad for the Ghoul's Diner.

I was prepared to tell him all about BatGN's plot with the tech-enhanced bats, so planning ahead, I had typed up a full explanation. I didn't want to scribble terse words on a notepad or shout at the top of my lungs.

As Russell watched the gathering twilight spread across the Quarter, he swayed along to the musical vibrations from below, humming deep in his throat. Bats swirled around him, begging for treats, but not as many as before. His paper sack was already empty, and he would soon have to go back to the diner dumpster to restock.

When I called out his name, Russell surprised me by twitching. He turned his angular face toward me, and he showed me more fangs in a smile. "Mr. Chambeaux."

I joined him on the belfry ledge, enjoying the view. "You can hear me this time?"

A domesticated bat landed on the gargoyle's dark arm, and I saw that it still had the electronic bling pasted to its chest, a silvery circuit board. Russell used a claw to pluck off the object, then he sent the bat flying away. He grimaced as he held the circuit between thumb and forefinger before flicking it out into the open air.

He tapped his hearing aids. "I can hear better now without all the interference from those jamming signals. I can't believe BatGN did such a thing to these poor sweet bats."

"I can't believe it either. It's a very unbelievable scheme."

"I've cleared most of them now," Russell said. "My hearing aids work fairly well."

"That'll make conversation easier." I pulled out my typed notes for reference and told him about BatGN's plan. Down below, the Banshee Tabernacle Choir launched into another number. The music was a pleasant background noise.

Russell and I sat together in comfortable camaraderie for a while, and I asked, "If the hearing aids work now, then you can understand what people are saying. You don't have to stay isolated up here anymore. Why not come down and join the rest of us? Chat with people on the street, make yourself heard?"

Russell gave me a solemn look. More bats fluttered lovingly around him. "Not interested, Mr. Chambeaux—we talked about it in the diner. Too many people talking all the time and not saying anything important. I prefer it up here." He drew a deep breath and stretched his big leathery wings. "Nothing wrong with a comfortable silence."

He popped out his hearing aids and sat in his own little world, enjoying the view from the belfry.

I couldn't argue with what he'd said—mainly because Russell couldn't hear me anymore—but I agreed with him on a certain level. I left the gargoyle in peace and went back down to hear my vampire half-daughter sing.

AT BARNEY & CLYDE'S GROCERY, A CELEBRATION WAS taking place. Pink and yellow balloons floated from streamers that stretched from the roof to the asphalt. A humming air generator inflated a white fabric sock ghost with big happy eyes painted on the side. As the cartoony fake ghost wobbled and flapped in the air, several real ghosts circled it, snickering and taunting. Big painted letters on the windows announced, *GALA EVENT!!!* And the next window splashed out, *REGULAR PRICES!!!*

As I walked up to the automatic doors, the three still-headless bodyguards shuffled out, proudly wearing new smooth white mannequin heads as temporary substitutes while the search continued for their real heads. It was good to see they didn't need to resort to lettuce or cabbage.

Inside, Clyde worked the breakfast cereal aisle, standing on a stack of boxes as he restocked the shelves. That reminded me to pick up more Unlucky Charms for Alvina.

When the imp grocer saw me, he looked relieved and relaxed. "Thank you for helping my brother, Mr. Shamble! You were really there when he needed you—when we both needed you."

"Thanks." I felt myself smiling with pride, though I'm not very good at accepting compliments. "I came to finalize a few details. Barney's suspicions were correct. His bookie was indeed cheating, but the resolution isn't going to make your brother happy."

Clyde sniffed. "It'll make me happy if he stops betting on the nightmares." He gestured toward the stock room. "He's in back stacking crates."

Behind the swinging doors, Barney was lifting boxes of toilet paper that were larger than he was, arranging them in piles of single-ply, double-ply, and extra-abrasive. He let out a bright sigh and waved at me. "Mr. Shamble!" He created a mini tempest and used the wind to help him lift toilet-paper boxes even higher onto the stack. "Are you here to wrap up the case? Did you find any more of BatGN's criminal activities?"

"It's like a spiderweb untangling. We've looked into all of his interference at the Ucky Derby, and Goldfanger is cooperating. Since many of the races were thrown, the results are no longer valid. It'll cause quite a shakeup in the Underground Downs."

"Did you get my money back? Everyone gets a full refund, right?"

"That's uh, not how illicit gambling works, Barney. No guarantees."

When the imp pouted, the breezes around him turned into a little storm. "If there are no guarantees, then what's the point of gambling?"

That wasn't a conversation I could win, so I changed the subject. "I wanted to give you something—a token of the case." I pulled the twenty-sided die from my pocket. "This belonged to BatGN. Keep it as a souvenir so you can do more research on actual probabilities."

Curious, he stepped away from the toilet paper and took the die, trembling with delight. "What a cool memento!" Cradling it in his palm, he stared at the numerous small faces. "It's my lucky day." He gave me a sly look. "And there's no better time than now to use that luck. I've been waiting to try these."

He fished in the pocket of his grocer's apron and pulled out a stack of lottery scratchers. He used his sharp fingernails to scrape off the silver covering. "I've got to win one of these days. I've got to win!"

I knew it was time for Sheyenne to close the case.

CHAPTER 41

Now that my case load was settling down, I enjoyed a leisurely Sunday afternoon walk with Sheyenne out to the park and the pond. I felt classy in my freshly pressed jacket and crisp fedora.

We were both feeling happy and content, until a loud caterwauling erupted from the bandstand. Overlapping voices rang out, not in harmony but at war. I cringed and pulled my hat down to cover my ears. Sheyenne paled as if she wanted to disappear into the ether. "What's that noise, Beaux?"

I listened to the wailing and screeching—two shrill feminine voices and a growling male bass—and I finally made out the words. "It's 'Memories,' I think—from *Cats*."

Fascinated yet appalled, like someone drawn to a disastrous accident scene, we detoured into the park. We bumped into quite a few people. I was surprised at the size of the crowd, until I realized they were all fleeing the vicinity.

On the bandstand, a trio stood together, needing no microphones as they hurled out their wreck of a song: Ivory in a form-fitting white cocktail gown, backed up by Sheila the banshee and Stentor the ogre.

I turned to Sheyenne, astonished. "Oh no—they formed their own band!"

The vampire, the banshee, and the ogre wrapped up

their song in an avalanche of a grand finale, then bowed, waiting for applause, but anyone within earshot was either stunned or half deafened.

Noticing us as the crowd scattered, Ivory waved from the bandstand. Unfortunately, because most of the people had dispersed, there was no place for us to hide. "Thank you, thank you, sugar."

Stentor waved a meaty, thick-fingered hand. If the banshee recognized me, she gave no sign; her mood was as dour as ever.

In the nearby pond, numerous fish were floating belly up among the reeds and cattails.

"We hope you enjoy the performance," Stentor bellowed out. "This is our only appearance on the bandstand. After today, we're forbidden to sing inside the city limits, thanks to Unnatural Quarter noise ordinances."

Ivory shouldered him aside, recapturing center stage. "This next song goes out to my dear, dear friend Sheyenne." I stiffened with dread. Ivory pressed her fists against her cleavage as she crooned out the opening lines of "The Lady Is a Tramp."

We didn't stay for the encore.

No more nightmare races, no more mail-order necromancers, no more corrupt mutant bookies. With César Marici reunited with Francine, most of my official cases were resolved.

Robin finished the paperwork and closed out the files on her Ear L. Thrombins gravestone typo case and the lava monsters versus the neighbor's sprinklers case. Since she was a passionate crusader for the rights of unnaturals, she was pleased with the week's work.

Sheyenne turned on the office TV, so the local talk show could keep us company. "It's time for the Sunday edition of 'Conversations with Dick the Head.'"

"He always has interesting guests," Robin said.

Dick the Head ("Don't forget the 'the!'") had been one of Robin's first clients after the Big Uneasy, when a gang of rowdy, heartless rednecks thought it would be fun to tie a disoriented zombie—Dick—between two pickup trucks and pull him apart. Dick's case had aroused great sympathy for the plight of all monsters who just wanted to live their unnatural lives in peace. After his impassioned plea in court, Dick's disembodied head had landed many gigs on the talk-show circuit, and his afternoon program on WRIP was a hit throughout the Quarter.

"Today, friends, we need your help!" Dick said from a presentation platter with a microphone in front of his mouth. "It's a lost-and-found case, and we need your eyes." He chuckled. "Not literally, folks. Keep them in their sockets or on their stalks."

The camera pulled back to show the guests for the show: six shrunken heads, leftover novelties that had been retrieved from Alterro's product display case.

"These little heads have lost their bodies," said Dick. "It's a tale that will pull on the heartstrings of anyone who still has a heart. Victims of a heinous crime, these poor heads were shrunken and detached from their bodies to be sold as cute souvenirs. Now, they're looking for their bodies back."

The shrunken heads all began to talk at once. "I want my

body back."

"Die! Die! You'll all die!"

"My brain hurts."

"Where's my neck?"

Dick said, "We also have several headless zombies looking for their matching parts." The camera pulled back to reveal three decapitated figures still wearing their business suits from Vincent Galdi, though they had ditched their temporary mannequin head substitutes for dramatic effect on the show. They loomed behind the host.

"Leaving no stone unturned, this station has even taken out ads on milk cartons." Dick rolled his eyes up and to the left. "Go on, show them."

One of the headless bodyguards held up a milk carton that showed one of the shrunken heads. *Have You Seen My Body?* But the headless figure was disoriented and faced away from the camera. "Turn around a little," Dick said. "No, to your left."

The headless zombie rotated slowly in a confused state until Dick told him to stop. The milk carton finally faced the camera. I knew there were quite a few other headless zombies wandering the streets.

"If anyone can help reunite these poor souls, please call WRIP. Our local philanthropist, Vincent Galdi, has offered a reward."

"Way to go, Goldfanger," I muttered. I wondered if the wealthy vampire was also financing Ivory's new band. If so, I hoped he would send them on tour soon.

On Monday, well before the first classroom bells rang, McGoo brought Alvina to our offices with a proud grin plastered across his face. He had watched her the night before.

Alvina had a fresh pink sweater and the new backpack from Lester's Flea Market. Her golden hair had been brushed and put into cute pigtails. "Better hurry! I don't want to be late for class."

Sheyenne glowed. "Ready for your first day of school, honey?"

The vampire girl was bubbling with energy. "Can't wait! I've got my papers and notebooks and school supplies."

McGoo worked open the top zipper on the backpack. "I gave her some snacks and candy, even some of those chocolate-coated espresso beans to help her concentrate in class."

"I love them!" Alvina said.

McGoo gave a hopeful look to Sheyenne. "Maybe you have a few snacks that are more appropriate?"

Sheyenne flitted into the kitchenette and returned with a blood box and a baggie filled with dry breakfast cereal for the kid to snack on.

After the first session with Dr. Schrank, the black mold had grudgingly agreed to a truce. The fungus promised to make an effort to work out its issues, and Sheyenne also agreed not to provoke it, at least for the duration of the counseling sessions.

"Let's all walk her to school together," I said. "It's a milestone for everybody."

Robin decided that none of her pending cases were more important than Alvina, and we all headed off toward

Nosferatu Academy. I was always proud of my half-daughter, but this day felt particularly special. Alvina had a personality so perky it verged on hazardous. She was a ray of sunshine, and it didn't matter to me that vampires avoided bright sunshine.

"You'll do great," Robin encouraged. "With a good education, you can be anything you want—even a lawyer."

"Or a private investigator," I said.

"Or a policeman," McGoo added, not wanting to be left out. "Uh, police ... person."

"She could be a great singer," Sheyenne added. "You've heard her voice."

"Francine says I'd be talented as a bartender, or a chemist," Alvina said.

"Anything you want, kid," I replied.

At the freshly painted crosswalk, we waited for the orc crossing guard to wave us forward, and soon we were standing in front of the stone structure that looked like a towering mausoleum. *Nosferatu Academy*. Unnatural kids ran around on the grass and on the playground. Some climbed the dead trees.

Alvina giggled, eager to join her new friends. She waved back at us, and we stood together as she ran to her first day of unnatural school.

"Every day has been a learning experience for me too." I looked at McGoo, Sheyenne, and Robin. They nodded.

"For all of us," Sheyenne said.

"Every day," McGoo agreed.

We watched Alvina run among the other unnatural schoolchildren. No doubt, before long she would be smarter than all of us put together.

ACK!-NOWLEDGMENTS

This zombie detective shambles again, with the help and enthusiasm of many people. I want to thank Hannah Sheldon and Jeri Goodkind, first readers extraordinaire, my wife Rebecca Moesta, the fabulous artists and designers from Miblart, and special Kickstarter backers Lloyd (TxCigarPirate) Lively, Sean Anthony Smith, Tracy Eire, James Johnston, and Gary Iber.

ABOUT THE AUTHOR

Kevin J. Anderson has published more than 175 books, 58 of which have been national or international bestsellers. He has written numerous novels in the Star Wars, X-Files, and Dune universes, as well as a unique steampunk fantasy trilogy beginning with *Clockwork Angels*, written with legendary rock drummer Neil Peart. His original works include the Saga of Seven Suns series, the Wake the Dragon and Terra Incognita fantasy trilogies, the Saga of Shadows trilogy, and his humorous horror series featuring Dan Shamble, Zombie P.I. He has edited numerous anthologies, written comics and games, and the lyrics to two rock CDs. Anderson is the director of the graduate program in Publishing at Western Colorado University. Anderson and his wife Rebecca Moesta are the publishers of WordFire Press. His most recent novels are *Clockwork Destiny*, *Gods and Dragons*, *Dune: The Lady of Caladan* (with Brian Herbert), and *Slushpile Memories: How NOT to Get Rejected*. For information on upcoming projects, appearances, free books and stories, and general fun stuff, sign up for Kevin's newsletter at wordfire.com.

facebook.com/KJAauthor
twitter.com/TheKJA
instagram.com/TheRealKJA

Read All the Cases of
Dan Shamble, Zombie P.I.

Death Warmed Over

Unnatural Acts

Hair Raising

Working Stiff

Slimy Underbelly

Tastes Like Chicken

Services Rendered

Double-Booked

OTHER BOOKS BY KEVIN J. ANDERSON

Alternitech

Blindfold

Captain Nemo

Climbing Olympus

Clockwork Angels: The Comic Scripts

War of the Worlds, Global Dispatch

Edited by Kevin J Anderson

Hopscotch

Million Dollar Series

Million Dollar Productivity

Million Dollar Professionalism for the Writer

Slushpile Memories: How NOT to Get Rejected

Worldbuilding: From Small Towns to Entire Universes

Writing As a Team Sport

On Being a Dictator

Mr. Wells & the Martians

Resurrection, Inc.

The Saga of Seven Suns, Veiled Alliances

The Saga of Seven Suns, Whistling Past the Graveyard

The Saga of Seven Suns: TWO SHORT NOVELS: Includes Veiled Alliances and Whistling Past the Graveyard

Three Military SF Novellas

Short Story Collections

Selected Stories: Science Fiction, Volume 1

Selected Stories: Science Fiction, Volume 2

Selected Stories: Fantasy

Selected Stories: Horror and Dark Fantasy

By Kevin J. Anderson & Doug Beason

Assemblers of Infinity

Craig Kreident #1: Virtual Destruction

Craig Kreident #2: Fallout

Craig Kreident #3: Lethal Exposure

Ignition

Ill Wind

Lifeline

The Trinity Paradox

By Kevin J. Anderson & Rebecca Moesta

Collaborators

Crystal Doors #1: Island Realm

Crystal Doors #2: Ocean Realm

Crystal Doors #3: Sky Realm

The Star Challengers Series

Star Challengers #1: Moonbase Crisis

Star Challengers #2: Space Station Crisis

Star Challengers #3: Asteroid Crisis

Kevin J. Anderson & Neil Peart

Clockwork Angels

Clockwork Lives

Drumbeats

TO ORDER AUTOGRAPHED PRINT COPIES

of this book and many other titles
by Kevin J. Anderson
please check out our selection at

WFS
WORDFIRE SHOP

wordfireshop.com